SWANSONG

SWANSONG

Pauline Bell

Chivers Press • Thorndike Press
Bath, England Waterville, Maine USA

This Large Print edition is published by Chivers Press, England, and by Thorndike Press, USA.

Published in 2003 in the U.K. by arrangement with Constable & Robinson Ltd.

Published in 2003 in the U.S. by arrangement with McIntosh & Otis, Inc.

U.K. Hardcover   ISBN 0–7540–8992–4   (Chivers Large Print)
U.K. Softcover   ISBN 0–7540–8993–2   (Camden Large Print)
U.S. Softcover   ISBN 0–7862–5432–7   (General Series)

The text of this Large Print edition is unabridged.
Other aspects of the book may vary from the original edition.

Set in 16 pt. New Times Roman.

Printed in Great Britain on acid-free paper.

British Library Cataloguing in Publication Data available

ISBN 0–7862–5432–7 (lg. print : sc : alk. paper)

In memory of
Maureen Arthur

PROLOGUE

September 2001

It was on a September evening, a whole year before the murder of Rosanne Goldsmith, that Detective Constable Caroline Webster arrived home at the end of her shift to find her promised supper was not on the table. It was not even in the oven. She found the errant cook, her fiancé, Cavill Jackson, immersed in that day's edition of the *Cloughton Clarion.*

He looked up guiltily. 'I'll take you out instead. To the Fountain?'

Caroline sank on to the comfortable sofa that she was determined to keep until its present near-disintegration was complete. 'Pour us both a drink. A glass of Shiraz might even persuade me to do the cooking for you. You did do the shopping, I hope.'

He nodded and disappeared into the kitchen. Caroline took up the paper, curious to see what had so absorbed him. Her eyes widened as she read the banner headline.

GOLDSMITH, CRANMER AND STEIGER TO PERFORM IN CLOUGHTON

Mr Lewis Blake (41), self-styled leading light of the Cloughton Amateur Opera Group, has persuaded three internationally renowned singers to take part in a production of Bizet's *Carmen* in twelve months' time. The opera is to be performed in the Victoria Theatre with Mr Blake as producer/director.

Miss Rosanne Goldsmith (mezzo-soprano, 29) is to sing the title role. Mr Miles Cranmer (tenor, 36) will be her lover, Don José and Miss Ursula Steiger (soprano, 27) is cast as Micaela.

Cavill appeared in the doorway, handed Caroline a glass and put down his own. 'Leave it a minute. It's not warm enough.'

Caroline indicated the article. 'Isn't "international renown" a bit of an exaggeration in the women's cases?'

Cavill considered. 'Steiger hasn't done much yet. Rosie Goldsmith's the business, though.'

'Do you know her? You called her Rosie!'

'I adjudicated in a tin-pot musical festival over in south Lancashire a few years ago. She was head and shoulders above the competition. She must have been nineteen or twenty then—and in those days she was plain Rosemary Smith.'

'Was she plain?'

'As a matter of fact, physically she is a bit like you. A couple of years later I played for a *Messiah* with her in Cologne. She doesn't do much oratorio now she's making a name in opera. She's done Despina for Welsh National

2

and Gilda for ENO. I saw that. She was delicious. And she did a fabulous Mimi in Sydney last year.'

Caroline grinned. 'You're selling her hard. I'd better get Mr Blake to let you write the programme notes. Where's all the money coming from to bribe them here?'

'Read on.' Cavill indicated the paragraph half-way down the page.

All expenses of the projected production will be met from Mr Blake's £2 million lottery win which the *Clarion* reported in February. 'Maybe, before long,' Mr Blake confided to our reporter, 'we shall have opera flourishing in Cloughton that will be financed, not by a lottery win but with lottery grants. May our *Carmen* be the first of many.'

Caroline looked up. 'Sounds as though the Vic is going to host a succession of rival productions of the same opera.'

'That would be taking specialization a bit far.'

'It would save on sets and costumes.'

'Oh, no it wouldn't.' He handed her her glass, nodding his approval of its temperature. 'Actually, I could almost see it happening. *Carmen* has been a set piece for years. Directors nowadays are seeing it as a bit of a challenge—they have to "put their seal on it".

I should think your scheme would soon tire an audience, though.'

Caroline drank gratefully. 'Do you like it? The opera, I mean.'

He shrugged. 'Yes. No. Plenty of good tunes but no real magic—not for me anyway. I wonder how Blake got Miles Cranmer to come.'

Caroline was not short of suggestions. 'Enormous fat fee? His dear old mother lives near here? Or, maybe, he's having a red hot affair with one of the two women.' She let her eyes run down the remainder of the article.

Cloughton Amateur Opera Group's last production, *Cavalleria Rusticana* with *I Pagliacci*, was presented in March this year. Principals were chosen for these two operas from the Group's Opera Chorus and the orchestra was drawn from the Cloughton Symphony Orchestra, augmented by some of Mr Blake's friends. Mr Blake refused to speculate about whether the same instrumentalists will play for *Carmen*.

There followed exhaustive curricula vitae of the three rising young singers.

'If it's money that's bringing the singers, do you think he'll bribe a decent orchestra as well? How much would it take to get a good one to commit professional suicide?'

4

Cavill declined to guess. 'If he can't offer enough, he'll lose his singers. They aren't going to give their all with the Cloughton lot vamping along half a beat behind them.'

Caroline passed her glass for refilling and asked with a deadpan face, 'How much are you going to hold out for when he comes to you?'

'They don't need an organist for *Carmen*.'

'No, but they need a children's choir, don't they?' He was silent for a long time and she added, 'Tempted?'

He thought about it. 'Depends whether the idea appeals to the boys—and how the whole affair shapes up. Anyhow, I haven't been invited.'

Caroline smiled as she got up to inspect Cavill's shopping. 'Oh, you will be. He'll not let the local celebrity off the hook, you can be sure of that.'

CHAPTER ONE

October 2002

On a Friday evening in October, outside a Cloughton supermarket, several shoppers took a break from stowing their purchases away in their car boots to appreciate the entertainment provided by Detective Constable Adrian Clement. Apart from a grin and a salute, Clement ignored them and continued to apply himself in earnest to his bending and stretching. He knew that his young running partner, when he turned up, late, as always, would complete their allotted miles marginally more quickly than he would himself.

It was only a few months since he'd winkled Jonathan away from the crowd of young troublemakers that haunted the central precinct each evening and taught him the basics of good running. At first, the lad had moved stiffly, pounding along with gritted teeth, tense shoulders and hands punching the air. Embarrassed by the barracking of his former friends, he had wanted to give up.

Clement had taken his problem seriously. 'OK. After tonight, we'll switch to early mornings. Your pals won't be up and, with any luck, my work won't have started.' This had been a big sacrifice for the DC. The hours between first light and breakfast were precious time when he did his serious training. He had received two rewards for it. One was a genuine delight in seeing the boy realize his natural ability. The other was a torrent of information from the lad's artless chatter about the petty and sometimes not so petty crimes perpetrated by his mates in 'the gang'. It had led to at least one arrest to his own credit.

Looking up from an impatient consultation of his watch, Clement saw Jonathan limping towards him across the supermarket car park, their habitual meeting place. When the boy's painful progress brought him near enough, Clement saw that he was sporting a bloodshot and swollen eye and a split lip. He kept his enquiry low-key. 'In the wars, were you?' Jonathan nodded, seemingly unperturbed. 'Did you ask for it?'

Now the boy was indignant. 'Me dad didn't do it.' Clement knew that the Stepney parents were genuinely fond of their son and concerned for his welfare. Jonathan appreciated this, even though, in Mr Stepney's book, the good parent's remedy for any erring or straying on his offspring's part was 'a bloody good leathering'. 'It were Shaun.'

'So, what does *he* look like now?'

Jonathan was tempted to describe an epic struggle, then thought better of it. 'You know he's a better scrapper 'n me.' Clement bit back further enquiries, knowing that the whole story would follow. 'He knows I'm your nark, see.'

8

Clement was a little alarmed, but asked, merely, 'He's never done it before. Why now?'

'Because he thinks I'm on to summat.'

'And are you?'

Jonathan looked glum. 'Wish I knew as much as he thinks I do.'

Clement deactivated his central locking system and reached into the car for cans of Coke, handing one to the boy. 'So, what exactly do you know?'

Jonathan pulled the can's ring and drank noisily. 'He's flush,' he announced, between mouthfuls. 'Chucking it around as though there's no tomorrow.'

'So where did he get it?'

Jonathan shrugged, then winced and rubbed his bruised shoulder. 'Don't know.'

'I thought you were going straight now, not seeing him.'

Jonathan glared. 'I am! I have to see him at school, though—when he's not laykin', that is. Then I saw him Wednesday night. I was doing the ten-miler I do with you, with the last four along the canal bank. I came down that snicket to it, going past that posh pub, the Silver Swan.' He tossed his empty can to the ground, felt Clement's glower and bent painfully to pick it up. 'There's a bog in the far corner of the car park there. I nipped in and there was Shaun with a fat roll of tenners. Shoved it in his pocket sharpish but when I first saw him he were counting it.'

'So, you asked him where he got it and he slapped you about a bit?'

Jonathan shook his head cautiously, rubbing the protesting muscles in his neck. 'Nah! Never opened me mouth. He just did it as a warning.'

'But you're still telling me.'

'Well, you asked.'

Clement's misgivings increased. He'd been grateful for Jonathan's loose tongue but so were the embryo villains who were his friends. Clement had been careful never to discuss any aspect of a case with the lad, other than the particular piece of information he wanted to establish or disprove. Now he began to realize that Jonathan saw the two of them as on equal terms. The boy's naivety had its advantages and disadvantages for both sides.

'You're my running partner,' he said, at last. 'Why did Shaun call you a nark?'

'He says even somebody as stupid as me wouldn't play games with the filth if there wasn't any money in it.'

Clement blinked. 'Are you asking me to pay you?'

Now Jonathan was insulted. 'I've never asked you for owt! Besides, you teach me running and buy me Stellas.' Clement grinned and ignored the hint. 'If you ask me, I think he's jealous.'

'What of?'

'He wants to do a bit o' tale-telling himself.'

10

'We couldn't pay him rolls of tenners.'

Jonathan's nose wrinkled. 'No, but he likes being cock o' the walk, both sides lickin' 'is boots, like.'

Clement shied his own can into a refuse bin. 'So, what do you want to do now?'

'Well, not the ten-miler . . .'

'You're not running at all!'

'But I could, a bit . . .'

'What have I told you about running through injuries?'

Jonathan shrugged again, grimaced and rubbed his shoulder. 'OK. The old man's been goin' on about teaching me to play chess. Might as well keep in the good books.' Clement hid a grin. He would not have put money on Jonathan's giving Mr Stepney a good—or even a bad—game. 'But when can we start running again?'

Clement considered. 'I'll meet you Monday night. See how you're moving by then. Not a long run though. We'll have to work back to that.'

'Cheers, then.' The boy slouched off towards his home in the block of flats that could be seen above the row of houses facing the car park.

Clement stood for a few moments, musing on the chequered friendship between Jon Stepney and Shaun Grant. He didn't know exactly how IQ scores were measured, but his layman's estimate was that Shaun's would double Jon's. Both boys lived in Sainted City—police-speak for a notorious quartet of tower blocks dedicated to an obscure quartet of saints. Nominally, they both attended the Colin Hewitt Comprehensive School, where they were assigned to the same class.

He could think of little else they had in common. Shaun's father had deserted his family years ago and his mother had sought the consolation of a succession of uncles. Nowadays, the uncles were more afraid of Shaun than he was of them. His mother protected and cared for him to the extent of hurling abuse at any policeman who dared to accuse him. Shaun was content with this arrangement and used his considerable wits to turn this and all other circumstances to his advantage.

For some reason, the DCI had a soft spot for Shaun, and Clement had to admit that if you forgot his well-earned reputation for antisocial behaviour the boy was an amusing companion. He liked the idea of recruiting young Grant as an informer, though his intelligence would be a questionable advantage to the police. He would always know exactly what kind of villainy was going on but he was sharp enough too to fool both sides.

Clement also liked the idea of doing a bit of freelance detective work at the Silver Swan. He knew it would bring him further into disfavour with his sergeant who always played by the book. On the other hand, if even half of what he'd heard about the past career of Acting DCI Mitchell was true, he'd be safe. As a detective chief inspector, he'd have to recommend sending an officer Shaun didn't know to gather intelligence at the pub. However, if Clement could sort out what Shaun Grant was involved in and present it to him with everything sorted out, the DCI would be a bit—no, a lot—of a hypocrite if he made trouble for him with his superiors.

The Swan was by the canal, surrounded by an upmarket estate of 'executive' houses. Clement had been there before, his object then being to annoy its smug, middle-class clientele with his steaming, sweaty, post-run person. They'd only think he was doing it again. Drugs seemed the obvious things to look for but he couldn't believe the management was aware of any dealing that might be going on within its hallowed walls. They were making far too much money legitimately to risk closure.

Since by now he'd cooled down again, Clement repeated his warm-up exercises and contemplated a satisfying evening's entertainment. Ten miles to log in his training book, the pleasure of annoying the nobs again, a couple of pints of excellent draught bitter and, maybe, an opening into the local brown trade.

*　　　*　　　*

That same evening, in Cloughton's Victoria
Theatre, the dress rehearsal of the town's
amateur opera company's much-vaunted
production of Bizet's *Carmen* was about to
begin. The *Cloughton Clarion*'s editor liked to
refer to himself as a 'culture-vulture', and he
had insisted that the paper's weekly arts page
should faithfully report every stage of its
preparation. Lauren Hardy, who had formerly
sung in the company's chorus and whose
charge the *Clarion*'s arts section was, had done
the reporting personally. It had been an
enjoyable assignment and she was sorry that,
as the first night approached, it was drawing to
its end.

She smiled, remembering the interview with
her editor in chief. 'You'd better tell the
morons what the show's about,' he had advised
her. 'Most of 'em won't know *Carmen* from
Carmen Jones—or Carmen Miranda, come to
that.'

Lauren had determined—and remembered
—to find out about Ms Miranda, but had not
asked about her at the time. Mr Flynn had
been in garrulous mood and Lauren had had
work to do. She had also refrained from
pointing out that *Carmen Jones* was an
adaptation of Bizet's opera and that a
knowledge of its plot would serve admirably as

14

background for the pieces she was about to write.

Sharing his opinion of the *Clarion*'s readers, she had tried to summarize the action sufficiently briefly to accommodate their short concentration span. All her attempts had been unsatisfactorily confusing. In desperation, she had resorted to the music section of the public library and a fat dictionary of opera.

Never having considered plagiarism a sin, she had been well pleased with her plunder. 'The gypsy girl Carmen at first attracts, then discards the young officer, Don José; when he cannot win her back he stabs her to death.' Surely that was sufficiently short and simple. She had added three commas to the borrowed sentence and considered she had made it her own. It was a pity that this bald statement of the two, possibly three, facts would give her readers no idea of the vital, colourful, passionate creation that was *Carmen*. Nor would it give them any conception of the free-loving spitfire of a brazen hussy that was Bizet's gypsy girl.

As these phrases flickered through her mind, Lauren had liked them. She had jotted them in her notebook, planning to weave them in somewhere among the seven hundred and fifty words that Mr Flynn had allocated to that week's piece.

Tonight, after much thought, she had decided to observe the dress rehearsal from

15

the front of house. Tomorrow, the opening night, she would report from backstage. What happened from the audience's view would be pretty much the same both times. Any behind-the-scenes crisis with critics and dignitaries sitting in the front row of the circle would be more dramatic news than a mere dress rehearsal disaster.

It was still only half-past six—an hour to go yet. Someone in the orchestra pit was busy tuning the piano. Raising her eyes to the stage, Lauren re-examined the set. It resembled the inner view of half a gasometer. Ladders at intervals round it rose twenty feet or so from the boards. After eight weeks of rehearsal, she had still not quite fathomed out what it was supposed to be.

The stage crew was having noisy fun in the wings and someone was whistling off-key. The youth singing Remendado, whose name she had forgotten, walked on stage, clad already in the miserable khaki uniform of a modern soldier but not yet made up.

There was the sound of a vacuum cleaner and a workman was sweeping the stage, wielding a broom with a three-foot row of bristles. A pony-tailed stagehand brought the vacuum cleaner into view and cleaned up what the sweeper had left. Then, satisfied with the state of the boards, they departed. Now two shaven-headed men arrived to test the mechanism of the sliding gates that, at several

16

points in the performance, closed off the lower level of the 'gasometer'. Maybe dust had to be prevented from jamming the works.

In the pit, the piano tuner had departed and the conductor, Cavill Jackson, stood by his rostrum, conferring with two members of the orchestra. Cavill was demolishing a meat pie. After a minute he wandered up on to the stage, still eating, and Lauren wondered if his crumbs would necessitate a further assault with the three-foot broom. He was chewing the last morsel as Lewis Blake, the moving spirit of the company and this production, hurried on stage. There seemed to be a problem. The body language of the two men suggested that each was refusing the other's solution to it. Splendid. Now things were livening up. Lauren's ball-point scurried across her page.

*   *   *

Cavill Jackson pulled out a crumpled but clean handkerchief and wiped the grease from his lips and fingers as he contemplated Lewis Blake. He was surprised to see the man so agitated. At the beginning of this enterprise, he had expected Blake to be nervous. He was giving instructions to singers who were used to being directed by experienced professionals. Any amateur musician would have felt overawed. Instead, the man had been excited

17

and confident. He had also been much more imaginative, sensitive and proficient than Cavill had expected.

But then, rather than growing in assurance, he had become increasingly anxious. He appeared to expect, at every turn, that something would go wrong. Now he was in a flat spin because his diva had not reported to him a good hour before this final rehearsal was due to begin. Cavill put his handkerchief back in his pocket and a calming hand on Blake's arm. 'But none of the others is here yet.'

Blake shook the hand away impatiently. 'Miles and Ursula are. And Ashley.' Cavill remembered that Ashley was the spotty youth from the chorus who was making rather a fine job of singing Remendado. 'The principals very generously agreed to be dressed and made up early because most of the chorus and the minor roles are still at work till half-past five. Some of them have to feed their families even after that, so they can't be here till the last minute.

'Rosie agreed to be got ready first, bless her. The car was picking her up from her hotel at half-past five. There was no sign of her. No one has seen her since just after breakfast.'

'So? It's a lovely day. She probably went for a walk and forgot the time. Did you look in the hotel gardens? Who went to collect her?'

'Tim, and he looked everywhere.'

'Well, give her another ten minutes, then

we'll decide what to do. She'll have turned up by then, or, if she hasn't, then Deborah can sing again. For Act 1 she wouldn't even need to change. After all, the understudy is the one more in need of practice.'

Cavill could see that Blake was bitterly disappointed by this cool reaction. What on earth did the man expect him to do? Wave his baton and produce the errant prima donna out of the air? He grinned at him. 'If it makes you feel any better, spend the ten minutes rehearsing the dressing-down you'll give Rosie when she turns up.'

Blake was becoming angry as well as worried. 'She's not like that. It'll be something important that's keeping her. She's never messed us about. She's not temperamental at all!'

'Then try to be like her,' Cavill retorted impatiently and strode away. He resolutely ignored the mute appeal from the fifth row in the stalls for information about the disagreement. Lauren sighed, then scribbled an observation on first-night nerves and fraught atmospheres.

*   *   *

Clement's run had disappointed him. He had taken almost two minutes more than his best time for the course. The draught bitter, however, had been well up to standard and the

19

reactions of the clientele of the Silver Swan to his perspiring body had been exactly as expected. The bar had been crowded but, as he drank deep from his first pint, the stools on either side of him had been pointedly vacated. After that first huge swallow he had sipped contentedly, watching his fellow drinkers through half-shut eyes and without any obvious turning of his head.

After a couple of minutes, the stool on his right was occupied again and he turned to find Shaun Grant grinning at him. 'I was going to pinch a couple of bottles when the bar staff were busy down the other end, but, now you're here, can you lend me a couple of quid?' He was less roughly spoken than Jonathan. When in less benign mood than at present, though, he was much more fluent in obscenities and blasphemies.

Clement had returned the grin. 'For your cheek, I'll buy you one. A Coke.'

'Make it a shandy?'

Clement had asked for another pint of the draught for himself and a half of mild. 'Come on, we'll drink outside. Then, if my boss drops in, you can pour yours on the grass.'

'Like hell I can. Do you come here often?'

'Only when I smell bad enough to offend the punters.'

Shaun had liked that. 'Nice one.' They had drunk in companionable silence for a while and Clement had transferred his attention to the pub's prettified façade. The view was spoiled by an ugly but serviceable steel bridge across the canal that allowed the people from the 'executive' housing complex on the far side to patronize the bar without inconvenience. People from all over Cloughton, and from some districts a good way beyond, came by car and the parking area had been extended twice. The second 'improvement' had risked offending householders in the older, sought-after properties behind the inn by encroaching on their gardens.

The building was in fine fettle, covered in a pale cream wash which was freshened every few months. The sign was discreet, gold on black, running below a row of first-storey windows and just big enough to be easily read. The window sills all sprouted matching trailing plants. A lane and the canal path separated the building from the water but it was close enough for the upper storeys to be photogenically reflected. The general impression was of respectability and prosperity.

Clement turned back to his companion. 'So, what brings you here? Don't tell me it's because you like the way it's tarted up.'

Shaun's face was deadpan. 'Saw you chatting up Jonno outside Tesco's so I came to keep an eye on you keeping an eye open for me. Thanks for the drink. I'll just take these back. Save the barmaid's legs for better things.'

He grabbed their glasses and disappeared through the crowd towards the bar.

Clement made a vow to himself to tackle the youngster and find out who was paying him for what. In the meantime, having failed his ten-mile time, he felt restless, in need of immediate action. He decided to make an attempt on his flat three-mile record. He was reasonably rested and rehydrated, even though beer had not been the ideal liquid for the job.

Promising himself he would atone with several pints of water with his supper, he got up, stowed his wallet away in his bum bag and walked back the few yards to the ugly bridge. He had measured the three miles from there to Tesco's car park soon after his arrival in Cloughton. Quite a few of his habitual routes ended there and the supermarket manager and security staff were now used to ignoring his lonely vehicle.

It had been one of early October's gift days. After a week of autumn gales, the morning had dawned calm and bright. People had reopened their windows and got out their summer clothes again. Now, Clement paused momentarily, his back to the still-warm steel. Did he really want to do this? Above him, a sky like curdled strawberry blancmange inclined him to idleness. The canal water was still and clouded, but the sluices that fed it splashed and chattered and broke the surface, giving an illusion of flowing. He spoke to himself sternly. If his three miles broke sixteen minutes, he could forget the ten-mile failure and go to bed happy. He began to run.

Though the heat of the afternoon had lessened, perspiration streamed and Clement felt as if he were breathing in warm water. By the time he reached the marina, he knew he had overrun himself. His ears were ringing. Suddenly, blackness swirled. He reached out and held on to the trunk of a sapling as unsteady as himself. Doubling over, he fertilized it with his two pints of draught. He felt better then and his vision cleared. The ringing, though, went on. After a second, it dawned on him that the sound was not continuous. Two rings and a pause. It was a telephone.

He looked around for the owner. The Asian boatyard owner and his mate, who had been lying on the roof of one of the narrow boats when he'd passed in the opposite direction, had disappeared. The man and the girl who had been working on another had gone home. He thought the phone had rung six times now. Intrigued, he followed the sound which was coming from further up the bank.

The ringing stopped just as he had traced it to the back of a huge clump of brambles. Skirting the tentacles that reached out to rip his skin, he saw a rough wooden bench. He stopped and blinked, dazzled by the low sun. He had to step nearer before he realized that

23

the heap in front of it was the collapsed body of a young woman. Approaching, he grasped her shoulder, lifting her slightly. She was dead, her throat cut deeply and decisively.

His faintness returned and, for a few seconds, he rested his head, cushioned by an arm, on the hot wood of the bench. Flies buzzed around the two of them. A moment ago he had been suffering from the heat of the day and of his exertions. Now, suddenly, he was shivering with cold. After some seconds he forced himself to raise his head and look at the woman again. No, it wasn't her. Thank God.

Relief flooded him, incapacitating him for a moment longer, then he sat back on his heels. What first? He thought that most of the blood from the wound had been absorbed by the parched ground. Strawy grass blades were sticky but not wet. The murder had happened some little time ago. There was no point in looking for a killer to chase now.

The mobile phone began to ring again. He located it under the bench and placed it on top, picking it up by its cord. Better not press the receiving button with his finger. Fishing his car keys out of his bum bag, he used them to connect himself with the caller and found he was breathless. 'Yes?'

The strangled gasp had given him an advantage. It had not apparently sounded masculine. 'Rosie! Where the hell are you?'

He tried to prolong the gasping. 'On the

24

canal bank.'

'Have you had an accident? Oh shit! Will you be able to go on? I'll send the car. Where exactly . . . ?'

Clement cut in in his normal voice. 'Who's speaking, please?'

The babbling was succeeded by silence. Clement could hear the man thinking, trying to control his panic. 'You must know perfectly well who I am. What have you done to Rosie? Are you really on the canal?'

Clement spoke slowly and soothingly. 'I'm a policeman.' He gave his name and rank. 'Yes, I'm really on the canal bank. So is a lady who is a stranger to me. Can you tell me what Rosie looks like?'

'Everyone knows what she . . .' There was a pause, then the voice continued more calmly. 'Rosanne Goldsmith is singing *Carmen* for me at the Vic tomorrow. She should be singing at the dress rehearsal now. The *Clarion*'s been full of pictures of her.'

'I'd still like you to describe her.'

'Very striking. Long dark hair and sort of hazel eyes, greeny brown, a bit slanting . . .'

'How tall is she?'

'Five five, five six? She seems taller because she walks like a model—or a ballet dancer. What's *happened* to her? We've started the rehearsal with her understudy.'

'Are you at the Vic now?'

The voice became impatient. 'I'm *Lewis*

25

Blake!'

Clement remained patient. 'Mr Blake, are you at—'

'Of course I am! I'm directing the confounded rehearsal—or I'm supposed to be. All I've actually been doing is ringing Rosie's mobile number non-stop.'

'Right. Please will you continue your rehearsal, preferably without telling anyone you've spoken to me. If it finishes before our officers arrive, please ask everyone to wait for us.'

'But will I have Rosie back for the opening?'

Clement sighed. 'I wouldn't count on it.' He pressed the button on Blake's rising hysteria and took his own cell phone from his bum bag to summon his colleagues.

CHAPTER TWO

On that Friday evening, since he was not on duty in his official capacity, Acting Detective Chief Inspector Benedict Mitchell had volunteered his services as nurse. He knew that he was hardly an ornament to his temporary profession. On the other hand, he knew that Hannah would be satisfied with the best that he could do for her whilst her daughter and son enjoyed a rare free evening and her husband slept off one of his migraine attacks.

Mitchell was fond of his mother-in-law and she of him. The cruel disease had first attacked her more than a year ago and he and she were now beyond the embarrassment caused by her increasing dependence on others for her physical needs. He would cheerfully wash her and prepare her for bed when the time came. He was thankful though that his brother-in-law, who was a qualified nurse, had given her the last meal she would require today, so that he was spared coping with one of her alarming episodes of choking.

He had ejected, with commendable tact, at least for him, an insensitive visitor, though not before she had upset Hannah by revealing shock and revulsion at the deterioration she could see since her last visit. When the woman had departed with a crass, 'Hope you'll feel better soon,' Hannah had produced a travesty of a laugh and averted Mitchell's explosion of anger.

She spoke to him through the computer software that the family between them had provided as soon as Hannah's speech therapist had mentioned it. He had warned that in less than a couple of months she would be beyond using even that but it would not matter. The device would have served its purpose.

Mitchell was wondering whether it would tire Hannah too much to be wheeled out into the garden to enjoy the evening air, when the

27

call from Clement came through. For the first time ever, he listened to his summons to a murder scene with a sinking heart. Usually, it was a welcome call to action. Not that he had ever wished anybody dead, but once a murder hunt had begun, that was never any longer an issue. The deed was done and the hunt for a killer was on.

He listened carefully to the information that Clement was giving him, then made the calls that would set the whole procedure of an investigation in motion. He noted ruefully Clement's evident puzzlement at the news that Mitchell himself might be delayed. Now he picked up the phone again and rang his own home number.

'Ginny? Adrian's found a woman with her throat cut . . . On the canal bank.'

Virginia was silent for a moment, absorbing her disappointment. Then she was assuring him that his absence could be covered, that the tasks for which he'd volunteered could be delegated. He left for the crime scene with grave misgivings.

It was ten minutes' drive from his in-laws' to the spot that Clement had so precisely described. For five of them, Mitchell worried about his family. For the other five, with his personal troubles far to the back of his mind, he mentally rehearsed the procedure his team was about to follow. The habitual excitement was rising.

*   *   *

Although it would mean a late finish to everyone's evening, Lewis Blake had decreed that the dress rehearsal, as well as the public performances of his production, should have a full twenty-five-minute interval at the end of Act 2. His singers would need a rest. The two professionals were not using full voice but saving themselves for the first night. Blake had bidden his company members to do the same, but they were used to giving him their all and, as he had expected, were having difficulty in restraining themselves tonight.

Now the curtain had come down on the killing of Zuniga and Don José's desertion, from the army into the smugglers' band. The show was half over and the orchestra, cast and officials retired to the rehearsal room, where willing volunteers had prepared suitable refreshments.

Lauren Hardy went with them. She knew that Blake's version of the plot was a far cry from the text that Bizet had actually set to music. She had carefully checked it out at the beginning of her assignment. Then she had decided that the *Clarion*'s readers would have no interest in her research. They were concerned only with the performance that would take place in their own theatre. They would have no truck with Mérimée's novelette

29

which had become the versified libretto by Meilhac and Halévy that the composer had used. Nor would they care about the 1990s adaptation into English which Lewis Blake had chosen, not so much to use as to take liberties with.

She compared the grim scene she had just witnessed with other, more traditional productions she had seen. The music here supported the traditional interpretation. It was light-hearted, the phrases, praising the freedom of an outlaw's life, much repeated as the characters, in high spirits, threw the tune from one part to another. Then, all wanting to speak at once, the voices joined in bars of joyous chorus. The musical mood Bizet had established was totally at odds with the black and sordid world Blake had created, with the smugglers cutting Zuniga's throat in cold blood on the stage.

Deciding it was a good job that Bizet was long dead, Lauren nodded her thanks to the chorus member who had brought her a glass of orange juice. He beamed at her. 'Are you giving us a good write-up? We're good, aren't we?'

Lauren suddenly realized that the singing and acting of these amateurs had been exceedingly good. Their *Carmen* was far better than their last production which she had reviewed the previous year. Had they learned from watching the three guest professionals, or maybe been challenged by them? Possibly they were lifted by the inspired direction of their leader. Blake was now unfettered by financial considerations and able to give free rein to his conception. She smiled at the youth who was waiting for the praise he had demanded and assured him that he would be pleased with her review.

In their intoxication with their own excellence, some of the chorus had quite forgotten the mysterious disappearance of their guest singer. Not so her replacement, of course. Deborah Murdoch was surrounded by a complimentary crowd which now separated to allow Blake to pass through to offer his own congratulations. He had a different message, however. 'Whatever you do, Debbie, don't oversing tonight.' Some of her friends were offended on her behalf, but Deborah saw the half-promise in his words.

Lauren watched the girl trying to conceal her excitement at the prospect of singing a leading role in the presence of distinguished critics. Then she sat back and let her eyes wander. This place had once been the Assembly Room. In the first decade of the twentieth century, when Cloughton's Victoria Theatre had been richly patronized, those patrons had retired here, during the intervals of performances, so as not to have to mix with the hoi-polloi in the public bars. Now the hall was sadly shabby. Since the original stained glass windows had been vandalized and boarded up, the huge room was lit only by broken chandeliers with approximately a third of their bulbs working. Panelled walls and a ceiling ornate with bands of gilded fruits, leaves and ribbons, indicated something of the makeshift rehearsal room's former glory.

She looked up and smiled as she saw that Miles Cranmer, also afforded passage through the mêlée of chorus members, was congratulating a dazed-looking Deborah. The company's substitute Carmen was not, Lauren knew, the only woman to make a bid for his attention in the hope of promoting her career by becoming intimate with him.

Cranmer had not been flattered by these attentions, nor by those of Ursula Steiger. Ignoring them, he had made it plain that, at least for the duration of this production, his affections were engaged by Miss Goldsmith. He'd be unlucky there, though. Lauren had overheard Rosie telling Ursula, 'You're welcome to him. He's too small and well fleshed for me—and,' with a wrinkle of her lightly freckled nose, 'not sufficiently washed.'

Lauren sighed, reminding herself that her evening's work was only half done. She finished her juice, pencilled some more hieroglyphics, then, in obedience to a warning bell, went to resume her seat in the stalls and speculate further on Rosie Goldsmith's absence.

*   *   *

On the canal bank, Clement was not anxious for his colleagues to turn up promptly. He had a bit of business of his own to see to before any other officers arrived. He finished his conversation with his DCI, then punched the buttons again. 'Shakila? It's Adrian. Wherever you are, get down to the wharf beyond Crossley Bridge. There's a boatyard there, below the industrial estate. You can park up there and hop over the wall that skirts the canal.' He cut through her questions. 'There's a body here with its throat cut. No one mentioned you, but if you're on the scene before they start dishing jobs out, they'll set you on before anybody realizes . . . Think nothing of it. The pleasure's mine. Just get here.'

Whilst he was waiting, an elderly man approached him from the opposite direction, looking about him and whistling. Seeing Clement, the man turned and began to mount the grassy slope between them. 'You haven't seen my dog, have you? Small black and white mongrel, lot of terrier—'

Clement interrupted him. 'Keep to the path, if you don't mind, sir.'

The man was indignant. 'Why should I?'

Clement came far enough down the slope for his warrant to be recognized. 'Perhaps you'd . . .' He broke off at a sound from behind him and turned to see Shakila, standing on the wall he had described to her and peering around in search of him. She climbed down and approached the two men by the route Clement indicated. It skirted the bench and the body which brambles screened from the older man's view. 'This is Mr . . . ?' He turned from Shakila to his companion on the path.

'Benton,' the man supplied. 'Harry Benton.'

'He's lost his dog.' Clement repeated its description until Benton interrupted. He spoke with his gaze fixed beyond the two officers, trying to see what they were hiding from him and seeming to spin out the conversation as he tried to guess what was afoot. 'I've been fishing all day, then called in at the Sovereign. Thought I'd round things off with a couple of pints. Josh sits beside me in the passenger seat. Don't suppose you lot approve of that. Anyway, as soon as I opened the door, he slipped across, between my legs and was off . . .'

By now, Shakila had her notebook out. 'Why did you think he'd be down here?'

'Because most nights he comes with me to meet my son and granddaughter. Hal, my son, is renovating Mr Patel's fleet of narrow boats. It's hard work and, generally, I meet him with the car. When it's wet, I park in the industrial estate.' He gestured up the bank. 'Hal and Gracie come over the wall, in the opposite direction to the way you did. When it's dry, I park at the Swan and walk along the towpath as I am doing now. It's a proper quagmire here on a wet day with this slope draining down into the canal.'

'So, where are they now, Hal and Gracie?'

Benton repeated patiently, 'I told you. I had a day's fishing. I said, if I wasn't back in time, that they had to make their own way. But the dog wasn't to know that . . .'

Shakila was pleased. 'So, you walk along here regularly? What sort of time?'

'Teatime.' He grinned. 'Grace has her face on all night if they're late and the tea spoils.'

Shakila grinned. 'Sounds like my mum. Who do you usually meet?'

Mr Benton rolled his eyes. 'Have you been listening? I meet Hal and Gra—'

'I hadn't forgotten that.' Hastily, Shakila made her question more precise. 'I just wondered who you passed, spoke to, maybe. You'd know about other people who might have been around here earlier this afternoon.'

Clement had wandered off and was squatting on the grass. Shakila glared at him as she noted all the information that Mr Benton offered, including his address. She was grateful for being alerted to the present situation, but impatient with her colleague's apparent lethargy and curious about his reason for involving her. Asking her witness to wait on the path until her inspector had had a chance

35

to speak to him, she wandered across to Clement. 'There's nothing much to do. Why don't you have a rest?'

Clement flushed. 'You were doing a good job on him. I didn't want to butt in.'

Shakila tossed her head and grabbed his wrist and he let her haul him to his feet. 'Right, let's look round. Look, dozens of condoms here. This is a favourite summer spot for prozzies. Not that she looks much like one.' She regarded the hunched body appraisingly. 'Too ladylike. Come on, we're modern archaeologists.'

'We're mucking the place up for the SOCOs—at least, you are.'

Ignoring him, Shakila continued her exploration. 'Somebody's had a fight with this sapling—and thrown up under it.'

Shamefacedly, Clement muttered, 'That was me. But it was nothing to do with the corpse. I hadn't seen it then.'

'Just drunk and disorderly?'

'On two pints? Oh, leave it. It's not important.' He made an effort to respond to her enthusiasm, pointing to the camera with its complicated-looking telephoto lens that lay on the grass on the far side of the body. 'That looks an expensive job. Let's hope the film's still in it.' With relief, he saw the Home Office Pathologist coming along the path. 'Ledgard's here.'

Shakila followed his gaze. 'And DS Taylor,

just turning out of the snicket.' She knew Clement would not be pleased and his sulky expression confirmed it.

'Trust her to be first off the mark.'

'She isn't, usually. Where's the DCI? Rumour is he gets a speeding ticket for every corpse he's called to, trying to beat everyone.' Shakila examined Clement more closely. There had to be some reason for his disorientation. 'Adrian, what on earth's up with you?'

'I thought it was Caroline. Same hair, same grey trousers, similar checked shirt.' Immediately, Clement wished he had remained silent. He turned on his heel and went to meet Dr Ledgard, indicating the body, face-down in front of the bench.

Ledgard was a man of few words. 'Touched it?'

Clement shook his head but qualified the negative. 'Checked for a pulse and I raised the head a bit—by the hair—to see if I knew her.'

Ledgard blinked. 'Thought I did myself, for a minute. Something of a likeness to one of your colleagues. Good job I was wrong.'

Clement nodded, swallowed. 'Caroline Webster.'

'That's right. Well, move over and give me room.'

Clement, gratefully dismissed, turned to face the equally unwelcome attentions of his sergeant. She checked with him what time he had discovered the body and asked for his observations so far.

Shakila covered his confusion, stepping forward with her notes on her conversation with the lost dog owner. Jennifer Taylor listened, approvingly. 'You seemed to find him interesting. How do you think he can help?'

Shakila considered. 'Not with what he's seen today—but he comes to meet his son most evenings. He's thinking about the people he sees who might have been there earlier, making a list for us. I don't think he's told us everything. He was annoyed because we didn't tell him what was going on, possibly keeping something back to bargain with. Or, maybe, he only pretended to.'

Jennifer Taylor nodded. 'Give him time to consider then. Send him home for now. Can you go back there later?'

Shakila nodded happily. 'Tonight?'

'No, leave him till tomorrow. Ah, here's Benny.' She turned away and up the hill to greet Mitchell who was arriving via the wall. He was followed by a quartet of beefy uniformed men bearing bales of luminous tape. They set about using it to mark off a sizeable area round the body, attaching it to convenient shrubs and a quantity of the stakes which the last of them carried.

More officers arrived, from both over the wall and along the path. Scene of Crime appeared in the form of a stooping, greying man and a trio of apparent teenagers, two of them female. A photographer prowled and his camera flashed.

Shakila watched Jennifer confer with them all and wondered how to busy herself. The sergeant was the detective most likely to notice and challenge her presence. She fumed inwardly as she watched the other officers milling awkwardly round the perimeter of the technicians' busyness. They reminded her of customers for a Sunday school trip whose coach had failed to collect them. She moved unobtrusively towards Clement. 'Where's DCI Mitchell been? What's more important than a corpse on a canal bank?'

'He's been as quick as most of the others. Anyway, it's personal.'

Shakila's jaw dropped. 'You're not telling me that the DCI's henpecked!' She had met Virginia Mitchell briefly at a recent sports meeting, expecting her to be Mitchell's age and shapeless from producing their four children. The woman had been a surprise to her, young, slim and marginally taller than her husband.

Shakila's musings were abandoned as Mitchell came over to his team. He offered neither apology nor explanation. 'We'll need lights here in half an hour or so. Can you see to that, Adrian?' He watched Clement break away from the group and take out his phone. 'The super won't be back from Wakefield till late. I'll have a look at the body and a word with Ledgard . . .' He paused, reviewing their options. 'We can't start the usual house-to-house.'

The team appreciated his point. The canal in front of them was separated on the far side from a busy road by a fringe of shrubs and unhealthy-looking trees on a steep slope. Behind them was the stone wall and the maze of the industrial estate where Jennifer had already set half a dozen uniformed officers to search before the fading light gave out completely. Mitchell nodded in the direction out of town. 'The towpath doesn't hit civilization till it meets Swan Lane, in front of that fancy pub.'

'The Silver Swan?'

'Right. We'll send Adrian and Shakila up there. Tell them to order a drink and socialize first, see what the punters have noticed. They can interview the staff formally later on. A lot of people will have been drinking outside tonight.'

'So what are we doing?' Jennifer demanded.

Mitchell grimaced. 'When we've finished here, it had better be the Vic, little though I fancy listening to the life histories of a lot of prima donnas.'

Jennifer nodded her head towards the victim. 'Well, you'll have to follow up this one. Cheer up, Cavill will be there, and, with luck, Caroline as well.'

Mitchell beamed. 'Caroline's certainly there. I've spoken to her. She's looking and listening and saying nothing till we arrive.'

*   *   *

Virginia Mitchell did not resent her husband's defection to a murder scene. For all her twenty-six years, she had been a policeman's daughter and for eight of them a policeman's wife. Philosophically, she rang the friends with whom she had planned to spend an evening at the Grand Theatre in Leeds, glad, at least, that the party had consisted of three so that neither of the others had to go alone.

She gathered together the things she would need for her replanned evening, half listening to her mother-in-law's footsteps across the floor above and half reviewing her husband's cancelled programme to check whether there was anything she could not manage in his place. Unless her father had recovered sufficiently she would have to put her mother to bed.

Her mother-in-law came downstairs and into the kitchen. Virginia turned to her. 'I don't think I can lift Mum on my own.'

'Won't Alex help—if your father's no better?'

'He's playing tonight at the Swan. He'll have left by now.'

'Well then, either your father will get up or

Benny will have to stay and help you.'

Virginia was changing out of her theatre clothes into jeans and a sweatshirt and drinking the tea her mother-in-law had poured. 'The twins are sound asleep. You've put your Irish 'fluence on them. Could you have Caitlin and Declan in bed by half-past eight? I'd like to take them with me—they cheer Mum up, but they're too tired after a week at school.'

'You can entertain Hannah by telling her about Benny's new case.'

'Except that I know precious little about it.' This sounded ungracious, and Virginia continued hastily, 'The kids will be happy. They much prefer your Irish tales to the stories we read them.'

'I could have them tomorrow, give you a break. You're looking tired with all this worry about your mum.' The elder Mrs Mitchell patted her daughter-in-law's arm.

Virginia cringed. Her mother-in-law had made a career of raising three sons and three daughters and was always ready to extend her mothering to anyone else she considered in need of it. The Brownes had been a much less tactile family, expressing their genuine concern for each other in practical ways.

'Actually, it's Dad and the children that I'm concerned about. I don't exactly worry about my mother. The MND has progressed more quickly than the doctors expected. She's going

42

to die in a few weeks. There's nothing I or anyone else can do about it. It's hard to bear, but it's not a worry.' She grinned. 'I haven't time to get philosophical. I'll have to go. Thanks again for being here.'

Niamh Mitchell watched her daughter-in-law dash down the path to her car and drive off rather more quickly than was wise for a police wife. Then she gathered up Virginia's discarded finery and replaced it neatly in the wardrobe. She had often wondered, as he grew up, what sort of woman would settle for her outspoken, intelligent, impatient, intolerant but well-meaning third son. She hadn't expected her to be a slip of a girl, just out of school, Benny's CI's daughter. Nor had she expected him, with his good Irish Catholic upbringing, to seduce her so that she came down pregnant from her second term at Oxford—and both of them unrepentant. It had worked, though. He had turned out to be a good picker, after all.

*   *   *

A stagehand waited to let Mitchell, Jennifer and several constables into the Victoria Theatre. He gestured towards the main auditorium before disappearing into the nether regions. Jennifer's eyes followed him. 'They obviously picked someone not agog for all the gossip—or else he's needed for scene shifting.'

Mitchell shook his head. 'He'll have been ordered to warn the director chap that we're here.' This was confirmed immediately. Lewis Blake came towards them from the stairs leading up to the circle. He asked, without preamble, 'She's dead, isn't she?'

Mitchell was making a mental inventory of the man. Late thirties, probably. Perspiring heavily—not surprising, considering his leather jacket and crew-necked sweater. Receding hair. More like a mechanic than a musician.

When it became obvious that her DCI was not going to answer, Jennifer said, 'I'm afraid she is.'

Immediately, Blake turned on his heel and disappeared back up the staircase. Mitchell nodded to one of the uniformed men to follow him. He spoke quietly as the man passed him. 'Hole him up somewhere apart from the rest and keep him on ice.'

Loud music told them the rehearsal was still under way. The two senior officers slipped into the back of the stalls, unnoticed in all the comings and goings, except by DC Caroline Webster, who got up from her seat beside Lauren Hardy and came to speak to them.

Jennifer asked, 'Are we letting it run to the end?'

Mitchell considered. 'We might have more co-operative witnesses if we do. How much more is there? Is this the end?' he added, hopefully, as the majority of the people on stage disappeared through the exits, right and left, leaving just two singers to face each other.

'Only another few minutes.' Caroline was placating. 'Carmen's nicely fixed up with her new bloke and now the old one's come to get her back.'

'So, does it all end happily?'

'No, he kills her.'

'Bad loser, eh? They're making a meal of it.' Mitchell cheered up suddenly as the chorus reappeared on the top tier of the odd-looking piece of scenery to sing a snatch of the toreador's music. 'Hey, I know this bit.'

'Most people can hum chunks of *Carmen* without knowing what it is.'

'There, he's got his ring back. Curtains!'

Caroline laughed. 'Not yet, I'm afraid, but we are getting to the dying groans. He gets arrested for killing her—and the death penalty. There's a flourish from Cavill's fiddlers, then it's over.'

Mitchell grinned. Caroline was as deeply into all this stuff as Cavill was, but she was reasonable about it, used terms everybody could understand. Now, at last, the curtain fell, the lights went up and he hurried forward to issue his orders.

CHAPTER THREE

Mitchell had no problem in collecting the whole company into the rehearsal room when the performance ended. They gravitated to it instinctively, as the centre of their last few weeks' activities. He sent Jennifer to begin interviewing Blake, set the rest of his officers to collecting names and addresses, then approached Cavill Jackson. 'Is there somewhere quiet and comfortable?'

Cavill nodded without speaking, then led him down a steep and narrow staircase to a corridor flanked by dressing rooms. The doors were open and none of them looked hospitable. Cavill took the nearest and they seated themselves in lumpy chairs. After some seconds of silence, he asked, 'What do you want me to tell you?'

Mitchell shrugged. 'I'm not sure yet. I'm in a foreign country. Tell me whatever you think is interesting or relevant.'

'You've read the *Clarion* pieces?'

'Some of them.' Mitchell could see that Cavill was not finding his attitude helpful.

'All right. For a start, there's no way that Blake's going to achieve the ambitions he claimed in those articles—not without another massive cash input, anyway.'

Mitchell was surprised. 'He's got through

two million already?'

Cavill smiled. 'It's a standing jump he's taken. The money would have gone further if he'd already been running. The bribes had to be big. Basically, I think he's just on a huge ego trip.'

'So, what's your excuse?'

Cavill thought about the question. 'Partly the chance to conduct. I've never tried it, except with my church choir.'

'Was it a secret longing?'

'I'm not sure. I'm thoroughly enjoying it though, and the norm is to go on doing it into your eighties.'

'Can't you play the organ till then?'

'In theory, but you'd do it less well. You lose flexibility in your fingers before you lose your rhythm and timing and your ability to wave your arms about.' Cavill remembered Virginia's mother and bit his lip.

'Go on.' Mitchell's anxiety to put Cavill at his ease had complex causes. His first conversation with this talented, likeable—and innocent—man had been in the course of his duties and with Cavill in the role of a murder suspect. Now, he was the person most likely to have his finger on the pulse of this whole enterprise. He was also the person who would, in the near future, become the husband of one of his much-valued DCs.

'Most of my family who're older than me have become arthritic and I suppose it'll happen to me.'

'You don't think there's enough public support for Blake to continue as he hopes?' Cavill shook his head. 'So, what's the point?'

'I've just said. He's in the news. The press loves him. He saw himself able to name-drop at dinner parties for the rest of his life— "When I engaged Goldsmith and Cranmer for my *Carmen* . . ." I'm not sure he'll want to now, of course.'

'Are you sorry you got involved?'

Cavill shook his head. 'Oh no. The boys have had an exciting time and a lot of good experience. I, personally, have just got keen on giving Cloughton one hell of a musical experience.'

'Pity, they'll miss it now.'

'No way. Blake's planning to go on tomorrow.'

Mitchell sniffed derisively. 'Claiming it as a mark of respect, I suppose. "This one is for Rosie."'

'You've quoted him exactly. You aren't going to stop him, are you?'

'I can't, at the moment, see any reason to. It seems you've spoken to him since we told you Miss Goldsmith was dead.'

Cavill was irritated. 'Why not? It's surely his business. According to Amanda, Mrs Tyler, in the ticket office, it's now a sell-out for tomorrow and Tuesday. The other performances are filling up too.'

'Why isn't it a straight run of consecutive evenings?'

'To give their voices a rest, especially the non-professional ones. They aren't trained to sing at full throttle night after night. Also, our run has to avoid a *Gerontius* that Ursula's singing in Leeds, a modern French recital Miles is doing in London and a Baroque recital that Rosie should have been doing in York Minster on Friday with me playing the interludes.'

'I imagine I'll be asked to turn that into a straight organ recital.' Cavill smiled. 'It'll be interesting to see whether I'm confirmed as second best by the punters wanting some of their money back. Blake's scared stiff now that all the critics from the national papers won't turn up.'

'Will they?'

'Who knows? Not many reporters, however arty and specialized, can afford to ignore sensational news. We'll probably even get a few extra, but they might be more concerned with the dramatic circumstances than with the quality of the music.'

Mitchell heaved a silent sigh of relief as, after a tap at the door, Caroline's head appeared round it. Cavill had given him a useful bit of background to Blake, and probably had more to offer, but keeping the conversation from sounding like the third degree whilst simultaneously keeping him from slipping into incomprehensible technicalities was wearing.

Caroline addressed him rather than her fiancé. 'They've sung themselves dry. They're willing to hang around but they want to open the green room.'

Mitchell beamed. 'Good idea. Can you go and persuade them to bring some coffee in here, then come back and join us.' He turned back to Cavill. 'How do you rate the substitute Carmen?'

'Deborah? Rather good, actually, though not on a par with Goldsmith as she is now. I heard Rosie in a local competition when she was about Deborah's age but I can't remember enough to compare them.'

'She didn't impress you back then?'

'Oh, she did. I can remember quite clearly my reaction to her songs—but that's all I remember, my feelings, not the details of her performance. She was Rosemary Smith in those days.'

'So, Rosanne Goldsmith is a professional name?'

'You're getting quite quick on the uptake for a copper.'

'So, who'll know about her?'

Cavill leaned back in his chair and closed his eyes to think. 'I'd start with her agent. Blake will have the details.' After a pause, he opened his eyes to add, 'He's a canny beggar.' Mitchell's expression invited an explanation.

'He's rehearsed the understudies almost as much as the principals. Rosie got a bit annoyed about it once or twice.'

'Just her?'

'I thought Cranmer was having second thoughts about the whole business.' Cavill's eyes were closed again and he spoke almost as if he were in a trance. Mitchell could see that he was exhausted. 'S'funny. It was almost as if Blake knew something was going to happen.'

Suddenly, he jerked awake. 'Hey! It was only a passing fancy.'

'It's all right. I'm not going to accuse him of anything—yet. Wasn't Miss Steiger annoyed?'

'Ursula's a lazy little cow. The fewer rehearsals there were the better she liked it. Lovely soprano but she won't go nearly as far as the others. No dedication.'

He was interrupted by a scuffling at the door. Mitchell opened it to admit Caroline and her well-stocked tray. She examined Cavill's face, then poured coffee, sending Mitchell a reproachful glance as she passed his cup.

'Nearly finished,' he promised.

Caroline knew it was meant as an apology. She found herself a chair as Cavill roused himself and drank. 'Blake must have spent a chunk of the loot on looking after his big names. He hired three cars for the duration of the rehearsals and three members of the chorus to drive each of them whenever they wanted to go anywhere.'

Mitchell sniffed. 'Hadn't the chorus anything better to do?'

'Those three probably hadn't. Gwen used to be a driving instructor. Ashley, the chap singing Remendado, has just been laid off by a mobile phone company and Tim's a student who's taking a gap year.' Mitchell scribbled the names. 'I suppose he was terrified one of them might find the novelty of slumming with amateurs was wearing off and would drop out.'

'One of them has,' Caroline put in drily.

Mitchell watched Cavill biting his lip. 'Go on, say what you're thinking you shouldn't say but you're really dying to tell me.'

'I've said it already. My impression is strengthening that Blake was half expecting something like this to happen. You'd expect a certain amount of greasing round big names, keeping them sweet, but he's nannied them like junior school kids. It's beginning to get Cranmer down. Ursula is lapping it up.'

'And Rosie?'

'I think she just accepted it. She was getting to the level when she got a bit of spoiling even from the old-established companies.'

Mitchell put his empty cup back on the tray. 'Which of the trio you mentioned drove Rosie about?'

'Tim did. I heard that Gwen refused to drive Rosie, didn't like her.'

Mitchell made another note, then spoke to Caroline. 'Have you been involved much in

52

this business?'

She nodded. 'Not as much as Cavill, obviously, but I've played at some of the piano rehearsals, done some of the odd jobs, helped some of the lame ducks.'

'Talked to some of the shy people, you mean?'

She shook her head. 'This has been an amateur set-up, so far. The chorus has some really good voices but they aren't necessarily musical people. Some of them can't read a line of music. They have to learn it by listening so I've done some note-bashing on the piano. Actually, there was a shyness problem about my having to do that. All the children we're using are in Cavill's choir and can sight-read very well, so the adults who couldn't didn't like to admit it.'

Mitchell nodded. 'And what impression did you get of how Rosie fitted in? Did the group like her? Did you like her yourself?'

Caroline wrinkled her nose. 'I could work with her, play for her. I wouldn't have told her my secrets, or suggested that the two of us went to the pub together one evening. Not that there were many free ones. Most of the chorus have day jobs, so a lot of rehearsals began at seven.' She grinned at Mitchell. 'And you found me one or two things to fill my time, in and amongst them.

'I think most of the chorus quite liked her. She helped them when Blake was asking more than they could manage. The other two tutted and whispered together that they should never have got involved in this amateur farce. They banked their cheques, though.'

Mitchell mulled over the information he had been given for some moments, then changed the subject. 'Did you see any signs of jealousy from people who had been the stars of past productions?' Mitchell turned to address Cavill. 'There must have been a few who felt their noses had been pushed . . .'

He left the question unfinished as he saw that Cavill, with his mouth tidily shut, was peacefully asleep.

*　　　*　　　*

Virginia had realized some weeks ago that her mother liked visitors who talked so that she could listen to something new. Chatting exhausted her. In addition, there was her mother's extreme frustration at the loss of her natural voice production. It made Hannah question whether she was still the person she used to be. Her voice was a part of what others made of her, one of the key markers, like body mannerisms. For her, these were severely compromised. She had been a very articulate woman. Her thoughts were still lucid, intelligent, original. Not being able to express them fluently distressed her.

For Hannah's entertainment tonight,

Virginia had taken along her collection of clippings from Lauren Hardy's opera diary in the *Clarion*. She settled to read them aloud. She could see that her mother was pleased at the idea, and that, as she continued Lauren's account, Hannah's interest was, from time to time, genuinely held.

'"... The truck that the children use in their mockery of the soldiers' parade is piled with ice-cream sellers' trays, old programmes, bags of oranges, a stack of folded white fabric, a pile of ashtrays, a coiled rope, a collection of PlayStation magazines, a football, a folded raincoat and a notice reading, 'Do not put anything on this truck.'"'

Hannah's face wore the slightly altered look that told her daughter that she was laughing. Virginia was pleased. 'She does have a nice turn of phrase, doesn't she? I'll find you some more choice bits.' She had marked them as the weekly instalments came out, knowing what Hannah would find amusing.

'"Escamillo makes his first appearance in the café. In leathers, with his shirt open to the waist, he looks like a cut price Elvis . . . Both sing out of tune, one slightly flat, the other slightly sharp—an interesting combination . . . 'Very, very good,' says Mr Blake. They haven't done anything as he asked. It is his form of capitulation."'

A metallic voice interrupted the selected passages. There was a triumphant gleam in

Hannah's eye. Her speaking device was not subtle but it was strident. It overrode any human voice, so that everyone gave place to it. 'I'm surprised she was not the victim and he the killer.'

'Blake, you mean? It's not all jibes. She makes some interesting points about what's going on.

' "Every rehearsal is different from every other, including the standard of singing. Presumably, every performance will be too. Then, each member of the audience at each repetition sees just one and thinks of it as 'this production' ... Rosie begins the Habanera but stops after a few bars to comment, 'The timing's not more than ninety-nine per cent right.' For whom is this exactitude? For God? For Bizet purists? For Cavill's self respect? Probably just for Rosie the perfectionist." '

'Does she not like her?' the machine demanded.

'Lauren not like Rosie? Oh, I think she did.' Virginia's finger moved down the column in search of another of her underlinings. 'Listen!

' "As soon as she moves, Rosie is Carmen, even in white trainers, jeans and a pink T-shirt." And there's another bit. "There is a protracted discussion on how some of the names, particularly Escamillo and Don José', should be pronounced. Rosie brings an element of common sense to it. 'Since we are doing a French opera, set in Spain, in an

English translation, I should think we could please ourselves.'"'

'Not quite the style of . . .' Hannah considered the options for expressing her thought from the machine's meagre resources.

'A provincial rag like the *Clarion*?' Virginia supplied. 'No, it's *Guardian* stuff. Lauren's obviously hoping to be read by one of the powers behind a national paper, one of the broadsheets. You do wonder that the *Clarion* printed it, though. It's not for the man in the Cloughton street. Still, I suppose not many of them look at the arts page, whatever's on it. I've never seen one of its issues raised in the letters column.'

She turned back to the cuttings that were now in wild disorder on the table. After a moment, she found the one she wanted. 'I like this bit.

'"I've added an extra dimension to the whole proceedings just by being here. In that sense, I'm not seeing it as it would be. It matters less as time goes on, but it's still significant."'

The machine interrupted again. 'You could do that.'

Virginia blinked. 'I could do what?'

'Writing. Journalism.'

'Mum, you're a genius. It'd be exciting. I might give it a go when all the tribe are at school.'

Hannah's face resumed its version of a

smile. The mechanical voice ordered, 'Start now or I'll miss it.' The slight twinkle in the eyes disappeared though the voice did not, could not change. 'I've probably missed it already.'

* * *

As he allowed Shakila to enter the bar of the Silver Swan in front of him, Clement fished for his wallet. It was now in the inside pocket of his sports jacket. Shakila had waited for him to shower and change, agreeing that questions to casual drinkers would be more welcome if the nosy parkers were sweet-smelling and respectably clad.

Clement fished out a note. 'I hope this is on expenses. We're only obeying orders.'

'I'm buying.' Shakila strode ahead of him towards the bar, arriving, with a pint of draught bitter and a glass of white wine, almost as soon as Clement had managed to find empty seats at a crowded table.

'You'll have to drive,' he warned her. 'This is my third.'

She smiled at him unkindly. 'No, it's not. You're starting again.'

Clement hoped she had not noticed his angry blush. 'What's this generosity in aid of?'

'Paying you back, saying thanks. I was grateful that you gave me the shout. Now I don't have to be.'

'Yes, but . . .'

Shakila understood at once. 'Ah. You had something else for me to do in payment? You can get the next round, then.' They drank in less than companionable silence as he worked out how to make his proposition attractive to her. She sipped her wine, refusing to help him. Really, he seemed to her to be two people. When he was off on some hare-brained scheme of his own, as now, he could be energetic, full of enthusiasm, sometimes almost manic. The rest of the time he tended to be apathetic, hangdog, soon offended and easily discouraged. He was intelligent enough. Why couldn't he just pitch in with the others as she longed to do herself?

She was pleased with her progress in the force so far, but, having worked seriously hard to get into uniform, she was now working even harder to get out of it. A few months ago, because of her fluent Urdu, she had become a temporary member of his squad and knew she had earned the DCI's respect for her work. She knew too that one case was all it had taken for Caroline Webster to worm her way into CID. Now, since Clement was giving her no lead in the present case, she got up from the table, taking her glass and mingling with the casually but expensively dressed patrons of the Silver Swan. Shamed by her example, Clement stirred himself and began a conversation with the drinkers who remained at their table.

By the time the bar staff came out into the floodlit garden to begin clearing tables, the two officers had met up again and had gone into the lounge bar. The landlord was anxious to be helpful but neither he nor any of his minions had noticed anything unusual as they had attended to the rush of customers brought out by the balmy evening.

It was late when Clement finally managed to lay his proposal before Shakila. They sat in an all-night transport café on the Leeds road, over huge mugs of instant coffee, made even more revolting by its lacing with heat-treated milk. At midnight, it was still warm outside and the grills and sizzling hotplates made the interior of the wooden shack overpoweringly hot.

Seeing that she was tempted, Clement fired his arguments in quick succession. 'You know we've got drugs on our patch. We've all been dying to be the ones to put a finger on something. I should have thought of the canal before. It's lined with pubs. It'd be a doddle to fill the cabin of a longboat or whatever they're called and tootle off—'

'Hang on a minute! You think this opera girl's mixed up in it? She's doing all right in her own line, probably making a bomb. Why should she be so stupid?'

'No one with a taste for money ever has enough, but that isn't what I meant.'

Shakila drained the gritty dregs at the

bottom of her mug. 'I wish you'd explain, briefly and clearly, what you do mean. It's after twelve. I'm being roasted alive in here and I've a busy day coming up, trying to force my way on to this enquiry. If you've really got a theory, cut the build-up and spit it out.'

Clement produced his trump card. 'You know I thought at first that the body was Caro's? I think the killer thought the same.'

'Why?' After a second, she began to answer her own question. 'She's been running on the towpath with you. Everybody knows you're a cop because Jonathan Stepney has no more sense than to tell everyone, so they at least suspect that she is.'

Clement's theory was becoming more convincing to her as she worked it out. 'This woman appears and sits half behind a bush. She's got an expensive camera with a telephoto lens. They didn't get a close enough view of her and they thought she was taking pictures of them with the boat and its cargo . . .'

'I rest my case.'

But Shakila had known he would not. She listened for a while longer to Clement's account of Jonathan's injuries, Shaun's new affluence and the expression he didn't like on the boatyard owner's face. At one o'clock, when she had failed to stem his flow of persuasion, she left him in mid-sentence.

CHAPTER FOUR

When she came into the incident room, early on Saturday morning, Shakila had still not decided whether or not to co-operate in Clement's plan. He was definitely going out on a limb. The manic glitter had been in his eyes as he had urged her. She did not care for being brow-beaten and she was not sanguine about their success, even if Clement's theory should prove to be well founded.

She had half an idea that they would be tangling with the drug squad. She agreed with Clement that, if they had their eye on the boatyard, then following up their own case in that area would certainly be vetoed by the superintendent, even if it appealed to DCI Mitchell and they could get it past him. And, if they took Clement's theory to Mitchell, he might well give such a sensitive job to DS Taylor rather than to the two of them.

The arguments were chasing one another round her head and she deliberately put them aside. Fetching coffee in a paper cup from the machine in the corridor, she sipped it, burning her fingers and her tongue as she studied the picture of the murdered opera singer that someone had pinned to the noticeboard.

A first glance showed a striking resemblance to Caroline Webster. Both were tallish. Both had below shoulder-length darkish brown hair, a broad brow, slightly hollowed cheeks and a full mouth. Then, as Shakila continued to examine the face, the likeness disappeared. Even in the flat picture, it was obvious that this woman had a poise that Caroline never attempted.

Rosanne Goldsmith was sitting, cross-legged, on a floor cushion. She was dressed in cream tailored trousers and a cream woollen sweater that had the kind of neckline that annoyed Shakila. It had no ribbing, so that the thin knitted fabric curled over into a roll that gave the garment an unfinished look. On this woman, though, it looked right. She would have looked right, Shakila suspected, whatever she wore.

The harder she stared at the pictured face, the less she could see anything of Caroline in it. These brows were delicately arched, not unruly, and the hair was darker and heavier, falling straight with an aristocratic carelessness. She turned away from the board as Sergeant Taylor came into the room. 'I was just thinking, they're hardly alike at all, really.'

Jennifer Taylor blinked. 'Sorry?'

'Adrian thinks the victim looked like Caroline.'

Jennifer seemed to be consulting a picture in her mind, rather than the one on the board. 'I suppose she is, rather. It's not in the face particularly, though. It's the body shape and the way they move. They both have a sort of grace. Caroline's is careless but Rosie's was more studied.'

'Did you know her?'

Jennifer shrugged. 'Not really. I met her a couple of times at Caroline's flat, just casually.'

Shakila ended the exchange by wandering away to the window. She looked down on the roofs of the few cars in the parking area below without seeing them. Another aspect of her dilemma had struck her. If she and Clement disrupted a major drugs investigation she would lose the approval and goodwill of Sergeant Taylor who was the DCI's good friend. Close association with Clement, even if their venture were successful, would put her at odds with Jennifer Taylor. There was no love lost between the sergeant and the DC. She'd also be risking disapprobation and possibly disciplinary action from more senior officers.

Maybe she should be satisfied with the rest of the shift taking her presence for granted as Sergeant Taylor seemed to be doing. Clement, after all, was speculating in advance of the facts. There were plenty of reasons why Jon Stepney and Shaun Grant might come to blows, and Shaun's proven skills as a burglar easily explained his possession of a few tenners.

She would have to keep away from the towpath and away from her colleagues if she were to strike up an acquaintance with the boatyard owner, as Clement was asking her.

But her imagination was already suggesting an assortment of wild schemes to obtain an introduction. This long debate with herself, she realized, was all play-acting. She had known almost as soon as Clement began his appeal, that she was going to go along with it.

She'd hedge her bets, though. As soon as she had a spare minute, after the briefing, she would go to the central library and borrow a CD of this opera. She might as well take a look at the computer while she was there and get herself a print-out of all the articles that the Hardy woman had written about the company and its notorious production.

She turned back into the room to find that the rest of the shift had found seats and that DCI Mitchell was coming in with Superintendent Carroll. They were a formidable -looking pair, the superintendent an inch or two over six feet, spare but muscular, Mitchell almost six inches shorter and built like a circus strong man. The DCI looked a little unlike himself this morning and Shakila tried to pin down what was different. He was as scrubbed-looking as usual, his clothes as spruce, his manner and bearing as perky.

Perhaps, she thought, the bearing was being maintained with a bit of an effort lately. The spring in his step had become deliberate. It was the hair, though, that was the real change. Usually it was subject to the relentless discipline of an army-style barber. Now, the thick brown locks on top were three inches long and the back of Mitchell's head was furry in areas where it used to be shaved.

Shakila knew that Mitchell's wife's mother, still only in early middle age, was dying of some horrible neurological disease. She was being nursed at home and his family life centred round her needs. He'd have little time for his usual meticulous attention to his person.

She thought the change in his appearance was an improvement, softening his blunt, serviceable features. If it weren't for the lines of tiredness and the grey cast to his skin it would make him look younger. She watched him take his place in front of the huge white pinboard and noted that his voice, as he addressed his officers, was as brisk as ever.

Mitchell was painfully aware of Shakila's scrutiny. The previous evening, he had been reluctant to sanction Jennifer's use of her and he was unhappy now with the assumption that the girl should have another temporary assignment to CID on this case. They had been glad enough to use her Urdu when a Pakistani girl had been missing. She had acquitted herself well on that enquiry and impressed the team with her common sense and quick thinking. In fact, he had encouraged her ambition to be moved permanently to CID until he had gradually become aware of her inconvenient preoccupation with himself.

He thought he could trace it back to his helping her conceal her discomfiture at her first post-mortem examination. To begin with, it had amused him but, over several months, it had become first an irritation and then a worry. Now, he deliberately avoided catching her eye.

Since she seemed determined that he should, he tried to avoid looking in her direction at all as he brought the collection of officers in front of him up to date with the overnight occurrences, as far as he understood them. 'I want to know,' he told them, 'everything about this woman. I want to know her birth weight, her O-level grades, her grandmother's maiden name and her favourite vegetables. Nothing is too trivial. When we have suspects I want the same treatment for them.

'And what one person finds out, I want everybody to know. As we're not Midwich cuckoos, that means learning the file by heart. There's just a bit more that hasn't reached the file yet. DS Taylor?' He turned to Jennifer, inviting her to come forward, and found himself the object of Shakila's black-eyed stare. He fixed his own gaze on his sergeant.

Jennifer kept her report on her interview with Lewis Blake to a few sentences. Having summarized her exhausted witness's few observations, she concluded, 'I'll get more sense out of him this morning, I hope. It struck me, when we talked about Miss Goldsmith, he seemed frightened about what had happened but not surprised. He didn't want to talk about it—kept digressing into how resentful his parents were about his money. Apparently, his father is dead set against gambling and thinks he shouldn't have it at all and his mother's theme song is that charity begins at home.'

'Maybe she's bumped off the singer then, to put an end to the drain on her son's resources.'

Mitchell grinned at Clement. 'You can be the one to chase that up. Not this morning, though. I want you to talk to Deborah Murdoch, Miss Goldsmith's understudy.' Quickly, he distributed action sheets. He had mixed feelings about the large number of them, grateful that the status of their victim had brought him such a large number of extra DCs and uniformed officers but irritated by his knowledge that they were not made available for all his victims.

He signalled to the regular members of his team to stay behind as the rest of the men departed. As he had expected, Shakila remained with them. Mitchell made no comment but turned to Jennifer, handing her two sheets of closely written notes. 'Have a look at my jottings from talking to Cavill last night. They should give you an agenda for your session with Blake. Was there a particular reason he wrapped his singers in cotton wool? Was he expecting some harm to come to them? Get some details . . .'

'Blake?' Caroline re-examined her action sheet. 'It says Blakes senior—the parents.'

Mitchell nodded. 'See what they say about him and how it compares with what he has to say for himself when we get round to him.' He stopped at Clement's indrawn breath. 'Go on, Adrian.'

'I've just remembered. I told you Miss Goldsmith's phone was ringing when I found her. When I asked the caller—we know now it was Blake—who he was, he said I knew perfectly well. He said what had I done to Rosie and was I really on the canal.'

Jennifer tutted and glared at Clement. 'Well, better late than never, I suppose.'

Mitchell rolled his eyes. If Jennifer and Adrian were going to fight their way through another investigation it was time for some strong words. For the moment, he turned to Clement. 'You mean he thought someone known to him was having a mindless joke?'

Clement shook his head. 'It was no joke. He sounded frightened.'

'Well, thanks for mentioning it.'

Mitchell frowned at his sergeant but kept his tone calm as he asked her, 'Would you have asked him about that last night? It might be more revealing to throw it into the middle of your questions about something non-threatening—like how he set up the company.'

'It would have been nice to have the choice.'

Mitchell was puzzled by Jennifer's attitude. He was familiar with her low opinion of Clement but she was not usually petty. He decided he would not deal with either of them in front of the superintendent and changed the subject. 'We aren't sure about next of kin. Cavill suggested we should try her agent.'

'I'll do that. It's Maria Gonzales.'

Mitchell nodded his thanks to Caroline. 'Got a number for her?'

She shook her head. 'Lewis will know.'

'Has the film turned up?'

'Did the uniforms find anything in the industrial estate?'

Clement and Jennifer spoke simultaneously, then each offered to give way to the other, not wishing to continue their dispute in public. Mitchell had heard both questions. 'Scene of Crime are sending a bag of rubbish to the lab but I think they'll probably be wasting their time. No sign of the missing film. One of the girls said you could get it out of the camera just by pressing a tiny button so we aren't likely to get lucky with prints, except the victim's. Did you and Shakila get anything from the Silver Swan, Adrian?' He looked up to see Clement shake his head. 'I've an idea Ginny's brother's group does some of its gigs there. Right, you'd better all go and earn your keep. Caroline, I want you to talk to the other two big names when you've finished with the Blakes. They'll be waiting for you at their hotel.'

He handed her one of its cards but she shook her head. 'Been there, to Rosie's rooms anyway.'

'Rooms plural?' Jennifer's lips formed a whistle. 'See what you mean about the cotton wool.'

Mitchell shuffled the remainder of his papers into a neat pile. 'Right. The four of us back to eat our sandwiches in my office at one.'

Shakila, to whom Mitchell had pointedly not given an action sheet, hung back. This time she spoke to Mitchell without raising her eyes. 'Sergeant Taylor told me to see Mr Benton again this morning.'

'And what about your own sergeant's plans for you?'

Shakila bit back a triumphant smile. 'I'm on a fortnight's holiday, starting last night.'

Mitchell had to admire her persistence. 'In that case, I can't see any objection to your doing what Sergeant Taylor asked.'

Her eyes still downcast until she was out of the door, Shakila left.

Superintendent Carroll's face showed that the arrangement did not meet with his approval, though what he asked was, 'What are Midwich cuckoos?'

'They were in some science fiction thing Ginny was keen on. Kids with gold eyes. When one of them learned something, the rest knew it by telepathy.'

'Mm, we could make use of that. Benny, I think you're out of line with Constable Nazir.'

Mitchell blinked and, perversely, sought to defend Shakila. 'She's the only one who'll come back having looked it up.' Carroll nodded, admitting that he had seen her make a note. 'I wasn't looking at her.'

'Yes, I saw that too. You're taking on this case with enough background difficulties. A PC with a schoolgirl crush on you is one you can do without, not to mention her calm assumption that she can manipulate her way to where she wants to be. Get rid of her.'

'She's good.'

'Yes, I agree, but, until she grows up and learns to work through the proper channels, we'll dispense with her. I'll see to it—to save her face rather than yours.' Carroll forbade further argument by walking to the door, where he paused. 'Rosanne Goldsmith's in your hands. I've plenty of other business in mine, but keep me briefed.'

Mitchell glared after him for some seconds before realizing, unwillingly, how thankful he felt to have the problem of Shakila removed.

*　　　*　　　*

PC Smithson, with Caroline in his passenger seat, drew up outside the Blakes' house. It was an ordinary, slightly run-down, semi-detached

72

bungalow in a respectable street.

Smithson stood with his hand on the gate. 'What are we supposed to get the old couple to tell us?'

'The DCI wants some background on the son before we approach him directly. He's asking Cavill Jackson as well. Says the more we know about the good Lewis the less chance he'll have to tell porkies.'

Smithson raised an eyebrow. 'Does that mean he thinks Blake's our man?'

Caroline lowered her voice as they walked up the path. 'It's a bit early to pick on anybody yet.'

Smithson had dropped behind her to admire a row of late dahlias. 'Surely the producer of the show is the last person to want disaster to fall on it—unless it's going to be a terrible flop and he wants an excuse for it. With Miss Goldsmith dead, no one's going to point a finger at him when everything starts to go wrong.'

Caroline shrugged and rang the bell. The door was opened promptly by a long, lugubrious-looking man with a neat beard but a droopy moustache. His bald dome had a fringe of grey hair round it, closely trimmed. As Mr Blake senior showed the two officers into a sitting room, his wife, smaller but fatter, followed them in. She seemed not to be comfortable in their presence and kept patting herself as if to be sure that the various parts of her anatomy were all present and correct.

When tea had been offered and refused, Caroline turned the conversation to the purpose of their visit. 'This production of *Carmen* is quite an undertaking for your son. It was very brave of him to take on professional singers.'

Terence Blake sounded unimpressed. 'I suppose so. It didn't seem to bother him, actually directing them. He had more of a problem with looking after them.'

'Treated them like royalty, then was on pins in case there was something else he should have done for them. Whole lot of rooms that Goldsmith woman wanted—and cars to take them all over—'

Caroline cut short the mother's diatribe. 'I suppose if they were happy with their living conditions they'd be more co-operative. Did you or your husband take any part in the proceedings?'

Terence Blake answered for her, glaring at her as though she should have waited for his permission before entering the conversation. 'No. Lewis took us in one day to show us round the theatre. He introduced his captive celebrities. Two of them were very civil. The German girl was quite rude—or not a good English speaker.' Caroline did not contradict the excuse and he went on. 'So, there's not much more we can tell you. What did you want to know?'

Caroline controlled herself and gave him the nearest she could manage to a charming smile. 'I suppose the only question it would help to ask is if anything in the least unusual has occurred. You'll have been watching things from the beginning, if only through your son.'

Ignoring her husband's glare, Edna Blake asked, 'Like Lewis suddenly getting rich? Like splashing money around on famous singers? Life's been a bit too unusual.'

'Yes. Everyone's told us about the big things. What we need is observant people to tell us about little differences because they're better pointers to what's going on. People are careful about the big things they do, their deliberate actions. They don't think to watch themselves for changes in their manner, slight differences in their usual routine, small things that are hard to explain.'

'Like the Thursday letters?'

'Thursday letters?' Caroline held her breath and dared Terence Blake to interrupt his wife.

Her chins wobbled. 'Lilac-coloured envelopes they came in with a typed address.'

Terence Blake seemed more anxious to help with the story than to silence his wife. 'They had him dancing on hot bricks every week. Demands for his gambling debts, I suppose. Someone after him, and serve him right— though he could afford to pay them off now, so perhaps not.'

'Not at the rate he was throwing money away on this daft opera scheme. Anyway, he's not deep into gambling. He used to do the pools as a youngster, before the lottery was started. Then, after, he only bought a couple of tickets a week. Lewis and I used to imagine what he'd do if he won. He never mentioned the opera caper. Talked about making his family comfortable, giving something back for all his education and being looked after. Huh! Easy to talk when you've nothing to do it with. Fat lot of benefit we've had from it.'

Her husband snorted. 'He can keep it as far as I'm concerned. He didn't earn it, so he's no right to it and neither have we. Still, I agree with Edna about the way he's showering it around. Just proves what I say. Easy come, easy go. If he'd had to graft for it, he'd . . .'

Caroline saw that Smithson was busy with his shorthand and stopped listening. She didn't think they had found their murderer here but there was an interesting trail to be followed to a series of purple letters.

*   *   *

As she entered the Silver Swan Hotel, Caroline was still undecided. Should she arrive at Miles Cranmer's rooms unannounced, hoping to surprise him into honest answers, or should she ask the commissionaire to warn him?

The latter would generate more goodwill—and ensure that she did not find him in bed. After his trauma of the night before, an international singer might well need to cosset himself a little before being expected to do himself justice in performance. But she would send up her name only, without her official title.

When he opened his door to her, Cranmer was hospitable but wary. 'I'm delighted to have your charming company, but I don't want you to play for me. I never do more than a few warm-up scales on the day of a performance, especially a first night. Come and sit down and I'll ring for some coffee. We'll have to be quick, though. I've been told to expect the police during the morning.'

Caroline produced her warrant card and watched his eyes widen. She studied the man as he readjusted his attitude to her. She had heard Rosie Goldsmith describe him as scruffy, but his casual clothes were immaculate and his shoes as well polished as her own. She analysed the 'unclean' impression as the result of dyeing his brown hair a shade or two lighter than his complexion could accommodate.

He dropped into an armchair, inviting her, with a gesture, to occupy the other. 'You're a copper? Cavill never said.'

'He'd better not! It puts your friends off and puts your enemies on their guard.'

'I suppose it does. So, how come you're such

a good accompanist?'

Caroline sighed. 'I'll tell you some other time. It's no secret but it's a long story and I'd better get down to business. What can you tell me?'

'About Rosie?' He shrugged. 'She's practically a stranger to me, except by reputation. I've read her reviews, heard her name mentioned in high places in the last couple of years, so I knew she'd arrived, so to speak. Not how or where from, though. I've sung with her once before, Elvino to her Amina. That's in *La Sonnambula*, Bellini . . .'

Caroline smiled sweetly. 'It was one of our college productions. I sang Theresa.'

Cranmer blinked. 'Well, anyway, even then, I didn't get to know much about Rosie. She slapped you down if you got even mildly inquisitive about anything she did before, or outside singing.'

Caroline was suddenly curious. 'What did you do before you got into opera?'

His expression was mock rueful. 'I'm afraid I'm one of the boring ones—cathedral school chorister, then music degree, then my teachers used their contacts for me. No romantic stories, I'm afraid, no lucky breaks—being heard by the right people as I swept my factory floor and sang to amuse myself.'

'So, when you heard about this caper, you thought you'd go slumming for a bit of fun?'

He grinned. 'Reprehensible but true.'

'Not the money?'

'Is that something you were sent to ask?'

'No. It was rude. Want to get your own back?'

He considered. 'Yes. Don't you wish you'd gone on with the piano, especially now you're with Cavill?'

She nodded. 'Occasionally. Maybe I'll wish it more often when we're married.' Caroline knew she had been pushing this idea to the back of her mind for some weeks but her interviewee was not the person with whom she wished to discuss her misgivings.

Her expression obviously forbade further probing, since it was Cranmer who switched back to their present situation. 'Right, so what can I tell you about Rosie?'

'My boss suggested her grandmother's maiden name and her favourite vegetable.'

'No detail too small, eh?' He grinned. 'Well, I noticed she had big feet, size eight. Blake wanted her to dance on a table in the scene at Lillas Pastia's but it drew attention to them . . .'

Caroline felt she was being mocked. 'What was she like to work with?'

'Easy on the whole. She loved the music, wanted the whole show to be a success, not just her own part in it.'

'You call an opera a show?'

He smiled. 'One of our affectations.'

Caroline nodded. 'How much time did you

79

spend with her yesterday?'

'I had breakfast with her in the dining room here.'

'Notice anything unusual?'

He shrugged. 'She didn't talk much, seemed preoccupied.'

'Did she mention her plans for the day?'

He shook his head. 'Not in detail. I know she was having a costume adjustment. She tripped when she was dancing on Wednesday. No disaster but she decided she wanted her skirt shorter at the back.'

'Was she worried about it?'

'I don't think that was what was bothering her. She didn't flap about details. Actually, I invited her out for a drive in the afternoon and an early supper together in one of your hilltop pubs. She refused, wanted to walk.'

'Where?'

'Obviously on the canal bank, but she didn't say.'

'You didn't feel like walking with her?'

He shook his head. 'I got the feeling she didn't want company and I didn't want to press. You shouldn't make an awkwardness with your leading lady with a first night imminent.'

'So, what did you do with your afternoon?'

'Ah, alibi time. Nothing useful to offer, I'm afraid. I listened to some music and fell asleep. This production has been no holiday. You've seen the heavy rehearsal schedule we needed with none of the chorus being pros.'

'Did that annoy you?'

He looked surprised. 'Not at all. I was glad that both Blake and his singers realized it was necessary. Not that they were all that bad. Musically, there were very few problems. As far as sound goes, this production is up to the standard I usually have from my chorus. The acting's still wooden, though. They're used to belting out their stuff just standing there. I think this is the first time they've had a theatre stage rather than a miniature one in a church hall, so they've never had room to act.'

'It doesn't sound your scene.'

'Well, no, but—it is a *Carmen*. I've always wanted to sing Don José. There was no sign of it on the horizon, and I'm not quite at the peak yet when I can dictate the programme to any company lucky enough to engage me.'

'What's so special about *Carmen*?' She allowed him three minutes of enthusing before she brought him down to earth.

He was amused by Cavill's children's choir. 'At their first rehearsal they stood to attention like my old cathedral choir. Now Blake's turned them into a gang of street urchins.'

Caroline smiled. 'That's what they always were. It was Cavill who gave them their Sunday manners.'

'And an excellent musical education.'

'That too,' she agreed. 'How do you find Blake as your director?'

Cranmer gave her a hard look. 'These are funny questions from a policewoman.'

Caroline sniffed and scowled. 'It is the death of an opera singer we're investigating.'

'Fair enough. I was surprised in some ways. He has the complete co-operation of his company and he's a better musician than I expected. I don't like his production, though. The music is being sacrificed to his craving to be original. It dictates a much lighter, less nasty atmosphere than Blake is trying to create...'

Caroline blinked as he broke off. 'Have you just remembered something?'

'The bottle.' Caroline waited. 'One rehearsal, early on—it was dropped from the top level, nearly brained Rosie. The warning cry was more than a bit late.'

'Anyone hurt?'

'No. It hit the floor with a thud and didn't break.'

'Who was up there?'

He paused, recapturing the scene. 'About half the chorus . . . oh, and one or two technicians. They looked like a class waiting for their teacher to explode. And there's something else I've thought of. We played a lot of games in the first week of rehearsals.'

'Games?'

'Sort of psychological exercises crossed with party games. Supposed to make us all familiar and comfortable with each other, but,

82

sometimes, it was silly and embarrassing. In the one I'm thinking about, we all had to give three pieces of information about ourselves, two true and one false. The idea was to see if we had learned enough about each other to be able to guess which one wasn't true.'

'And Rosie's three?'

'Ah, that's it. I can't remember, but Lauren will have a record of it. If one of us sneezes she writes it down.'

'That's Lauren Hardy, the *Clarion* journalist?'

He nodded. 'She did a feature on the history of what she called the three big names. It won't help you, though, because Rosie refused to see Lauren. Told her to apply to her agent for a handout if she really had to include her in the piece.' He laughed. 'Not so Ursula. No childhood incident was too trivial. She only got the same number of words as we two did though. I kept my piece to the main events. I'm sure people are more interested in my career than my babyhood, though I did think it was relevant that I sang my first *Rigoletto* at seventeen . . .'

In her detective constabulary role, Caroline would have cut him short there and departed. As it was, she lingered until there was a natural break in the man's boasting and she could leave tactfully. After all, in a few hours' time, her husband-to-be had to coax a triumphant performance from him.

83

CHAPTER FIVE

PC Shakila Nazir leaned against the cold corridor wall outside Superintendent Carroll's door and tried to still her shaking limbs. Once she had taken in the gist of his communication to her, her attempt to conceal her embarrassment had manifested itself as a difficulty in controlling her physical movements. When she was dismissed, in spite of her determination to walk to the door in a dignified manner and close it quietly, her hand had slipped and the door had slammed.

Blinking back tears of humiliation and frustration, she tried to tell herself that she hated the superintendent. Her fury, though, was directed against herself. She was twenty-two years old. Not only had she indulged in stupidly adolescent imaginings concerning her DCI, but she had so failed to control her behaviour that her feelings had been apparent to the people who had the power over her advancement. Worst of all, they had been obvious to Mitchell himself.

She had better move away from here before Carroll came out and saw the state to which he had reduced her. She straightened her shoulders and turned in the direction of the canteen. After a few steps, it occurred to her that she might have to face another member of the team before she had managed to compose herself.

Turning back, she descended the staircase to the station's rear exit and, reaching the street behind it, she dived into a coffee bar. She would meet no police officers here. The place was scruffy and the coffee poisonous, so that her colleagues wondered, half-heartedly, what illicit trade kept it open.

Having learned better than to order coffee, Shakila asked for chilled fruit juice and watched as a girl with dirty fingernails poured it from a striped carton that identified its contents as the cheapest line at Tesco. Dispiritedly, she handed over seventy pence for a fraction of the amount of juice that had originally cost less than forty and carried her glass to the murkiest corner of the room.

Her face burned again as she considered the superintendent's comments. She would not, she decided, leave her report on her interview with Harry Benton on his desk as he had commanded her. She would not risk seeing him again. She could hand it to the duty sergeant in the foyer, explain that she was on holiday and ask him to have it sent up. And she could spend that holiday in any way she wanted, couldn't she?

For the first time in a couple of hours her lips twitched into a smile. She picked up her orange juice, held the glass up to the inadequate light, examined its smears, then marched with it to the counter. Showing her warrant, she expressed herself forcibly on the price of the lurid-looking liquid and the condition of both its container and the room in general. Then, conscious of a resurgence of her customary buoyant mood, she strode to the door.

As she walked in the mild air and fickle sunshine, she discovered that her unhealthy attachment to Mitchell, whatever its cause or nature, had not survived condemnation. Under Carroll's judgement and her own shame, she found it was no longer there to be scrutinized, analysed, even renounced. She supposed she should be grateful to the superintendent for liberating her. Now Mitchell was merely a respected senior colleague whose team she was still determined to join. She had made the task extremely difficult for herself, but she had had to rise above the results of her own rashness before. She would go to the library now, as she had determined to do before the morning briefing.

The central branch was just a couple of minutes' walk away. Its bright walls and thick, sound-deadening carpets were a considerable improvement on the sleazy café, though, on such a mild day, the central heating had produced a fuggy atmosphere. Shakila's custom was to face unpleasant tasks straightaway and now she settled at a table in the reference section to write her report on her conversation last night with Harry Benton.

When it was finished, she might go to the boatyard incognito and get into conversation with his son. He might even introduce her to the boatyard owner. Maybe she would pretend to want to hire a boat. She could invent a friend who had to be consulted so that she would not need to commit herself on the spot. She began to consider the idea of actually taking one. It would be a good reason to be hanging around the canal and the canal-side pubs.

She finished the report, put it away, then looked around her, considering the white-faced, sun-starved people, both staff and readers. Shakila could not have contemplated an indoor job. She knew she had found her purpose in life when she had been accepted for police training. She had felt that life could offer her nothing to match the triumph of being chosen as the best student of her intake.

After her parents had both died in a typhoid outbreak in Lahore, she had come to England at the impressionable age of fourteen to live with her older married brother in Leeds. Twice, she had watched part of her new neighbourhood burn down around her in racial attacks. Once the part had included their own house.

She had decided after the latter incident that she had to try to find some way to change things. She had, proudly and boldly, put on her uniform and set out to bridge the gap between a mainly white police force and her resentful fellow expatriates.

Her hopes of swift success were soon dashed. She had found that, at a local level, only murders and rapes were adequately investigated. Perpetrators of racial violence and vandalism escaped because of a lack of manpower, an even greater lack of willing witnesses and the laughable punishments that were inflicted on the few who were caught. Public opinion and the media were not on the side of the PC in the street.

Murder was seen as the worst crime—and she had no quarrel with that. The police had to give it a good chance of being solved and received the most glory when it was. You never saw an aid case on a cop show on television, such as a PC getting someone to hospital who had been trying to jump under a bus. So, now Shakila was no longer satisfied with being a rank and file PC. She had both personal ambition and ambition for her own community. She wanted to represent it in a way that was acknowledged by the English media.

She could see nothing wrong with such aspirations. She utterly rejected the superintendent's condemnation of her 'pushiness'. She deserved to be on this case, justified by the way she had conducted herself on the last one. Caroline Webster had made the transfer into CID by exactly the same method, taking advantage of a temporary assignment to make herself invaluable.

Shakila's own conduct with regard to Chief Inspector Mitchell was another matter. She spent a few moments now, regretting that she had ever met him, then she stood up and pushed her library chair back impatiently. He was a good DCI, the sort of boss who would go out on a limb to crack a case and understand if she did too. And, considering her present state of disgrace at headquarters, along that shaky limb was the only way for her to go.

*   *   *

Clement felt puzzled and slightly anxious when a radio message from Mitchell sent him to an interview that should have been Shakila's. Had she been to the canal already, giving it priority over Mitchell's instructions? And, if so, what had happened to her?

He had better do his own job before he investigated that. First the Bentons, then Deborah Murdoch. A glance at the map showed him he would have to cross town and pass the busy Saturday market. Quicker to walk than drive.

On the Swayneside estate, most houses were rented and only a few were owner-occupied. The latter tended to be marked out by newer and brighter paint than had those maintained by the council.

Number 17 was one of these. Like all the others, it was separated from the road by a small garden. This one was immaculate. Someone had cut geometrical flower beds out of a tiny lawn. The grass had been razored so that no stray blades blurred their lines. The miniature rose bushes were still in flower. Each had been recently dead-headed and there were no fallen petals. Clement wondered whether the plot was the handiwork of Henry Benton senior or junior. Then, remembering his recent equal-opportunities course, he added the as yet unknown Grace and Gracie to the list of possible gardeners.

Number 17 had a shining maroon door. The two numerals screwed on to it were brassy bright. The door opened at his knock to reveal a formidable woman of uncertain age. Not young was as precise as Clement could be. As the two of them stood and weighed each other up, Clement could hear the sound of a flute. It played the same phrase repeatedly and with increasing speed and facility.

The woman smiled and was no longer formidable. She invited Clement inside, then yelled a resounding 'Harree . . .!' which produced the witness he had met on the canal side the previous evening, this time with his dog in attendance. It barked its objections to Clement's presence until it was dispatched to the back garden.

Whilst the old man tied it up, the woman explained that the family had heard the bare facts about the murder that had been released to the media. She herself was horrified that it had happened so close to where her son and her granddaughter had been working. She wanted to hear no more about it!

When Harry Benton returned, the woman, presumably Grace, shooed both men into a small sitting room and disappeared back to her kitchen. Clement established that his witness had read the *Clarion*'s account of the *Carmen* production. 'We aren't musical folk,' Harry Benton had hastened to assure Clement, as though there were something not quite respectable about it, 'except for the lass. She's in this opera affair, though she's not officially in Mr Jackson's choir. He only takes boys, but Gracie plays the flute, you see, so Mr Jackson takes an interest in her. He's got a few other girls in his street gang who play other instruments.'

'His street gang?' Clement had looked puzzled.

'In the *Carmen* story. There's a gang of youngsters on the street who mock the soldiers at the beginning, then they come on again at the end, during the bull fight. That time, they're pickpockets, stealing from the crowd. Young Gracie'll tell you all about it.'

Clement thought it would hardly be necessary to trouble Gracie but now he reconsidered. Intelligent children were shrewd and observant. There was no telling what she might have noted. Mr Benton's information about the usual teatime traffic along the canal path was disappointing. 'I often see another chap walking an alsatian. It used to fight mine but now they just play. Who's there depends on the weather. There might have been more than usual yesterday.'

Clement settled himself more comfortably in the armchair his host had offered and looked around the room. It was decorated with an abundance of photographs, on walls, mantelpiece and tables. Most of them featured a slight, dark-haired girl, following every stage of her development from babyhood to early teens. There was also one of his witness as a younger man, dressed in military uniform. Clement enquired and Harry Benton answered briefly, 'Ex-marines.'

'Are you still in the army?'

Benton shook his head. 'Loved the action. Got too old for that and couldn't settle for a desk so I got out.'

He offered no small talk, waited for Clement's questions. He had been much more garrulous last night. Obviously, he had heard the news since then, realized the seriousness of the matter and was behaving appropriately.

The flute playing had finished a moment or two before. Now the door was pushed open and the much-photographed girl came in. She was followed closely by her grandmother who dismissed her. Gracie was noticeably surprised and disappointed, probably used to grandmotherly indulgence.

'You must have some homework to do, Gracie.'

'I got it all done last night, Gran, so as to get it out of the way.'

'What about your lines for the show?'

Gracie thought this must be a joke. 'If I don't know them now it's a bit late.'

'Well then, finish your flute practice. You'll be too busy later.' The woman's sharp tone seemed to startle her husband as well as the girl, who left the room obediently without sulking. Grace placed her coffee tray on the table, removing two photographs to accommodate it.

When she had left the room, Benton went over to the sideboard, took something from a drawer and handed it to Clement. It was a neatly typed list. 'I thought a good while about what you asked last night. I've put the name of everyone I can remember passing whilst I was looking for Josh—or a description if I don't know the name, those young lads on their bikes for instance. I've ticked the ones I see regularly.' Clement grinned and decided that it was Harry Benton who was responsible for the design and maintenance of the little garden.

When he left, some minutes later, he saw Gracie out in the street. She was obviously hoping to waylay him but not daring to come within view of the front window. Clement drove slowly along the gutter until she was standing by his passenger window. 'You seem rather anxious to speak to me.'

She gave him an assessing glance. 'Can I sit in the car?'

Clement shook his head. 'That would count as interviewing you.'

'But I'd like to be interviewed.'

'That's fine by me, but we'd have to fetch one of your parents or grandparents to make it legal.'

Her expression told him that this would not do. 'I haven't got a mother, anyway. She died when I was little.'

Clement nodded without comment. The girl did not seem to be sympathy-gathering. 'You will be given a chance to have your say. DC Webster will be talking to all the children's chorus—you know? Caroline?'

She nodded. 'Yes, but . . . You see, you've come to our house so they'll all expect me to know something. They'll think I'm stupid if I haven't heard something to pass on.'

Clement understood her problem. 'Look, I can't either tell or ask you anything right now. On the other hand . . .' The girl's face brightened. 'You could tell them you helped us. If there was anything you feel like talking about now, I wouldn't feel I had to stop you. And, if it included anything we haven't been told already it could quite likely help the enquiry.'

'Something only us children know?' Clement waited hopefully. 'I know Miss Goldsmith liked us girls better than the boys.'

'Oh.' Clement monitored his tone so that the remark was not a question.

'We all liked her back. We don't like Miss Steiger. She calls us "you children". Miss Goldsmith knew all our names. She soon learnt them. There are fifteen boys in Mr Jackson's choir and us three. We're in because Mr Blake wants a mixed choir and Mr Jackson knows us because he teaches us the piano.'

'Not the flute?' Clement asked, in spite of himself.

'No, but he found my flute teacher for me. He says I need another piano teacher because he's away too much, but he'll always give me special extra lessons when he's around. He plays the organ all over the world. His favourite one is in Frankfurt . . .'

Clement was beginning to wish he had driven away without taking pity on the child. He opened his mouth to excuse himself when she said, 'Once Miss Goldsmith asked us girls to tea at her hotel. We had to take our instruments to play to her.' Her face fell. 'I wasn't allowed to go.'

'That was a pity for you.'

'Well, I suppose it's not quite fair to say that. We'd been invited to Uncle Simon's, but

95

I'm sure he wouldn't have minded for something like that. But . . .' She gave a gusty sigh. 'Grandad said it'd be rude to cancel. He made a big fuss about it. He's always on about good manners. The other two went and had a super time. Miss Goldsmith said I could go on my own later, to make up, but now I won't be able to.'

Suddenly, Gracie darted away through a gap in the terrace and round the back of the houses. Clement saw that the maroon front door had been opened and her grandmother's head was peering round it. Clement grinned to himself. Oh for the hearing of a thirteen-year-old. He drove round the corner, then opened his notebook and noted down as much of the one-sided conversation as he could remember.

He saw little point in it, but the DCI's instructions were always to take everything offered. Only when the case broke did it become apparent what had and had not been relevant. Naturally Rosie had preferred talking to the girls. They were a year or two older than the boys and easier for her to relate to. Still, if he failed to put the ramblings of any witness, in full, in the file, Sergeant Taylor was certain to ferret it out and use it against him.

* * *

Caroline had little stomach for her interview with Ursula Steiger, having taken an instant dislike to the girl at their first meeting in an early rehearsal. She knocked on the door and, after some seconds, heard a shout of 'Come in.'

Caroline opened the door for herself and saw her interviewee slumped on a sofa. She offered her hand but, when the girl still refused to get up, she dropped it and settled herself, uninvited, on an upright chair.

The room was immaculately clean from the efforts of the hotel staff, but cluttered and untidy. The girl's hair gleamed, probably the result of a hairdresser remunerated by Lewis Blake, but she had made no attempt to arrange it. Most of it hung down her back, but a heavy section obscured the right side of her face and, probably, the vision of her right eye. The mouth, painted in a dark plum colour, pouted. Her slouching position emphasized the meagre bust and the disproportionately spreading hips. Caroline wasted no time in small talk and Steiger answered her questions in a strong German accent, promptly, but in a tone that made her resentment of them clear.

She found fault with every aspect of the production. The rehearsal area was uninspiring. 'Most of the windows are boarded up. All you can see through the filth is an advertisement on the wall across the street for the "Ultimate Skin Tattoo Studio".' She gave an exaggerated shudder. Her fellow principals were overrated and miscast. 'When they stand together at their first meeting, she's four inches taller than him!' The workload was excessive. 'The ridiculous schedule is killing me.'

Steiger's version of Rosie's refusal of Cranmer's invitation for the previous afternoon differed somewhat from his. It included greater persistence on Cranmer's part, irritation that became anger on Rosie's and an unpleasant scene in the foyer before Rosie rushed out through the main door.

For Steiger, Bizet himself was found wanting. 'It irritates me that *Carmen* contains so many excellent musical ideas that are undeveloped.'

'Well,' Caroline countered, 'he didn't have the chance to write, rewrite and adapt, like Andrew Lloyd-Webber. He died soon after the first night.'

Grudgingly, Miss Steiger admitted that Ashley, the production's Remendado and her personal driver, had a basically good baritone as well as some skill behind the wheel. Caroline decided that this unexpected positive note was her cue to depart.

*   *   *

Lewis Blake met Sergeant Taylor with a resentful expression. 'I answered all your questions last night.'

Jennifer smiled at him. 'Correction. You

answered my preliminary questions.' She followed him into the narrow hall, noting that, on this mild morning, he was wearing his leather jacket in the house. Maybe, she decided, it was his form of armour. He seemed to have banished his parents from their house during his further interrogation—or maybe they had chosen to be absent.

Blake settled Jennifer in the minute sitting room and interrupted her first question by one of his own. 'I want to know what you are doing to protect the other two.'

Jennifer blinked. 'Have you any reason to believe they're in danger?'

'Well, we didn't think Rosie was, did we?' He scowled at her, then dropped his eyes.

She waited in silence till he raised them again. 'We have the distinct impression that you did, Mr Blake.' Satisfied that she had disconcerted him, she moved on. 'We have a slightly clearer picture of your arrangements than we had last night so I have one or two more questions.'

He managed a half-smile. 'Surely. Ask away.'

'Could you explain in detail the extremely extravagant travelling facilities you offered your guest singers?'

'I hired a car for each of them for the duration of their stay in Cloughton.' His tone was grudging. 'And I asked three chorus members to act as chauffeurs when they were

99

required.'

'Isn't that rather unusual?'

Blake shrugged. 'Everything about this production is rather unusual. I expect some rather unusual things happened when Scottish Opera was first set up, and ENO and Welsh National.'

'Well, it's very generous. I hope they were suitably grateful. Who drove which singer? Perhaps you could jot down the names and addresses for me.' He leapt up to comply, grateful to have moved on to a topic he felt comfortable with. 'I'm told someone called Gwen refused to drive Miss Goldsmith. Is that true and can you tell me why?'

He hesitated a fraction too long. 'It may be true. If so, I can't tell you why. I asked them to sort it among themselves. They'd be paid the same whoever drove whom. Tim drove Rosie. She'd asked to be picked up last night at five thirty sharp but she wasn't in the hotel foyer as arranged, nor in her rooms. Tim searched everywhere he could think of.'

'Then what?'

'He rang in. I told him to wait for another half-hour. Then, if she still hadn't shown up, to come back and get into costume and made up.'

'Later, presumably, you told Deborah Murdoch to take over Miss Goldsmith's part for the last rehearsal.' He nodded. 'How did she react?'

Now Blake's smile was genuine. 'Like

anyone else in her position would have done. Asked if Rosie was ill and tried not to look as if she hoped so.'

'And now?'

'She's probably feeling pretty mixed up—panic-stricken, excited. Not grief-stricken, perhaps. They hadn't got close enough for that, but she'll be very sorry about what's happened. Rosie was kind to her, helped without patronizing.'

Wanting Blake completely off his guard, Jennifer put her notebook down and sat back in her chair. 'Can you go back a bit? Have you always had this project in mind and then the lottery win made it possible? Or did you dream it up whilst you were wondering how to spend the money?'

He had to think about this. 'The former, I think. I've always been aware of how good my company is. A lot of the chorus are also in the Choral and some are in Cavill's church choir. He and Cavan Cully between them have made sure that the people in Cloughton with good voices know how to use them and that saved me a lot of hassle.'

He paused, perhaps waiting for Jennifer to protest that his own training had been crucial. When the silence dragged, he continued, 'I always thought it a pity that so few people heard them. I used to dream up schemes to bring them to the notice of a bigger, more discriminating audience. One of the plans was to get a big name to come and draw a crowd for them but I couldn't think how to tempt anyone suitable.'

He stopped, raised his hands and dropped them again. 'And now I'll just be notorious for letting one of them die.'

'And you think the other two might share her fate? You're going to have to explain yourself, Mr Blake.' When he made no response, she continued, '. . . otherwise I can only draw my own conclusions. You must have some knowledge of the death, or some reason to suspect that—'

'I was at the Vic yesterday!'

'All day?'

'Most of the afternoon.'

'Mm. As I'm sure they've already told you, Mr Cranmer and Miss Steiger last saw Miss Goldsmith leaving the hotel at about ten yesterday morning. Did you see her after that, or do you know that anyone else did?'

Blake shook his head. 'Why does the morning matter? She was killed in the afternoon, wasn't she?'

Jennifer eyed him sternly. 'Until we get the report on the post-mortem examination, we don't know that.' Jennifer made unnecessary notes in her book until she felt Blake was sufficiently frightened, then looked up again. 'In the meantime, perhaps you could explain to me why you expected DC Clement to know who you were when he answered Miss

Goldsmith's telephone? Who did you think he was? Why did you think he had "done" something to her and why did you doubt that he was on the canal bank when he told you that he was?'

For a few seconds, Blake sat, silent and immobile, staring at his scuffed shoes. Then, obviously coming to a decision, he got up and crossed the room. He moved stiffly, reaching for a volume from the small bookcase as though the action physically pained him. He took something from between the leaves. 'I can't think, now, why I didn't show these to your people weeks ago.' With fumbling fingers, he laid out on the table seven sheets of paper.

*   *   *

Clement was pleased that the DCI had sent him to talk to Deborah Murdoch. For several weeks, she had been preparing herself for the possibility of taking Rosanne Goldsmith's place. She had the most obvious motive for killing her. Moreover, whether or not she was guilty, she would have been observing the victim, trying to learn from her, in every way. She would have studied Miss Goldsmith's interpretation of their role, her approach to her career in general and the lifestyle which she almost certainly had every intention of acquiring for herself.

The house was large, imposing and well

kept—more so than most Victorian family residences that had been turned into flats. Deborah's was on the ground floor at the back, its windows looking out on to a pleasant garden. The sitting room, where she settled him, seemed appallingly untidy, until he realized that the clutter on every surface consisted of piles of school exercise books. He apologized for interrupting her marking, expecting her to say she was glad of a distraction from it.

She said, 'You want to talk about Rosie, I suppose?'

Clement shook his head. 'I want you to talk about her.'

Deborah had been making coffee for herself. Without consulting him, she reached for a second mug from the row hanging below a wall cupboard and brought them both to the table. 'Where do you want me to start?'

'With how she fitted in with the company and the production?'

The girl settled back in her chair, quite at ease. 'Rosie held the whole show together. When she was on stage, things lit up, and when she wasn't she chatted to discouraged people, soothed angry ones—she was just generally friendly and sensible.'

'Were there a lot of angry ones?'

Deborah frowned. 'Maybe that was the wrong word. Offended ones, people who'd made suggestions that Lewis turned down,

104

people who'd had their lines cut—you know?'

Clement did not know, but nodded all the same. 'Were the other two different?'

She considered. 'Miles was all right, in a superior sort of way.'

'And Miss Steiger?' Deborah shrugged and wrinkled her nose. 'You don't like her?'

'I don't have any sort of feeling about her, except that she's useless.'

'Can't sing, you mean?'

'No, the voice is all right. She can't act, though. One morning she was practising finding a body in the smugglers' den in Act 3. Lewis said she wasn't showing any revulsion. She did it again, just the same, only singing louder. When he suggested some gestures, she told him she'd have to go away and think about it.'

'What sort of gestures?'

She grinned. 'Not rude. He told her to look freaked out, to imagine the waxen skin and the shock of seeing a body in that creepy place.' She sniffed. 'Ursula would manage "freaked out" better if someone whispered that she'd come to rehearsal with a curling pin left in! There isn't a body there, anyway, in the score. It's one of Lewis's innovations, to "make the atmosphere more black".

'When she's had a good look round the den, she kneels to pray.' Deborah gave a disgusted laugh. 'Looks as if she's taking time out from an aerobics class. She made a big fuss about that bit in a previous rehearsal. Said she was something between an agnostic and an atheist. She's supposed to be acting, for goodness' sake. Who cares what she really is?'

Clement wondered whether to lead the girl back to the point, but knew the value Mitchell put on letting useful facts slip out inadvertently. He let her continue.

'All that fuss about a prayer, then, the next minute, she's asking if she can wear a cross round her neck and hold it when she's speaking to God. She said there are so few excuses in opera to sing out and up and God is one of them.'

Deborah had forgotten her circumstances as her contempt overwhelmed her. 'Her mouth wobbles when she belts out her top notes—not a pretty picture. Bit of a voice wobble too. Still, the words are "I said I would not be afraid." Better give her the benefit of the doubt. Might be deliberate. If the rehearsal goes on a bit Ursula always gets tired first. Her voice gives out too. She's no discipline, you see. Actually boasts about never singing scales or practising alone to keep the voice supple . . .'

Clement had had enough. 'Seems to me you have quite strong feelings about her. Lucky for you it wasn't Miss Steiger who died.'

Deborah sighed. 'All right. She's not my favourite person. She genuinely is lazy, though. Rosie and Miles spend lunchtimes rehearsing spoken dialogue and testing their lines.

They're at the piano first thing, singing scales, though we're not called till half-past ten.'

'I thought rehearsals were in the evening.'

'Most chorus rehearsals are. The principals, under-studies and minor roles have to come during the day. I've been on school holidays during the summer and my head's keen on opera, so he's supported my request for some time off. I only got it without pay, of course. Anyway, it wasn't a problem for me. Some of us had to book time off work now instead of in the nicer weather earlier in the year.'

'But Rosie herself was not temperamental?'

She shook her head. 'Not at all. Rosie stamps her foot when she knows it's all gone wrong again, but it's nervous energy not temper. She grins and takes her share of the blame.'

'Give me an example.'

'Well, Lewis wanted her to dance on a table. She thought it was dangerous. The table was small and her feet are enormous but she gave it a go and fell off still without getting annoyed. Then Cavill ruled it out and Lewis gave in.'

'Right. So she was easy to work with. Did you see her yesterday?'

She shook her head. 'No, I . . . Wait a minute. Yes, I did, very briefly. I was walking up Gerrard Street round the corner from the hotel and I saw Rosie waiting for a bus.'

'I thought Blake was having her chauffeured

around.'

'I know. Rosie told Lewis he was making too much fuss. I heard her saying to Cavill that she felt smothered and she was going to do her own thing. I still wondered why she didn't call a taxi, though.'

'Which bus did she want?'

'I don't know. There are three shelters and Rosie was at the end one, furthest from the hotel. I think there are several routes to each stop, though.'

Clement made a note and changed the subject. 'You teach, I gather?'

She nodded. 'Head of music at St Austin's. It's an eleven to sixteen comp with all the musical children in the area creamed off by that new place up the valley, one of New Labour's specialist schools. I can't do anything with my lot, though I bet Cavill would. Look at those kids he's got here. They're mostly from those run-down streets behind his church, but they're brilliant.'

'Copy his methods, then.'

'You'd need his personality and enthusiasm as well. To be honest, I don't really care whether my kids discover music or not. I just want to sing myself. I haven't got the contacts to do it professionally—and I don't know whether I'm good enough.'

'You'll pretty soon have a better idea.'

'I know. I'm trying not to look at it like that. It's heartless to be pleased and excited. I'm trying to think of it as filling in for Rosie so as not to let the others down. I'm going to have to get out of teaching. I'm not on fire like Cavill. Every day in school gets more of a drag.'

Anxious to stem a flow of self-pity, Clement said, 'I've read one or two of the *Clarion* pieces. Not over-flattering, are they?'

Deborah grinned. 'They're typically Lauren. She's always been a bit caustic. Not vicious, though. Always amusing and she mocks herself as much as anybody else.'

'Do you know her well?'

'Used to. She's an ex-member of the company.'

'Ah, she's getting her own back after being kicked out.'

'Oh, no. She was very ill—had weeks in hospital and lost her job at the *Yorkshire Post.* Now she's trying to get back into journalism but it's telling on her. I'm sure Lewis would have her back for the asking, but she can't manage both work and a taxing hobby yet.'

'How did the famous three react to her barbs?'

Deborah looked a little surprised. 'I've never heard any of them refer to it. They probably realize the *Clarion*'s just a rag.'

Clement supposed it was. He was glad to be away. He'd snatch another coffee at the little market café in his own more cheerful company.

CHAPTER SIX

There was a tap on Mitchell's door. The person who had disturbed his train of thought did not immediately enter. Not a colleague, then. He yelled 'Come in!' and Cavill appeared, looking sheepish. 'I have to apologize for my bad manners last night.'

Mitchell grinned. 'I was the one who demanded an interview when you were exhausted and then bored you to sleep. Never mind. I don't like apologizing so I accept yours with no more said.'

Cavill perched on Mitchell's visitors' chair as if prepared to answer more questions, but then glanced at his watch. He needed to remind Mitchell that the murder that was his first priority had created countless problems for himself and Blake. Adjustments to the production would take all day. 'I haven't got long and I really can't remember what I did or didn't tell you last night . . .'

'Tell me what difference it's going to make to tonight's performance that young Deborah Murdoch will be taking the lead.'

Cavill shook his head. 'I can't begin to measure it. Chiefly, it's that she doesn't seem capable of deep feeling. She seems much less nervous than you'd expect. That's maybe all a part of it. The voice is very good, though it lacks the techniques that she has never been taught. She'll offer us a rendering that's very correct but with no soul.'

'And you have to be full of drama and emotion for opera?'

Cavill's tone was admonitory. 'You need passion to perform any kind of music.'

'Will it affect the audience, do you think? The murder, I mean, not Miss Murdoch's failings.'

'You mean, will they all come? There'll be two who come as voyeurs for every one who stays away because Carmen isn't Rosie. To begin with I was worried about Cloughton providing much of an audience at all. Ordinary people feel uneasy about opera because they've never tried it. They've sung in choirs, school ones and church ones and local amateur ones, or at least they know someone who has, but only professionals put on opera. It's complicated and it's expensive. There are amateur operatic societies, but not very many, and they usually have a basic repertoire of musicals and operetta.

'Anyhow, I misjudged Cloughton. People turned out in force to book. They're coming from miles around too.'

Surreptitiously he glanced at his watch again and Mitchell asked quickly, 'As a musician, where would you look for motives in this murder?'

Cavill was silent for some seconds. Then he

spoke slowly. 'I can't believe that any of the folk I've been working with could have done it. In theory, I suppose I'd look for jealousy in the regular lead singers who've been relegated to minor parts. They perhaps wouldn't mind for a one-off performance. They're afraid now though. Lewis has money to spend and lots of important people have heard of him. He might not want mere amateurs again and singing is very important to some of them, even though it isn't their livelihood.'

'Important enough to kill for?'

'I don't know. Anyway, there are all the people who think there are better ways to spend money than on the society. Lewis has had plenty of hassle from his family and letters from charities.' He sighed. 'He's always whingeing about it—and about Lauren's articles. He says things like, "All publicity is good publicity" at rehearsals but he's livid about her really.'

Now, Cavill's consultation of his watch was overt. 'I'll have to go. You can imagine what today's going to be like at the Vic.'

Reluctantly, Mitchell got up. He was puzzled. Cavill's apology had not been really necessary, certainly not urgent. Then he had merely repeated information he had offered before. Mitchell had a feeling that his visitor had not yet worked round to what he had come to say.

Cavill reached the door and paused there.

'There's just one thing—a bit ephemeral, I'm afraid. I felt there was a change in Rosie, quite suddenly, at the beginning of last week. It's difficult to describe. She still behaved totally professionally, and no one else remarked on it. She was still technically good, and involved to a degree, but preoccupied. It was more noticeable when she wasn't actually in the scene being rehearsed. Before then she would spend spare moments chatting to the chorus members. In breaks, she'd fool around with them—or coach them—whatever they wanted from her. This last few days she's seemed withdrawn, tended to sit by herself, or even left the room until she was sent for again. Before she would watch the others, take an interest in the whole production.' He shrugged. 'It's probably nothing. Cheerio.'

Satisfied now, Mitchell let his witness go and entered his last remarks in the file.

*   *   *

Arriving back at the station just after midday, Jennifer went as bidden to report to her DCI. She paused at the head of the stairs, which she had taken at a run. As her breathing became more even, she watched with interest as a woman emerged from Mitchell's office escorted by a deferential PC.

In one swift glance, Jennifer summed her up—the carefully preserved complexion, the expertly blonded hair in youthful, casual style, though not so youthful as to be a bad mistake. The woman was slim enough to carry off her white sweater and close-fitting trousers, though she had taken the precaution of throwing over them a wrap of opulent purples and gold. Jennifer accurately surmised that here was Rosie Goldsmith's agent.

She tapped on Mitchell's door and walked in, as was her custom. Seated at his desk, he pulled a comic face as his comment on his last visitor.

'Maria Gonzales?'

Mitchell nodded. 'Though I bet that's not what's on her birth certificate.'

Jennifer settled herself on his least uncomfortable chair. 'Yes, she looked a bit stagey. She's got style, though. Did she say anything useful?'

Mitchell lifted a thick eyebrow. 'I suppose so, in a way. She's done the ID so we've got that out of the way. She's a bit of a poser. Kept telling me who else was on her books. I might have been impressed if I'd ever heard of any of them. She knew precious little about Rosie's personal life, just a few details about her childhood and a lot about her recent career.

'She—Rosie, not our pseudo-Spanish friend—was born in Accrington into a working-class family. Narrow, old-fashioned ideas but they weren't badly off.' Mitchell glanced at his notes. 'She was an only child.

She had piano lessons from her grandmother before she even started school and began to learn the violin when she was eight.'

'Did she want to? They sound a pushy lot.'

Mitchell shrugged. 'Don't know. She was auditioned for the National Youth Orchestra but turned down. She gave up the violin immediately, went back to the piano and began to do more singing. She started going in for local competitions and winning them—'

'Born in Lancashire, working-class, pianist and singer. Sounds like another Kathleen Ferrier.'

Mitchell blinked. 'If you say so. Wasn't she a contralto, though? Rosie was a soprano.' It was Jennifer's turn to blink. 'Rosie then met up with someone called Felling, who used to be a singer herself. She gave Rosie some coaching for a while. We'd better try to find the woman, see what she's got to tell us.'

'The next bit's interesting. Gonzales thinks there was once some trouble with a man. Apparently she was permanently off them, except for . . .' He looked at his notes again for his witness's exact phrase. ' " . . . the frothy sort of carry-on that's expected professionally" Oh, and the woman offered me an alibi, though I didn't ask her for one. It involved loads more names I've never heard of. I'm sure someone will have a tedious day finding it all checks out.'

'How did you find her?'

'I didn't. She presented herself in the foyer. Travelled up from London in the small hours.' He waved a sheaf of notes at his sergeant. 'There's reams of stuff to go into the file about all her recent bookings. Ms Gonzales said Rosie was the least temperamental singer she'd ever dealt with. She was generous to other singers who were good. If they were bad, her sarcasm was equal to the best barbs of Carl Cookson. He, by the way, once wrote a letter to Rosie, criticizing one of her performances. She wrote back saying it was better to be insulted by an eagerly read critic than to be ignored by him.'

Mitchell shuffled his notes into a tidy pile and pushed them away. 'That's the total of my morning's work, for what it's worth.'

Jennifer grinned. 'It's no less relevant than the O-level results and so on that you were clamouring for this morning.'

Both officers looked up as a rapping at the door heralded the entry of two of the station's civilian staff, bearing trays of sandwiches and coffee. As though in response to this signal, Clement and Caroline arrived together to help consume them. Mitchell waited until all four of them were eating and drinking before demanding reports.

'BT are busy now,' he informed them, between bites of beef and pickle, 'putting direct lines and answering machines in the incident room. We haven't many proven facts

116

to put on the board yet—not even the name of a relative or her date of birth. There'll be photographs up in time for the debriefing tonight. I'm not hopeful that the bagfuls of gubbins picked up at the scene will help us much, but they're at the lab anyway. The victim's clothes might help us a bit more. Nothing more than the usual women's stuff in her pockets and handbag—'

'Handbag?' They all looked at Clement. 'I didn't see one. Mind you, I didn't look too vigorously. Didn't want to mess up the scene before the SOCOs got busy.'

Jennifer glared at him but said nothing. Mitchell shot her a warning glance. 'It was found about a dozen yards away. Possibly the killer threw it there—or took it with him, then thought better of the idea and dropped it.'

'Are we sure,' Jennifer asked, 'that we're looking for a he?'

Clement seemed very sure. 'Surely throat-cutting's a man's crime.'

Caroline, five feet six tall and muscular, bridled. 'I don't see why.'

Mitchell took another sandwich. 'We'll ask the experts, not waste time arguing.'

'When's the PM?' The question came in chorus from all three.

'This afternoon.' They waited, but Mitchell issued no invitations and they were relieved.

Caroline asked, 'Has Dr Ledgard told us anything useful from his preliminary examination?'

Mitchell grinned. 'He was muttering about Jack the Ripper. He pointed out the difficulty of cutting the throat of a struggling person. Said it's usually only done when the victim is either tied up or unconscious. We found no weapon, so, unless someone else took it away and said nothing, which seems unlikely, we can assume the killer took it with him. In any case, Ledgard said the cut was forcibly delivered with no tentative practice strokes, which those of us who got near enough saw for ourselves.

'The killer knew what he was doing. He made his main cut at the side of the neck which is easier and quieter. If he'd pulled the head back and cut across the front, the main arteries would slip back and be protected by the windpipe. Slicing through the carotid artery meant the woman was dead before she'd produced much in the way of choking noises.'

'No guess at a time of death?'

'What do you think? One of the SOCOs pointed out how the blood had pooled below the undergrowth. The ground was so hard and hot that the blood congealed before it could soak in. I'm not sure how that helps us but I've now passed on all the little secrets that the boffins have so far confided.'

'Why,' Caroline asked, 'did he cut her throat, rather than stab her in the back? Her clothes would have soaked up the blood. He needn't have handled her so much and there'd have been less chance of getting marked with her blood himself.'

Mitchell poured the last of the coffee into Jennifer's mug. 'That's just question one of a long list. All of you, put yourselves in the killer's place. Why kill this particular woman? Why on the canal bank? Why at this particular time, on this particular day? How did he protect his skin and clothing?'

'Answers in triplicate to be brought to the debriefing!'

Mitchell grinned at Clement, then asked, 'Any theories off the tops of your heads?'

'Might her throat have been cut because she's a singer?'

Caroline's offer was diffident but Jennifer took it up. 'You mean it's a matter of professional jealousy?'

'Perhaps. Yes.'

'We'd better stop talking about a male killer then.' They looked at Mitchell. 'If someone's jealous of Rosie's opportunities, it would have to be another soprano.'

Clement blinked. 'So, we're looking at Deborah Murdoch?'

'Only as one possibility,' Caroline reminded them. 'Debbie's going to sing *Carmen* tonight and I'm sure she's thrilled, but there are other people who would die for the roles Rosie had lined up for next month or even next year—people who have nothing to do with this

Cloughton production.'

'Besides,' Jennifer observed, 'if Deborah wanted to make sure she'd be taking the lead in front of all the eminent critics, she'd only have needed to put Rosie out of action for twenty-four hours or so. There wouldn't have been any need to kill her.'

They considered this in silence, until Clement observed, 'She was killed on the canal bank because that's where she was. Whoever did it could have been following her and picked that as his best chance of not being observed. The towpath had people on it but the bench she'd been sitting on was well screened.'

Mitchell was interested. 'How do you mean, following her? All Friday? All through the production?'

Clement shrugged and Caroline returned to her original point. 'I'm not disagreeing with Jennifer or the DCI, but I'm not sure that's the kind of jealousy I meant. Rosie could be quite caustic when it was called for. I was thinking of a sort of jealous anger. Maybe she'd advised someone to give up singing because they weren't good enough. Perhaps the someone was even angrier because they'd heard Rosie's singing recently, compared themselves and realized she was right.'

Mitchell nodded. 'Do you have anyone in mind?' Caroline shook her head. 'Right then. Superintendent Carroll is conveniently in agreement with our decision to let the opera continue tonight. As he says, it'll keep them all here and means they'll be preoccupied when we talk to them.'

'Not very conducive to accurate recall.'

'True, but I take his point. It's often useful to catch people off their guard.' Mitchell realized that Jennifer was staring blankly at the wall. 'Wake up, Jen. Where are you?'

She blinked. 'Still thinking about what Caroline said. Would someone want to destroy her own role model? Do away with just the thing she was aiming at?'

Caroline frowned. 'She might persuade herself that Rosie got where she was by—well, using means not available to everybody.'

'Did she have musical connections, then?'

'Not as far as I know, but she was very attractive, with a sort of presence even when she was just fooling around.'

'You're thinking of Deborah Murdoch, aren't you?'

Caroline took a pause to consider before nodding at Mitchell. 'Yes, I'm afraid I am.'

Mitchell turned to Clement. 'You've talked to her. What do you think?'

The DC summarized his session with the new Carmen, adding, 'I got the impression that it was Ursula Steiger who'd been giving her a hard time. She spent most of the time I was there bad-mouthing her. She was very approving of Miss Goldsmith.'

'Well, if she'd just cut her throat, she wouldn't be advertising the fact that she hated her.'

Clement glared at Jennifer. 'She's got an alibi of sorts for the afternoon. She went for a walk—no, not on the canal path, in Crossley Park. Met a few of her pupils there who were less than polite.'

'Did you ask for the alibi?'

Clement shook his head, turning back to Jennifer. 'We've got to go with Caroline on this one. She's spent weeks with the girl. Is she good enough to take the chance she's getting tonight?'

Caroline shrugged. 'She'll sing every note absolutely perfectly but with no impact. There's no passion in her personality so she can't put any into her music. The critics will admit she has a beautiful voice, but the audience will wonder what Don José could possibly have seen in her to make him give up so much for her.'

Mitchell was intrigued. 'Would a flat sort of woman like that be able to screw herself up enough to cut someone's throat?'

'Maybe not. I don't know.'

Clement's tone was contemptuous. 'She couldn't even screw herself up to change her job—just moaned on about how much she hated it.'

Caroline was not willing to give up on her favourite suspect. 'I think you can be too lazy or maybe too depressed to take any action on the things that bother you, but you could still be capable of violence when all the resentment you've been building up spills over. The last straw might be something quite trivial.' Mitchell grinned. It seemed to him very unlikely that his cheerful, capable DC was speaking from her own experience.

'I definitely got the impression that Deborah's praise of Miss Goldmith's singing and her generosity to the company amateurs was genuine.'

Mitchell looked at Clement in surprise. His tone had been confident, neither peevish nor aggressive. Maybe the young man was growing into his place in the team at last. He nodded his acceptance of Clement's opinion and reached for the phone. 'I'm going to order more coffee. You've more to hear before we all go out on the hunt again. This is Jennifer's story.'

Before the sergeant had a chance to begin it, Clement asked, 'Where's Shakila?'

'She's off the case.' Mitchell's expression forbade any further questions.

Even the bribe of more of Mitchell's excellent coffee did not prevent groans at the thought of further sitting and talking. The team was anxious to be out on the job once more. However, when Jennifer produced photocopies of the seven letters that Lewis Blake had reluctantly handed over to her that morning, their attention became more willing.

'This was the first.'

They gathered round Mitchell's desk to examine the scrap of paper. It congratulated Blake on his ambitious project and politely invited him to 'pay black rent' to ensure that it proceeded smoothly. Jennifer waited for the team to read and consider the letters before telling the rest of her story.

Blake, having turned them over to her, had been reluctant to describe his response to them. Only bringing him down to the station and threatening to keep him in an interview room until she had the whole story had loosened his tongue. 'Tonight's our first night! I've a million things to do. Can't we . . . ?'

Jennifer had shaken her head. 'The sooner you answer all my questions the sooner you'll be free to attend to your musical duties.' Taking his sullen silence for agreement, she asked, 'How seriously did you take this first letter?'

He had shrugged. 'No specific instructions were given, as you can see. I just put it aside and said nothing to anyone.'

'You thought it was a joke?'

'I didn't rate it any more unpleasant, at that point, than the begging letters I'd received from people who considered that their causes were far more deserving than my self-indulgence—as illustrated by the opera project.'

124

'It contained a threat. You should have brought it to us.'

Blake had given her a tired grin. 'If everybody did as they should the police would have nothing to do. Actually, I had a small but uncomfortable suspicion that my mother might have written it, maybe on my own computer whilst I was out.'

'Did you keep a record of the dates all the letters arrived?'

He shook his head. 'Not at first. The second one came after about a week's gap. I'd guess they came in the third and fourth weeks in April.'

'Through the post?'

He nodded. 'Addressed to me, care of the theatre. I threw the envelopes away.'

Jennifer nodded. 'So, what did you do when the second letter arrived?'

His grin was shamefaced. 'You've read it. All it wanted was a five pound note putting in an A4 envelope, to be left in one of the telephone boxes outside the Vic. There wasn't any specific threat, just that melodramatic row of dots after "Otherwise". For the sake of a fiver, I decided to be on the safe side. It was so silly that it cheered me up. I was convinced it was some teenager, who'd read the *Clarion* pieces, jerking me about.'

Jennifer waited. Blake stared at a cigarette burn on the edge of the scarred table at which they both sat and remained silent. She demanded, unforgivingly, 'And the third?'

He answered without raising his eyes. 'By then we were into September and the three principals had arrived. Before then, I'd just been rehearsing the company in the music. Before she'd even got to the first rehearsal, Ursula Steiger was laid low with food poisoning for three days. On the day the third letter arrived, Peter, who's singing Escamillo— he's the bullfighter, you know—twisted his ankle because one of the rungs of a ladder that leads up to the second level of the set had been unscrewed, or worked itself loose, whichever you choose to think.

'I thought that my correspondent meant business. I also stopped suspecting my mother. It wasn't very likely she'd fathomed out the computer or how to work the printer. She certainly wasn't likely to have got on to the set in the rehearsal room to fiddle with that. I've dated the letters since then. There's been one each Thursday since the second week in September.'

'And they all ask for trivial amounts of money, with the method of delivery getting more complicated and ridiculous.'

Blake looked up angrily. 'Twice they had to be delivered during rehearsal time. I had to leave Cavill in charge and think up some pathetic excuse to give him.'

'And the last one came this last Thursday, two days ago?' He nodded. 'So, you followed

126

instructions, put a ten pound note in a blue Basildon Bond envelope and went with it to the phone box on the corner of the precinct. Was that timed to hit a rehearsal?'

Blake sighed. 'No, but when I got to the telephone box there was a card taped to the door telling me to go to a shop in Bank Street—'

Jennifer frowned. 'Where's that?'

The constable leaning against the wall by the door spoke up, making Blake start in alarm. 'It's that grubby little alley behind the market leading to the old bus station.'

Something stirred in Jennifer's memory. 'Was the shop Porter's?'

Blake nodded. 'That's it. I'd forgotten the name. I had to ask for a letter there. It told me to buy a packet of envelopes from the same shop, put my original one containing the tenner in it, address it to "An Opera Buff" and leave it to be collected.'

Jennifer completed her note taking and looked up. 'I see what you mean about jerking you about. Why did you keep following such mindless instructions?'

Blake thumped the table with his fist. 'I've told you! Sorry, but what would you have done in my place? First there was Ursula's illness and Peter's ankle, and then the bottle—'

'The bottle?' Jennifer listened to Blake's account of its fall from the second level of the set. 'So, Rosie had a lucky escape.' Further questions had elicited no more solid facts and Jennifer had allowed her reluctant witness to return to his duties at the theatre.

Now, as she finished her account to the team, Caroline nodded. 'Cranmer told me about the bottle incident. He thought it was just a bit of dangerous fooling. By the way, that shop, Porter's, rings a bell.'

Jennifer reopened her notebook. 'It did with me too. I found it on the computer when I got back. It's the postal address for a couple of shady businesses uniforms are keeping an eye on for us.'

'Has Blake's letter been collected yet?' Clement wanted to know.

Jennifer shook her head. 'Haven't had time to ask. I'll see to it. Pity we haven't got Shakila to mooch around in there for us.'

Mitchell busied himself refilling Caroline's cup and thought aloud to distract them. 'So, Blake's been trying to supervise, either personally or by proxy, every moment of the three singers' lives. He wasn't just being specially hospitable to them.'

Caroline took her mug. 'One of the staff told me that Blake investigated the hotel security to the point where the manager threw a massive tantrum. He told him, if he wasn't happy, he could take his paranoid trio elsewhere.'

'What I want my paranoid trio to do,' Mitchell announced, blandly, 'is to settle down here with the file and know it off by heart by debriefing time—that's six thirty.' There was a dismayed silence, followed by an outbreak of counter-suggestions. He held up a hand to still them. 'Until you know what everybody else has found out, you can't make informed suggestions and you won't know what else to ask about. Settle down, children, and no quarrelling!'

'What about you?' Jennifer demanded.

Mitchell beamed. 'The delights of the PM. I promise to share every sordid little detail with you at our next meeting.'

As he disappeared down the corridor, Clement reached for a folder from a heap of them on the desk. 'I reckon we've got the best of the bargain. Let's get at it.'

CHAPTER SEVEN

Shakila was not as far off the case as her DCI and her superintendent had intended her to be. The gusts of anger that had carried her through the morning so far had abated. Her report was safely delivered to the duty sergeant and her spoils from the library lay on the coffee table beside her chair.

Coming back to her flat always lifted her mood. Now she looked around it with pleasure. Clement had remarked that it was painfully tidy. Certainly she liked to have everything in its place. Apart from the two huge, comfortable armchairs, the furniture consisted solely of a long modern unit in pale beech, built along one wall and incorporating all she needed in the way of storage and equipment.

Unframed prints of abstract paintings were the only patches of bright colour. Silver grey walls extended down to sage green carpet and all was restful. It amused her when her white acquaintances arrived, expecting Asian reds and oranges, but her furnishings had been chosen to please herself rather than to surprise them.

She adjusted the blinds to shut out most of the bright daylight and pushed the borrowed *Carmen* cassette into the video recorder. The cheerful and vigorous overture pleased her and she recognized a melody here and there, but she did not become engrossed in the developing action. The performance was in French and the subtitles intrusive. Her brother's more traditional Pakistani decor would have been a better setting for Carmen's wild behaviour than her own cool room. She wondered if the reason people seemed to dress up to go to the opera was an attempt to get themselves into the right mood.

After a few minutes, she switched off the tape, brewed coffee and made a cheese sandwich. She took them, together with the sheaf of computer paper the library had obligingly printed for her, to the raised flap in her 'unit' that served as a table. She read quickly, skipping over the technical phrases and appreciating Lauren Hardy's racy style of writing.

She had not realized until now the scope of Lewis Blake's undertaking.

To the layman, an opera begins when the conductor walks into the pit. To the company, the meshing of the diverse elements which that represents is not the overture but the final crescendo. 'All right on the night' is the result of planning and organization where there is little room for the haphazard and none at all for sheer luck.

Shakila read on. She thought she knew what Lauren meant by 'the conjunction of availabilities'. Or the lack of it! It was no use having a theoretically wonderful cast who weren't free at the right time. Opera was a competitive business and the good singers were heavily booked. She was startled to discover that what Lauren called 'stage hardware', sets, properties, costumes and wigs, could cost between twenty-five and fifty thousand pounds. 'This is apart from fees for designers, lighting designers and technicians, choreographers, stage manager, wardrobe people, the conductor and, probably the most expensive of all, the performers' wages.'

Shakila wondered what—or if—the chorus was being paid and began to have some conception of why the paper had been reporting on the progress of the production for well over a year. There would be a sizeable chunk missing from Blake's lottery win when the curtain finally came down on it.

She passed on to the diary of the rehearsals. Lauren had written a weekly piece until this last week. Sensibly, she had made no attempt to give a comprehensive description, but had enlarged on particular incidents that had appealed to her. Shakila's lips twitched as the merciless comments spilled out.

We are rehearsing the last scene today. Carmen arrives with her new love, Escamillo the bullfighter. The crowd waiting outside the ring goes wild. Don José (you remember? Carmen's cast-off soldier?) appears and manages to get close because he is in disguise.

As Escamillo triumphs in the bullring, Carmen and Don José act out their tragic fate. The chorus, Blake decides, are to be stall holders, selling to the crowds. He explains what they are to do with their wares. 'When you sing,' he yells, 'your item is visible.' He is affronted by the roar of laughter. 'Come and buy,' sings the chorus. Fans flicker, posters are flourished, children's garments waved and oranges roll all over the floor as chorus members prove their inadequacy as jugglers.

Chaos reigns. 'Brilliant!' says Blake.

Shakila laughed out loud, pushed the sheaf of computer paper into a drawer, drew back her curtains and went out into the sunshine. It might be pleasant, she decided, to take a walk along the canal side to the marina. And, surely, it would be churlish not to make a little conversation with anyone she might meet there.

*   *   *

Disappointed with the result of the post-mortem examination, Mitchell decided to drive home and have tea with his family. His four youngsters were due for a reminder that they had a father and he needed their cheerful company.

The pathologist's grisly and smelly labours had led him merely to confirm the suggestions he had made the previous night so Mitchell would therefore have little encouraging information for his disgruntled team members after their tedious afternoon with the case file.

His slight depression became extreme irritation as he parked in the road and entered his garden. Only a couple of weeks ago, he had made his annual end-of-season assault on it. Now, the untimely warm weather had set the privet hedge sprouting again and fooled the withered and pruned remains of a fence of rambling roses into producing three or four pink and white flowers.

He glared at the row of hanging baskets in front of the house. Virginia insisted that they were as attractive in their autumn shagginess as in their high-summer splendour. Mitchell accused her, in their traditional October argument, of making this her excuse for laziness.

He found her in the back garden with their two elder children, admiring the handiwork of an athletic spider that had bridged the considerable gap between a fuchsia and a newly-planted astilbe with a web that sparkled a little with the dew of late afternoon.

'We're going to see Granny Hannah after tea,' Caitlin informed him, then she skipped off down the path. Declan followed her with a long-suffering air and Mitchell assumed that he had been asked to keep an eye on her.

He stooped to remove a tuft of couch grass from the border and asked, without looking at his wife, 'Do you ever wonder if Hannah gets angry at our efforts to keep her alive? You wonder how she can face each new day—or each long night. Where can she find even the smallest thing to enjoy?'

Virginia gave the question serious consideration. 'She still loves her blessed Shostakovitch and she still feels she has an input in the children. Actually, I almost asked her the same question a few weeks ago.'

'And?'

'She was still talking then. She said that, however much she lost, there'd still be some point in carrying on—she couldn't have her relations suspected of putting her down.'

'That sort of remark was just a refusal to answer.'

Virginia shrugged. 'She's thankful that none of her five senses has disappeared and even more glad that her eye and bladder muscles haven't been impaired.'

'But she's always been so independent.'

Virginia was indignant. 'She still is. All right, physically she has to have everything done for her at this stage, but what she can control, she does. She doesn't look to us for encouragement. She doesn't often sink into depression and compel us to support her spirits. She takes a pride in that, and so she damned well should!'

They were unaware of Declan's approach until he spoke. 'What will I do if you and Daddy get neurone disease?'

Virginia's prompt answer told Mitchell that his wife had pondered the question for herself. Both children listened solemnly as she explained that, even if Hannah suffered from the strain of the disease that could be inherited, their father would not be affected. 'Besides, clever doctors are working all the time to find cures and treatments. By the time I'm Granny Hannah's age they might have found a way to make it better.'

'But will it make Granny Hannah not dead?' Caitlin asked.

Virginia shook her head but it was Declan who supplied an answer. 'No. Once you're dead, it's for good—but Granny Hannah in heaven will be pleased about the other ones who don't die.'

Suddenly, Virginia was sobbing against Mitchell's chest. He was bemused, both thankful that her iron control had broken and almost embarrassed, certainly ill at ease, to see his self-sufficient wife willing, for once, to accept his support. He put his arms round her tentatively. Would this acknowledgement of her need for comfort irritate and embarrass her?

He was distracted from the question by the sight of Declan's stricken expression. The child was aware that his remark had in some way triggered his mother's unprecedented show of distress. His eyes met his father's as he asked fearfully, 'Did I make Mum cry?'

Mitchell held out a hand to him. 'Yes, you did, and a good thing too. Mummy's very sad, like we all are, because Granny Hannah's going to die. When you're sad, it helps if you cry sometimes.'

'Like when my hamster died,' Caitlin suggested helpfully.

Declan said, after a moment, 'Hamsters aren't the same.'

Mitchell set them to transporting leaves from the lawn to the compost and took Virginia inside. He thanked a hazily conceived providence for his opportunities to see life again through a child's eyes—not that he had ever been a child anything like Declan.

He said as much to Virginia. 'He's definitely your child.'

Her blotched face creased into a grin. 'I do assure you, he's also yours.' Then, with a change of tone, 'You've never doubted that, have you?'

He began to brew coffee. 'I never thought you had a lover in Oxford that you didn't tell me about, but I've sometimes felt . . .'

As she often did, Virginia found the words for him. 'That he was born out of the miasma of Oxford and academia?'

Mitchell laughed. 'You've recovered then? Go and wash your face while I find the dictionary.'

She returned as he was pouring the coffee. 'That smells good. I do know what you mean about Declan. He thinks in abstracts like I do, and loses himself in what he's reading—for what that's worth.'

Mitchell sat down on one end of the sofa

and regarded her seriously. 'There's a whole world that you can walk in and out of and I can never find the door.'

'Very metaphorical.'

'Don't worry, I don't want to go in. I'm a bit jealous, though, that you can. Not that I want to stop you . . .' He tailed into silence, not sure what he wanted to say and lacking the philosophical vocabulary to express it even if he could have worked it out.

Virginia brought her coffee and came to sit beside him. 'I'm jealous of you too—though I don't think jealousy is quite what we're talking about. You've got your life together. If something needs doing, you do it—you don't agonize about it or put it off. You live in the real world and, sometimes, that's where I feel a stranger. You can opt to stay out of my world but I have to struggle in yours. I couldn't cope as well without you, not as a crutch, but as a mentor. You prevent my fecklessness becoming sordid filth. Besides, I'd starve. Neither of us gets fat on my cooking.

'Caitlin's like you. By your reckoning, she doesn't seem to be my daughter. She's chiefly concerned with where the next meal's coming from and how to do what has to be done, neatly and efficiently. Let's hope the twins have the good points from both of us.'

Mitchell rose to wash their cups. 'These days, Kat looks as if she needs to know how long it is till she's fed again.'

Virginia smiled at this thought as she listened to him splashing in the kitchen. Caitlin had been a fat baby who had grown into a squat, square toddler, almost ugly. During the last year, though, she had lengthened and fined down to become almost wraithlike. Her lank hair had darkened and thickened and so Virginia had let it grow. The child now had more grace and charm. Her face, though, still had her father's blunt features which usually wore his same uncompromising expression.

'She's better than any of us at dealing with my mother,' Virginia said, as Mitchell returned from the kitchen. 'She rushes in, shouting, "Do your funny voice, Granny Hannah!" My father thinks I should teach her to be more tactful.'

'But Kat doesn't do tactful.'

'True. Anyway, I know that she's Mum's favourite visitor. Caitlin accepts her as she is now. There's no embarrassment caused by comparisons with how she was. Mum finds it harder to deal with Declan. He's not embarrassed but he is distressed. His distress is embarrassing to Mum because she can't relieve it.' Virginia looked up and caught Mitchell's abstracted expression. 'What are you thinking?'

'I'm wondering if I can hand the debriefing over to someone else and come with you after tea.' He broke off, scowling, as his cell phone began to ring.

Virginia listened to her husband's side of the conversation and realized he would not even be staying for tea. 'Don't worry, we'll manage. Dad and Alex will both be there.'

Reluctantly, Mitchell obeyed his summons to the station. For once, he did not—could not—push his personal concerns from his mind and concentrate wholly on his job.

*   *   *

At the end of the afternoon, Jennifer, Caroline and Clement came into the interview room together, feeling virtuous and well informed. Clement surveyed the larger than usual collection of borrowed DCs and uniformed officers who had been drafted on to this high profile case. He regarded Mitchell gloomily. 'Will we have to spend tomorrow afternoon reading up what all these folk have been doing?'

Mitchell beamed at him. 'No. You'll be busy then. You'll have to do it in your spare time.'

Jennifer was studying the noticeboard, which now bore enlarged pictures of Rosanne Goldsmith's mutilated throat and a timetable of her Friday activities, so far as they were known.

Mitchell dealt with the latter first. 'Miss Goldsmith came down from her room at nine fifteen and found Cranmer having breakfast. At that time, the dining room was almost empty. Miss Steiger had had her meal delivered to her room.

'Just after ten, there was the quarrel with Cranmer who was forcing his unwanted company on Miss Goldsmith. We've got some widely differing accounts of this disagreement from Cranmer himself, Steiger and a couple of the waiters. Thanks to Smithson, who thought to hunt the waiters up, we know that one of them followed her when she stormed out. Blake had bribed him to keep an eye open for her.' Mitchell nodded approval in the elderly PC's direction.

'Miss Goldsmith walked right round the hotel, came in through the back door and went up the back stairs, presumably to her rooms. What next?'

Another PC raised a hand. 'I've been talking to Tim Watson, her driver. He rang her at ten or fifteen minutes past ten. She told him she wouldn't need him till rehearsal time. He tried to persuade her that she would enjoy a drive over the moors—'

'Why?'

'Because Blake's instructions were to stay with her. She got more than a bit shirty with him and then hung up.'

'Who can blame her?' Jennifer asked. 'What did Mr Watson make of his instructions from Blake?'

The constable grinned. 'Said he took his money and did as he was told. Then he unbent a bit and said he thought the money had sent Blake a bit mad. He hadn't been the same since he got it.'

'Right. Done your report?'

The young constable's tone was smug. 'In the file, sir.'

Mitchell nodded. 'Anyone else able to fill in any of these gaps?' No one volunteered. 'Have we had any joy from the bus company?'

Yet another PC gave details of the three routes, along one of which Rosie Goldsmith probably travelled the previous morning. One was a circular tour through a sprawling council estate, into the town and back again. Both the others were longer distance journeys, to Wakefield and Burnley respectively.

'She'd hardly have been going all the way to either, surely. Those buses go all round the houses and take hours.'

Caroline nodded agreement with Clement, and added, 'It doesn't seem likely either that she'd know anyone on the Swayneside estate.'

'Why not?' They jumped at the sharpness of Jennifer's tone. 'She might live in the lap of luxury now, but she was born into a little Lancashire town into a working-class family. From all we've been told about her, she wasn't a snob.'

'How near,' asked Mitchell, 'is Burnley to Accrington? Could she have relatives there? I suppose,' he added, 'she could have them anywhere.'

Jennifer regarded him sternly. 'Oh, no you don't. We know you like heaps of suspects, but be reasonable. We've got a score of people who wanted her out of the way so they could sing her roles. There's another dozen who want to stop the opera while there's still some of Blake's money left for them. Now you want to uncover a whole lot of skeletons in Rosie's family cupboard.'

Mitchell ignored her and turned to Clement. 'What time did Deborah Murdoch see Rosie at the bus stop?'

'Just before half-past ten.'

'Smithson, grab that timetable and find out the time of the first bus after that on all three routes. We'll get on to the drivers tomorrow.'

'Not tonight?'

Mitchell shook his head. 'It's Saturday. They'll all be in the pub if they're not on duty. Besides, tonight, most of us are going to the opera.'

The reactions of his officers ranged from delight to dismay. Mitchell dismissed those chosen for the privilege to change into appropriate clothing and was surprised when Clement stayed behind. The DC, wearing an expression of bashful smugness, sat back in his chair.

Mitchell raised an eyebrow. 'You've a theory to try on me?'

Clement nodded eagerly. 'Is it possible, sir, that Blake had some reason for wanting Miss

Goldsmith out of the way?'

'Blake?' Mitchell considered the idea and its implications, but allowed Clement to spell some of them out to him.

'He's covered his tracks well. Made it seem as if he was doing all he could to keep her alive.'

'Very likely because he was. And the letters?'

'Sent them to himself, done on his own computer. If we trace them to his machine, he's covered himself, planted the idea that his mother might have used it while he was out. If she could, so could other people . . .'

Keeping his expression solemn and his tone even, Mitchell asked, 'Have you now abandoned your theory about a drug-smuggling canal boat owner killing Miss Goldsmith in mistake for Caroline, or is your theory that he and Blake were in collusion?'

Clement's face fell. He got up and went to the door. 'It was just a thought,' he observed, sulkily.

He was turning the knob when Mitchell called him back. 'Adrian! Bags I don't tell Jennifer that we've added another suspect to the list.'

*   *   *

Some minutes later, Jennifer put her head round Mitchell's door. 'Do you really need me

144

at this beano at the Vic?'

'Not if you're needed at home. Has something happened?'

Jennifer shook her head. 'Actually, it was your home I was thinking of visiting.'

Mitchell was thankful that Ginny was not going to be alone tonight. 'She'll be with Hannah just now, but I'll let her know to expect you. She'll come back home in time to put the children to bed.'

'I thought I'd bounce a few of my ideas on the case off her.'

'Jen, she's got enough to think about. I've been trying not to use her as a sounding board myself.'

Jennifer was unrepentant. 'No, she hasn't. She's got enough on her mind—too much, in fact—but not enough to think about. She needs her friends and something to distract her from the home situation now and then. And I need . . . well, I need . . .'

'. . . the shock of Ginny's coffee to stimulate your brain cells.' He grinned. 'I have instructions to stop joking about it, though. She's decided it's irresponsible to go on half boasting about not being able to do something. When Hannah dies, she says she's going to take a cookery course.'

Jennifer laughed. 'That I must not miss. If she becomes a cordon bleu expert, I might get quite nostalgic about her dire coffee, but the transformation should be quite entertaining. I suppose it's pointless asking how Hannah is.'

Mitchell shrugged. 'Some weeks she deteriorates slowly, some weeks quickly. No one yet has dared to tell Ginny that it'll be a blessing when it's all over.'

'Well, I shan't be the one to do it.' Jennifer glanced out of the window at a sky patterned with scudding clouds. 'It's a pity the weather's broken tonight. I hope it won't keep the audience at home.'

Mitchell shook his head. 'No chance! Nobody who's set himself the ordeal of listening to three hours of the same piece of music is going to be put off by getting his overcoat wet. Anyway, those clouds are being blown across to Bradford. Cloughton might miss the rain.'

On that count he was wrong. As Jennifer parked outside the Mitchells' house, later that evening, huge branches were slapping against one another in the park across the road and the relentless wind drove chilly gusts of rain into the chinks of her garments.

She found Virginia composed and hospitable. The two women settled themselves, one each side of a bottle of rough Shiraz and, in spite of herself, Jennifer asked after Hannah's health. Good manners seemed to demand it and Virginia seemed to welcome the chance to clothe the exact situation in words.

Her mother was too frail now to go out

146

beyond the garden. Her breathing had become laboured and she dreaded being lifted by anyone but Alex. 'He's got it to a fine art. He's better than we are at feeding her too, though meals can still take up to an hour. Drooling isn't as culturally polluting as being incontinent but it's still very humiliating. Time now seems contracted into a concentrated present—and an anxiety-provoking immediate future.'

'Ginny, have you been planning that speech?'

Virginia blinked. 'How could I? I didn't know you were coming. What was wrong with it?'

Jennifer shook her head. 'Nothing at all. Anyone else would just weep. You don't have to because you can use words to contain it all, pin it down so that you can separate yourself from it. When you've some time to spare and this is over, you really should write something.'

'My mother said that this afternoon. She wants me to start today, though, for obvious reasons.' They were silent for some moments, then Virginia added, 'I hope I'll be as outward-looking and connected to other people when I'm dying.' Jennifer nodded and refilled their glasses. 'So, how's the case going?'

Jennifer grinned. 'So, you do want to hear about it?'

'Of course I do. Benny's stopped coming home high on the day's progress, waiting for me to throw in odd ideas. I miss it but I can't convince him he's not just "adding to my problems". Actually, I haven't got any.' Jennifer was puzzled but managed not to interrupt. 'My mother's dying, horribly. I wish she weren't but there's nothing I can do about it except try to see things from her side and do things as she wants. I'm good at that and glad to do it. We all wish things were different, but the way they are isn't, thank goodness, my responsibility.'

'But, all that and four small children . . .'

'Niamh has them as much as I do. That made me feel a bit guilty until I saw how much both sides were enjoying it. I try to remember that she's sixty-seven and that she can't go on for ever, stopping the gaps in our lives. Mum, though, will only go on for another couple of months at most. Then we'll have problems, of course.'

'Then? Why?'

'Use your head, Jen. Father-in-law, son-in-law problems for a start. Does Dad get his job back? What happens to Benny then? Mother-in-law problems too. Niamh's enjoyed taking the kids over, and I'll want them back.' She sighed, sounding depressed for the first time. 'And there's always Alex.'

'I thought your brother was getting on with everyone these days.'

Virginia nodded soberly. 'He is. Because of Mum's condition, Alex as a nurse is exactly what we need, so he's been forgiven for giving up his medical degree and dossing around for a while, then settling for what Dad sees as second best. He won't rub along so well with me either when Mum isn't here. She's always been the buffer between us and Dad, always valued us for what we are and talked Dad out of his big ideas for us.'

She looked up. 'Weren't you going to distract me from all this soul searching? No more wine till you've told me who killed Rosie Goldsmith.'

Jennifer grinned. 'I'll buy my own, then. I'm not staying dry till we've found out. Benny shot himself in the foot by getting rid of Shakila—well, letting the super do it. We could make good use of her.'

'Then let's hope she works through her schoolgirl crushes quickly.'

'Benny told you.'

Virginia shook her head. 'I've used my eyes at various social functions. I'm surprised he told you lot, though.'

'We've used ours too. I gather she did all the work at the scene while Adrian just stood there dithering. I can't weigh that bloke up. He's so erratic, lackadaisical, lazy. He can be quite good at getting witnesses to open up, then he'll suddenly sink back into himself again. Benny thinks he's still depressed but all his trouble was two years ago and more.'

'His wife died, Jen, and his baby.'

Jennifer accepted the reproof. 'If he's right about this murder and it proves to have nothing to do with the opera, it's even more stupid to have dropped Shakila. She'd be the obvious person to interview our friend Khan.'

'An Asian I gather, but who?'

'Manager of the marina.'

'The one Benny thinks might be trundling crack round the canal system?'

'And dropping it off at waterside pubs, yes. So, you're hearing about some of our exploits?'

'Only if I ask. But he doesn't think aloud any more, or rage about the super or explain how he intends going out on a limb to prove he's right and everyone else wrong.'

Jennifer laughed. 'That's got nothing to do with your home situation. There's no way you can complain about John Carroll without being grossly unfair—and being a DCI, even a temporary one, is making Benny relatively sober and respectable, nearly boring. He doesn't go out on many limbs these days.'

Virginia raised an eyebrow. 'Just turns a blind eye when one of his team does.'

'A rebel by proxy. Perhaps.'

'So, who's your favourite suspect?'

Jennifer considered. 'It's a bit early for choosing. Deborah Murdoch seems the favourite because she gets to sing Carmen in front of people it's worth impressing—but I think we should have a closer look at Steiger.'

'Why?'

'She was probably hoping for Carmen herself and thought being asked to sing Micaela was a bit of an insult. Micaela's the weedy ex of the hero. She loses out once he's met Carmen. Anyway, I just don't like Steiger.'

'So, who do the others fancy?'

'Caro thinks Deborah. Clement was keen on Patel—thought he'd killed Rosie, mistaking her for Caro taking pictures of his drug dealings. That's why he called Shakila in—to harangue the poor chap in Urdu.'

'Clement called Shakila in?'

'I find that easier to believe than that she was taking an evening stroll and met him by chance. Anyhow, he's changed his mind. Now he's busy haring after Blake.'

'Blake?'

'A bit fanciful, but you know Clement.'

Virginia considered the idea. 'It's possible, I suppose. He must be a very complicated character though, if—'

'Good. If Blake's been playing a lot of silly games, he's certain to have slipped up somewhere. A simple crime's much easier to get away with.'

Virginia grinned. 'Ah, but if you're devious by nature, you don't like simple.'

Jennifer was serious. 'What Benny's really worried about is whether Rosie's the killer's only intended victim. The letters to Blake implied that all three guest singers could be in danger. Still, it looks as though they're surviving the first night. Otherwise I'd have been called in again.'

Virginia divided the wine dregs in the bottle absolutely evenly between their two glasses. 'Oh, Benny wouldn't spoil our girlie chat for such a trivial reason.'

CHAPTER EIGHT

The audience had begun to trickle into the Victoria Theatre half an hour ago. Now they were arriving in the foyer in droves. All the lights were on. Gilt tracery sparkled on the crimson panelled walls and the wraps and gowns of many of the female patrons.

Mitchell's team stood in a close huddle at the foot of the grand staircase that led to the circle corridor. They were surrounded by theatre sounds, excited chatter, the clink of glasses from the bar, odd trills of music from regions beyond as instruments were warmed up and tried for pitch. The bouquets of the bar wines mingled with ladies' perfumes.

Impervious to it all, the police officers reviewed their situation and considered their options. Their smart clothes and glasses of wine fooled none of the theatre staff or the company members and not all the paying public. Here were the police, out in force and expected, variously, to ensure everyone's safety or to add to the occasion's excitement by arresting Rosie Goldsmith's killer as the climax of the evening's entertainment. They supported one another by offering facts, fears and speculations.

Caroline was more nervous than Cavill about his conducting debut. Sternly, she centred her thoughts on a suspect, settling at random on Miles Cranmer. How annoyed had he been by Rosie's snub? What was his opinion of this production now that it was being offered to the public? Was he regretting putting his reputation on the line? Might he have tried this drastic way of stopping the performance going ahead? If it had not, would he still have got his money? How much did he need it? They hadn't gone sufficiently into everyone's financial situation.

She thought Cranmer a very conceited man, not overtly boastful though, except by comparing his own performance with that of others. He had never been impertinent about them, merely benevolently contemptuous. It was interesting that he had worked with Blake now for almost two months but still referred to him only by his surname.

She turned to share some of her musings with Clement but his comments concerned only the two female principals. 'Deborah was so spiteful about Steiger. I'm sure she must have been belittled and humiliated by her.'

Mitchell for once ignored his officers' comments, being preoccupied with just one question. Was either of the other two professional singers in danger?

A muffled announcement over the Tannoy system brought the drinkers reluctantly out of the two bars and persuaded the gossiping throng in the foyer, still chattering, to drift along to their allotted seats. His own chosen position was the small box at the far right-hand extremity of the circle. It contained only two chairs, neither of them wide enough to accommodate him comfortably.

The management had willingly conceded the box since it afforded a restricted view of the stage. Actors and singers on his own side had to be recognized by the tops of their heads. Clement, stationed in the corresponding position on the other side, could be seen across the auditorium, settling himself and fussing with his belongings. Taller but slighter than Mitchell, he fitted his chair and sat at ease, his elbows resting on the padded velvet surface of the circle rail.

The boxes commanded an excellent view of the rest of the audience. Mitchell took a pair of binoculars from his pocket and fiddled with the focusing wheel. A strange face appeared as if immediately in front of him. He guessed the man to be in his late thirties. His hooded eyes were already glazed over with boredom and the mouth already chewing. Mitchell wondered what motivation had brought him so unwillingly along.

He trained the glasses on another face. A child this time, maybe ten years old, gazing round in wonder, then, as the orchestra began its final tuning, looking puzzled and disappointed. Maybe he thought the performance had already begun and was not impressed by it. Nor was Mitchell expecting to be enthralled. He was not intending even to listen.

He put down his binoculars on the empty chair and surveyed the auditorium as a whole, trying to concentrate on all that was happening there. In spite of himself, his mind wandered and he felt uneasy. Was there anything here that made his own presence necessary? He suspected that his reason for sitting in this box now was his love of being where the action was.

Would there be any action tonight, apart from what was happening on stage? Surely, their killer, if his murderous intentions had not yet been fully carried out, would not use this occasion, when the police presence was so apparent. Even if there was another murder intended tonight, it was unlikely that he personally could do anything to prevent it. Did he not trust his men?

He suspected he could not bear to miss being in at the kill—in this case, maybe, quite literally. It would rile him to have the news brought to him by Caroline or Clement. If his father-in-law were in charge of the case, he would, at this moment, be sitting in his office at headquarters, masterminding their operation.

He turned his mind to a check of the routine work still waiting to be done. He should by now have sent someone to interview the journalist who had written up a diary of this production in such detail. The woman could probably supply few facts that were unknown to Cavill and Caroline, but she would have her own viewpoint and should have been seen by now.

Mitchell pulled out a notebook and began to make a list. Steiger's account of her Friday afternoon should be checked. Someone must go to Porter's shop to find out how they came by the letter that Lewis Blake was given there. Personally, he felt that this jerking about of the newly rich producer had no significant connection with their murder, but the matter had to be cleared up. In any case, not all his team agreed with him.

No one had checked why the 'taxi-driver', Gwen, had refused to drive the victim and nor had he had a word with his brother-in-law about his gig at the Swan last night. He added these to his list, together with a reminder to see personally the men he had set to patrolling the canal bank in the late afternoons. Was it enough to have sent a couple of uniforms, rather than someone on his team of detectives? Would two men he hardly knew have asked the right questions? What might people have seen there on Friday? Someone behaving sanely and calmly after a carefully premeditated killing? No one would remember him. Someone shaken and frightened after giving way to a sadistic impulse, and blood-splashed into the bargain? Someone would have reported that already.

It occurred to Mitchell that a calm killer might claim to have been walking innocently on the towpath on Friday and deliberately feed them false information. A wave of panic washed over him. Was he really or only nominally leading this investigation? Was the blind leading the blind? If he could bounce all these questions off Ginny as he usually did, the answers would come to him before she even had time to speak.

Did the whole business hinge on Blake's money? His parents had been seen, but how many other relatives and friends had expected to benefit from his good fortune—and how much of the two million was left? That question at least he could answer without too much trouble.

He took up the binoculars again and focused them on another face, an interesting one. He thought this woman must once have been very striking, almost beautiful. The bones were good and the colouring vivid, but the skin was lined now, and, worse, the teeth disfigured with much dental work. The red-gold hair was lifeless and bedraggled and the woman pushed it impatiently off her face as she spoke into her mobile phone. She had been standing in the stalls at the end of a row, and now she put her phone away and departed through a door that led backstage.

A ripple of applause began, and he watched Cavill walk across the pit below him, ascend the rostrum and turn to greet the audience. The applause increased. Cavill held up a hand to still the clapping and collected the attention of his players.

Mitchell saw that the orchestra pit had been formed by taking away the first few rows of the stalls. If he shifted his chair to the far right of the box he could watch Cavill's face. Good. That would be a fair guide to whether anything untoward was happening on the stage. He wondered if he had left anything undone that could have helped prevent further trouble tonight. Uniformed men were patrolling the corridor of dressing rooms. Two men stood backstage, as far out of the way of the cast and the stagehands as was consistent with their seeing all that was going on.

The orchestra began to play. Oh well, all he could do now was keep a vigilant watch.

* * *

Cavill raised his baton and the orchestra leapt

into the lively overture, the beginning of an exciting journey until all the familiar tunes were introduced and the magic was lost, at least for him. He could feel the stir in the audience when the strings touched on the Toreador's song and its musically uneducated element recognized the one tune it had heard before.

In the text Bizet had used, Escamillo was a vain, empty fool with all the subtlety of an Elvis Presley. Hadn't Lauren made that comparison? His song, therefore, was swaggering and appropriately banal, marked in the score *'avec fatuité'*.

Cavill was not unappreciative of his audience. They were allowing him to experience the much rehearsed production afresh. Their excitement was dissipating all the staleness that had accumulated over the last few weeks. He paid silent tribute to his orchestra, which was rising to the full range of demands the music made on it—first the public blatancy of the municipal band, followed by a contrasting suggestion of raw intimacy and private tragedy. The same contrast was at the heart of the final act, with a bullfight background to the playing out of the personal tragedies of the two former lovers.

Cavill had determined to concentrate on Blake's production and put aside any personal feelings but he was finding that impossible. Apart from his sorrow that a talented young singer's life had ended so suddenly, so cruelly, he felt a bitter personal disappointment at having lost the opportunity to conduct Rosie Goldsmith as Carmen.

He was resentful because too many extraneous issues were distracting his singers. A first night was quite enough of a drama and this particular opera contained a double portion within its plot. They could have done without the scandal-mongering element in the audience and the badgering of the police and the press.

The orchestra finished the overture and the curtain rose on the towering set of circular balconies, full of armed soldiers, dramatically lit from above. Had Blake set this production in Seville as Bizet demanded, or in Santiago? Certainly, it portrayed a society where the military was in power. He smiled to himself, remembering a review of the dress rehearsal he had read that morning that pinned down his own sentiments. 'The long shadow of Pinochet seems to hang over the opening scenes.'

The soldiers' chorus plunged into their opening number and Eric, in his character of Morales, began to sing alone. Cavill's heart sank. The voice was sweet but weak, as it had been at the first rehearsal. Eric's Morales tonight was not the sergeant of the regiment, the stern disciplinarian who would mete out her punishment to Carmen and a more severe penalty to Don José for letting her escape.

Cavill saw that Eric was aware of his failure and in panic, approaching a major freeze. He decided on an encouraging beam, rather than an admonitory glare. He could think of no way though to make Eric, in centre stage, catch his eye to receive any kind of message.

Then, to his amazement, he saw Ursula Steiger make an early entry from where she was waiting in the wings. He watched her take Eric's hand and bring him to the footlights as he sang, close enough for his anguished gaze to meet Cavill's encouraging nod. Eric smiled and the smile entered his voice. The audience warmed to him, silently urged him on. Both men felt it, though not even Cavill could have said which of his senses absorbed the impression.

With the confidence it gave him, Eric began to project and Cavill relaxed. He saw that Ursula had vanished back into the wings. The audience noticed too. There was a ripple of applause for her, quickly quashed as the chorus continued.

Cavill wiped his forehead as the changing of the guard began. Now he could feel the waves of excitement from his choir, also waiting in the wings. He had no worries about projection here. Fifteen of the eighteen of them were quite used to singing together, sometimes in cathedrals that took more filling with sound than this smallish theatre.

He felt the children's disappointment when

their total of four minutes' singing in this act was over and the soldier chorus shooed them off stage. They had found this excursion into opera tremendous fun, but Cavill had been thrilled when one of them had declared that he preferred 'the stuff we do on Sundays'.

Now the girls were emerging from their factory, Carmen still lost amongst them. As the soldiers harassed them and flirted with them, the audience anticipated, with a mixture of hope and dread, the five minute aria they had all bought tickets to hear Rosie sing. Deborah rose from the centre of the group. Everyone on stage turned to face her. Audience and chorus alike willed her not to disappoint them, not to let herself down.

She responded. They lifted her. As the men sang their lechery, she taunted them. Her movements were still a little wooden, but her voice, as she began the Habanera, teased both them and the audience. At the portamento into 'Ah, Love!', Cavill melted with pleasure. She had almost everything still to learn, but here was a new English soprano. As Carmen, she was feeling a sexual power that miserable little Deborah Murdoch had never felt in rehearsal, probably never in life.

With her audience, both on and off the stage, mesmerized, she moved and gestured as she felt led, totally ignoring the blocking and actions that had been hammered out between Lewis Blake and Rosie. Just fancy! Cavill

162

shook his head to clear it. Little Deborah was an audience's singer, rising to the occasion they made for her. Cavill became increasingly excited, conducting the music from memory as his fingers fumbled the pages of the score.

Could he believe what he was seeing and hearing tonight? Selfish Ursula Steiger helping an amateur over an attack of stage fright? Seemingly inhibited, passionless Deborah Murdoch responding to the stimulus of a huge live audience? For the first time, Cavill realized how much Deborah had wanted this opportunity. Could she, possibly, have made it for herself?

He dismissed the thought and concentrated on the duet between Don José and his first love, Micaela. Caught up in the general excitement even Ursula sang with conviction and animation. Cloughton was having its 'hell of a musical experience' after all. He gave himself up to the glorious sound, using the enchantment the singers were spinning, controlling it and tossing the initiative back to them.

From her seat next to the aisle at the back of the stalls Caroline Webster watched her fiancé and realized that, throughout her married life, she would have to share him with countless performers, countless audiences. She saw his rapt expression and knew that, for tonight, she did not exist for him.

*　　*　　*

The curtain fell at the end of the second act. Against the crashing applause, Mitchell thought he heard a knock on the door of his box. Feeling slightly foolish, he yelled an invitation to enter and the door opened.

He was confronted by a vision in Technicolor. Short, mousy-coloured hair and a round, homely face had left his visitor little scope for first night operatic glamour. She had compensated by draping her stocky figure in a satin tunic that made blue and green mountains of her bosom and hips.

Mitchell invited his guest to be seated and her chair groaned in sympathy with his own. 'You are . . . ?'

'Amanda,' she supplied. 'Amanda Tyler. I've been looking after the ticket office. My brother's in the chorus. I'm sorry to keep you from your interval drinks, but you said if any of us remembered . . .'

Mitchell took the hint. 'No problem. You keep in mind what you've remembered and I'll supply the refreshments. G&T suit you?' She grinned and nodded. Mitchell spoke into his radio and sent one of the patrolling PCs scurrying to the bar. 'So, what have you got for me?'

'I only remembered tonight. Being back in the kiosk where I do all the ticket stuff reminded me . . .'

164

'What of?' She looked offended and Mitchell realized his tone had been impatient.

'A couple of weeks ago a man came to buy a ticket. Just the one, which was unusual. Most people come in pairs or big groups.' Mitchell nodded, accepting the significance of this point. 'He took ages to decide where he wanted to sit but, in the end, he decided to splash out and took the last seat left on the front row of the circle. I encouraged him to go for that one because I thought that it would stay empty. As I said, most people want two seats together, or even a whole row. When there are odd seats like that left unbooked, the manager grumbles as if it's my fault.'

Mitchell bit his lip and hung on to his patience. 'Why are you telling me about this man?'

'Well, he looked ordinary enough, just middle height and—'

'But there must have been something that struck you about him or you wouldn't be here.'

'Well, it was Rosie, you see.' Mitchell managed to contain himself until this cryptic statement was elucidated. 'She was called that morning—by Mr Blake, for rehearsal. Do policemen understand opera talk? Well, it was rehearsal break time. She was running up the stairs from the green room—that's the cafeteria where they'd all been having their coffee.' Mitchell assured her that he did indeed understand theatre talk. 'I saw her through the glass door. She'd half pulled it open, then took her hand away and let it shut again. I thought she was going back down for something she'd forgotten but after a minute I looked over again and I could see her watching us.'

'Maybe she thought you were having a private conversation.'

Amanda shook her head. 'She could have walked through the foyer with no need to come near us. Anyway, that wasn't all I had to tell you.' She looked up and beamed as a curious PC brought in a tray bearing a double gin and tonic and a tankard of beer.

The PC smirked. 'Will there be anything else, sir?'

Mitchell replied, straightfaced, 'Not for us, but get yourself a packet of crisps, sonny.' The constable caught his DCI's spinning fifty pence piece and thanked him solemnly.

Amanda sat nonplussed as the door swung shut behind him. 'Er . . . about Rosie. As soon as the man had gone, she came across to me and asked if he was a friend of mine. I said, "No. Why?" and she said we'd talked for so long that she thought he must be—sort of giving away that she'd been watching. She wanted to know what we'd been talking about. I thought that was a bit nosy, not like her.

'She must have realized what I was thinking. She said, all sort of airy, "Not that it's any of my business. Just taking an interest in our audience." She seemed a bit flustered. It was time to go back to the rehearsal room, but she went out through the main door and into the street. I think she was trying to see which way the man went . . .'

'Did she seem frightened of him?'

'Not that I noticed.' Amanda's eyes widened. 'You don't think he was the one that did it?'

Mitchell shrugged. 'I've no idea, but I do think I'd like to speak to him. Can you stay here till Act 3 begins and point him out to me?'

'But . . . he didn't book for tonight. Tonight's been a sell-out for ages.'

'So, which night is he coming?'

She shook her head. 'I can't remember. There's hundreds of tickets been sold. You can't expect me . . .' The voice was rising indignantly.

'It's all right. We'll watch that seat. Can you remember anything at all about what he looks like?'

She shut her eyes and sipped her gin. Mitchell hoped it would not make her even more discursive. She spoke melodramatically, a medium in a trance. 'Average height, brown hair, not sure about the eyes, clothes quite casual . . .' Mitchell despaired.

'. . . and the tip of the little finger missing on his left hand.' Her eyes had opened and her tone become triumphant. Was she mocking him? As he considered, she put her empty glass back on the tray and rose to go. As she reached the door, she spoke, without turning back to him, as if thinking aloud. 'Rosie dashed off so quick to see where this chap was going, I never got round to telling her what we were talking about.'

'And what were you?'

'About Rosie. He wanted to know everything I could tell him. A sort of one-man fan club, he was.'

*　　　*　　　*

By the time he was dismissed, at the end of the performance, Clement was in the disgruntled mood that came over him on any day when he had been denied a run. Suddenly, he decided he would take a short one now.

It was cut shorter by a phone call from Shakila, but just stretching his legs had restored his good mood. She had summoned him to the Swan and he quickened his stride, since it was not long to last orders.

He saw her as soon as he entered. She was sitting near to but slightly apart from several young bikers. As he queued at the bar, he could see her exchanging the odd joke or remark, but making it clear by her body language that she did not intend them to draw her or himself into the group.

Mindful of his experience the previous day,

he ordered a pint of bitter and a pint of tap water and drank from the latter first. The bikers were eyeing him, obviously having had him pointed out and claimed by Shakila. He saw their eyes cast up as, mopping his face, he came to sit beside her.

He grinned. 'They don't seem to think I'm much of a catch.'

She replied, seriously, 'It's only the gear. You can look quite presentable when you're cleaned up.'

Having dispatched the water, Clement turned with more enthusiasm to his beer. Jerking his head in the direction of the bikers, he remarked, quite audibly, 'They couldn't run further than to wherever they're parked up!' He dropped his voice. 'Drink up and we'll talk outside.'

'It's too cold.'

'In the car. I parked it here when I started and did an out-and-back.'

The car's upholstery struck chill. Clement turned the key in the ignition and switched on the heater. 'Who's going first?'

'I will.' She plunged eagerly into a description of her day, realizing as she relived it how much she had enjoyed it. The weather had still been pleasantly mild at eleven that morning. She had been surprised but thankful to see that the police tape blocking off the murder scene allowed single file traffic along the towpath. She had watched Hal Benton as he worked, totally absorbed in his painting, and been genuinely interested. She had expected to see paint being slapped on to bare boards. Benton, however, was a craftsman. He was carefully restoring each curl and flourish of the lettering of the boat's name.

Shakila thought the boat resembled a floating gypsy caravan. It had similar garish colours and ornate patterning.

When the man laid aside his brush and reached for a thermos flask she had moved forward to speak to him. Having paid tribute to his work, she had professed deep interest in oak hulls and elm bottoms and sympathized with his disapproval of modern boats made entirely of steel. She had been rewarded with an invitation to go aboard and look around.

She had been surprised by what she saw. The cabin would be warm on the inside whatever the weather. The boat also contained a full-sized cooker, a fridge and a hot-water shower. Benton obviously despised the holiday-makers who had obliged his employer to defile this traditional old boat with such modern contraptions.

Shakila had enquired about the possibility of hiring a boat so late in the year. Benton had reassured her. 'Oh, yes. Mr Patel doesn't have a closed season, though things are very quiet at the moment. It's quite busy at Christmas, I'm told. There are plenty of boats available just now, though.'

'I'd like to hire one, I think. Are they difficult to manage?'

'Not once you've got the knack. He'll send someone to show you how to steer it and all the rest. He'll be here in the morning. Come and see him about it.'

'So, I can't make a booking with you?'

He had shaken his head and glanced at the police tape that fluttered feebly in a slight breeze.

Clement was becoming impatient with all these details. 'I don't need a weather report and I'm not interested in whether you managed to get off with Hal Benton.'

Shakila tossed her head. 'OK, drive me home. On the way, you can tell me all that's happening at your end. One thing I could do for you would be to chat to the old man—Hal's father. Hal's busy working and takes no notice of passers-by but the old man often comes a bit early to meet him. He might have seen something whilst he was sitting and waiting.'

'I've already seen him. He was fishing all day Friday and Hal made his own way home. He told you that himself at the scene.'

'Did you ask him about the regular towpath walkers?'

'Of course I did, but it can't do any harm if you gossip to him—see if you can pick up anything else.'

'Will do, then, and I'll let you know how I get on with Patel in the morning. I haven't decided yet how I'm going to approach him. I could just be a customer or I could go all native and seductive in a sari and, to use your vulgar phrase, try to get off with him. What do you think?'

Clement grinned. 'Depends what you wear underneath. It's a bigger mystery than what a Scotsman has under his kilt. Wear whatever allows for hiding a mobile phone. I think, if you're more than a prospective customer, you'll be getting into deep water.'

'In the canal?'

Clement was serious. 'Don't try to be funny. Try to be careful.'

CHAPTER NINE

On Sunday morning, Shakila sat on her dressing-table stool in her painfully tidy bedroom. She stared, unseeing, at her reflection and tried to decide how to dress for her meeting with Minesh Patel. Almost all of the clothes in her wardrobe conformed roughly with the Muslim rules of dress. She owed too much to her brother who had taken her in and supported her since her parents' death to want to risk any offence to him.

Lately, however, she had interpreted the rules along Western lines, wearing smart trouser suits and the trousered form of police uniform when on duty. For her present purpose she wondered whether a sari might be more flattering. Her brother declared that it was certainly more sexy and she had to agree that, as a teenager in full Asian gear, she had attracted just as many suitors, both coloured and white, as her English friends had done by baring almost all. The filmy fabrics promised and suggested.

Almost decided, she changed her mind again. Perhaps Patel would not buy the idea of a Pakistani woman planning to go on a narrow boat holiday with an unrelated friend. She got up, opened her wardrobe and once more considered all her options.

Suddenly, a solution occurred to her. Last year, her short excursion into CID had happened because a Pakistani schoolgirl had disappeared from Cloughton. It was thought that Nazreen might have run away from an arranged marriage with one of her cousins and Shakila's chance had come because her fluent Urdu enabled her to get to the root of the family problems underlying their case.

Why not use the story? In Asian dress, she would approach Mr Patel and appeal to him to rescue her from a similar situation. She could ask him to moor a boat in some hideaway for her. Her imagination supplied more details. She'd declare her family's choice of husband for her was old and ugly, invent for him a string of other women.

She embroidered the story as she pulled out filmy garments from behind her everyday clothes. By the time she was satisfied that she looked the part, she was ready to play it. She smiled to herself as she tucked away her mobile phone, remembering Clement's speculations about where it would go. Then she set out in high spirits. She was going to make Superintendent Carroll eat humble pie.

*   *   *

Mitchell believed that an examination of her home would give the team a valuable insight into their victim's character. He had backed his belief by sending two constables with his sergeant rather than the usual one. PC Smithson she had requested. The female officer was a stranger to her, young and beautiful with a supercilious expression. The latter proved to be misleading. Kirstie McDonald had enlivened the journey to London with droll mimicry at the expense of most of the Cloughton station's hierarchy. Jennifer was well pleased with both her assistants.

Apart from its location in a sought-after area of the capital, there was nothing ostentatious about Rosie Goldsmith's flat. Everything was homely and much smaller than Jennifer had expected, though the building itself was imposing enough. A minute hallway opened off the main top floor corridor. Doors were in a row along it. Jennifer opened them, to find a bedroom, a bathroom, a sort of office with a daybed and a kitchen, all very tiny.

A wider door at the end, across the width of the hallway, led into the main room. This was twice the size of the others, with a huge window overlooking Lord's. Smithson wondered aloud if it would be possible to watch test matches from the little balcony. 'Not in October,' Jennifer told him and sent him to search the office. She decided that the living room, bathroom and Rosie's own bedroom would reveal more about their owner to another woman than to a man. Kirstie was allocated the kitchen and bathroom and Jennifer set herself to exploring the rest.

The main room was dominated by a huge sofa, well worn and heaped with cushions that made bright splashes against its washable cream cover. The cushion covers appeared to be hand-made of simple tapestry work with an endearing mistake here and there in the design. Jennifer had a sudden vision of Rosie busily stitching to while away long hotel-room evenings after exhausting days of rehearsal. The carpet was of reasonable quality but not luxurious, a little worn and faded in places. It seemed as though Rosie had been perfectly satisfied, in her success, with the place that had served as her refuge when she was struggling to establish her career.

Jennifer crossed the room, turned the key in the french window leading to the balcony and looked down. Matchbox cars, taxis and buses stopped and started, beeped and roared and belched out pollution below. She wondered how much of it reached this level. Singers, she had recently discovered, are paranoid about the care of their throats and lungs. Still, in recent years Rosie had had little time to spare to spend at home.

Jennifer could see most of the cricket ground, winter green now, with the pitches regrown almost to the colour of the outfield. It seemed unlikely that Rosie had watched a game from here. The players would be mere white dots and the ball invisible. Besides, no one had mentioned that she was interested in any sport.

Jennifer went back into the room and saw that Rosie's answering machine was registering four messages. She switched it on. The first voice was a man's, light and high, possibly a singer's.

Rosie? Roger. Care for a bite of supper after the show? Give me a buzz before twelve.

Click. Now a woman with a south London accent.

Oh . . . er . . . I hate these machines . . . well, just to say thank you, Miss G, for the birthday card and the chocs. I'll be in to do for you Friday as usual. It's er . . . Mrs Johns.

Jennifer smiled grimly. Someone had done

176

for Rosie on Friday but she didn't think it was her cleaning lady. She listened to the third message.

Rosemary? It's Henry. Oh, damn! Why did you have to be out? I should have written but I just sat in front of the blank sheet and didn't know how to begin. Rose, did you know we're all in Yorkshire? I'd like to think that's why you agreed to come and sing here, so we can meet again, see what we can sort out. There was silence for some seconds, then the voice began again. *I've taken good care of . . .*

Perhaps this caller had decided that leaving his message had been a bad idea and hung up. Or had someone come into the room when he didn't want to be overheard?

There was another click, whirring and several beeps. Jennifer realized that the fourth caller had hung up when Rosie's recorded message had begun, declining to state his business. Might it have been the third caller again, with courage renewed? She called Kirstie from the bathroom and played the tape again. 'Why did the interesting one stop?'

'Some machines only allow a limited time for each item.'

'Yes, but they give you longer than that. I wonder how old these messages are.'

'Presumably since before Miss Goldsmith came to Cloughton, so she never got them. If she had, she'd have wiped them.'

'How do we know that? You can ring your

own number and hear messages on your tape. Anyway, even if she was still here she might not have. I come in and listen to mine as I'm hanging my things up and putting the kettle on. Usually the messages run out whilst I'm still busy.'

'I suppose so. And she might have wanted to listen to that third person again.'

Jennifer shrugged. 'OK. Carry on where you were.'

Kirstie departed and Jennifer returned to her search of Rosie's sitting room. A Bang & Olufsen music centre of an old design was surrounded by racks of discs that represented a very catholic taste in music. They were efficiently sorted into alphabetical order within types—jazz, heavy rock music, chamber music, choral singing including oratoria and several John Denver compilations. There seemed to be no recorded opera.

The bookshelves along one wall contained, unsurprisingly, technical books on music, especially singing. There were also a good many paperback thrillers, a set of Dickens' novels with matching bindings and an unmatching set of books on various painters. Jennifer pulled a couple of them out and found they contained coloured plates and the volumes had obviously been chosen individually. There were no pictures, however, on the walls which were an unbroken white and gave the room its cool, calm atmosphere.

The books and music were there to stimulate but they had to be taken up, deliberately. Nothing forced itself on the occupant's attention.

Cupboards and drawers contained conventional domestic equipment, financial documents and business papers, including insurance and a sealed, unlabelled envelope that Jennifer thought might contain a will.

She moved to the bedroom. Drawers and the wardrobe there contained the few garments Rosie had not taken to Cloughton. Like the ones found in her hotel rooms, they were good quality but by no means new. Beneath shoe boxes, in the bottom of the wardrobe was a small, leather bound album of photographs. The pictures were mostly of a chubby baby who, after a page or two, became a toddler. One picture included a young man who seemed faintly familiar. In another, a much younger Rosie held the infant on her lap. She appeared ill at ease with it and the child seemed to be struggling to be put down. Not a close relative, obviously.

Jennifer slipped the album into a plastic bag as PC Smithson tapped on the door and came in. 'I think I've got all I can from the study.' He handed over his own plastic-sealed booty and glanced with interest at his sergeant's. 'She kept all her letters neatly filed, according to who they're from and in date order. A lot of them are short notes about the arrangements for her work, concerts and rehearsals and such. They're all recent. Looks like she had a clear-out as soon as the engagement was over.

'There are some notes and letters from various friends, and then these.' He indicated a fat bundle of envelopes. 'They're all in the same handwriting. From someone called Jane.'

'Someone who wrote regularly?' Jennifer beamed. 'Smithson, I think you've struck gold.' She turned to Kirstie who had joined them. 'So, what did you find?'

'Photographs.'

'In the kitchen?' Jennifer went to look. The snapshots were on most available surfaces, pinned to the cork notice board which was otherwise empty, blu-tacked to the kitchen units and propped on various ledges. Their subjects were many and various. 'Probably all casual friends,' she decided.

'Shall we take them?'

'Why not?'

Smithson remarked in his deliberate way, 'I thought the place would be full of opera stills and publicity photographs. We haven't found any books of cuttings and reviews either, but she might have them with her.'

Jennifer shook her head. 'We didn't find anything like that in the hotel rooms.'

'Have we finished then?'

Jennifer thought that, probably, they had. She collected up all the evidence bags they had filled, waiting for Kirstie to scrabble the last of

180

the pictures she had gathered from the kitchen into a large one. She left the two constables waiting in the hall whilst she had a last slow walk through the rooms, taking Polaroid shots from many angles and, thankfully, remembering to extract the tape from the answering machine.

The end volume of the set of Dickens was slightly out of alignment. Irritated, she went to straighten it. The book would not close completely because of an envelope slipped between the leaves. Jennifer removed it and slotted *Dombey and Son* neatly back into its place. The small manilla envelope was addressed to Rosie. It contained a scribbled note and a handful of elderly snapshots, mostly rather dog-eared. The slip of paper was not headed. 'Found these when I was having a spring clean. Thought they'd bring back a few memories. Julie.'

A summer garden was the background to all the pictures. Here was Rosie again, aged about fifteen. She was surrounded by other youngsters, in various silly poses and with stupid expressions. Someone's birthday party? In the last shot, several girls dangled striped ties, whilst a boy knelt, applying what looked like a cigarette lighter to the end of one of them. Now Jennifer understood. Dimly, she remembered taking part in a similar ceremony. These kids had just left school. This was the celebratory party and they were symbolically disposing of the despised uniform.

She turned to the much younger Kirstie. 'Did you do this when you left school?' She splayed the snapshots as though they were a hand of playing cards, then suddenly snatched one out of the fan. 'That is Rosie, isn't it?'

The other two officers examined the picture and agreed. 'It's the only one where she's standing up. To me, she looks . . .'

'Pregnant?' Kirstie nodded. 'Mm, that's how it looks to me.'

*　　　*　　　*

Since she knew all the children involved in the opera at least by sight, Mitchell had sent Caroline to talk to them. She had occasionally led the boys' choir practices in church from the piano when Cavill had been giving organ recitals abroad and each of the three girls had come to his house for piano lessons at some time when she had been there.

She knew they were all talented. Otherwise Cavill would have passed them to other teachers. She had known little about the girls before the opera rehearsals had begun, but, over the last few weeks, she had got to know them well enough for them to feel comfortable with her and to talk freely. All the same, she did not feel hopeful that any of them would be able to help the case along.

She had elected to speak to the girls together rather than individually. This was not only to put them further at their ease but also in the hope that she would learn as much from their asides to each other as she did from their answers to her questions.

She had seen that Rosie Goldsmith had taken trouble with the girls, but she had not known about the tea party at the hotel until Clement had mentioned it at a recent briefing. She asked about it now. The two who had accepted the invitation had been much taken with the 'posh' hotel and the elaborate cakes that had accompanied their tea. Caroline asked what the three of them had talked about.

Gracie bit her lip and listened. Kate, pretty and stage-struck, eagerly began to tell. 'I asked Miss Goldsmith—Rosie—about how a singer could get started, and how she'd got famous herself.'

'What did she say?'

'Well, she didn't really answer the second part. She said she'd broken all the rules but she'd been lucky to get away with it. She said what I should do is get good exam results and try for the Royal Northern College or the Royal Academy.'

'Boring.' Amy, strapping and sporty, who just happened to have a good voice and whose parents had insisted on the piano lessons, was contemptuous. 'The food was scrummy but the talk was really—'

'Boring. Right.'

'Rosie's only interested in people who want to take up music for a career so Gracie missed nothing.'

'Well, I do, so I did miss something!'

Caroline looked at Gracie reprovingly. 'You need to take things more seriously if you really mean that. Cavill tells me you have a lot of musical ability but you don't practise nearly enough.'

Gracie coloured. 'It's Gran's and Grandad's life ambition to stop me. Every time I go upstairs to get my flute out she calls me down and gives me a job to do.'

Caroline gave her a hard look. 'Every time?'

'It feels like it.' The girl's voice expressed distress rather than indignation. 'I know Gran's turned sixty and it's hard work having Dad and me to look after. I do help.'

'Have you told Cavill about this?'

Gracie shook her head. 'Grandad thinks I should go to an ordinary university and do a course that leads to a job. He says music's too chancy for a career. It's better for a hobby.'

'What about your father?'

She smiled. 'He pays for my lessons with Mr Jackson. They cost a lot and we're not very well off, so he can't be against it. He sometimes gets worried himself when jobs aren't coming in. Then he half wishes he belonged to a big firm, but usually he says he likes working for himself.'

'That doesn't make you safe, in any case,'

Amy cut in. 'My dad's big firm made him redundant a couple of years ago.'

'If you're born to be a performer,' Kate volunteered, melodramatically, 'you just have to do it. You won't be happy if you don't, however rich you might be.'

Gracie had no more to say but she nodded firmly in agreement. Caroline tried to turn the conversation back to the murdered singer, but the girls seemed to have nothing useful to add. She left them, determined to persuade Cavill to look into Gracie's family situation. Kate had voiced frustration but it was Gracie who was suffering it.

She thanked Kate's mother who had sat in on the interview as the girls' chaperone and had had the self-control to remain silent. Now for the boys, who were waiting in a dressing room with Cavill. She had still not quite decided how to approach them. They were mostly much younger than the girls as they left the choir when their voices broke. Some of them were as young as twelve when this happened, though Mark, Cavill's best boy at present, was almost fifteen and older than all three girls.

He had a sweet and powerful soprano and she knew that Cavill had offered him privileges, denied to the other boys. He wanted to keep the voice for his choir but was not willing to embarrass the lad by herding him with much younger children. When their voices broke, the boys were advised to take some time out from singing until they settled again. Cavill kept in touch with them, anxious to have them back as young tenors and basses, though not all excellent boy sopranos sang well as men.

At present, Cavill's youngest choir member was only six. She began to chat to them informally. Only if any of them seemed to have something important to contribute would she ask specific questions. She would make Mark the exception, though.

After half an hour which yielded nothing that seemed relevant, Cavill dismissed the younger boys to the parents who waited in the theatre foyer. Mark waited self-importantly. Caroline was amused at the idea of encouraging him to gossip. Cavill was wont to say his choir consisted of fourteen small boys and one old woman and spent a good deal of time telling Mark to stop talking and sing. Today, he disappointed her. He had hardly spoken to Rosie throughout the weeks of rehearsal and had had no interaction with her on stage.

Mark proved, however, to have taken a shine to Gracie and was quite prepared to gossip about that. He seemed to have been slower than his friends to show an interest in girls, especially since they avoided him. Now he had spent eight weeks in close contact with three. Kate's veneer of sophistication put her out of his class and the hoydenish Amy frightened him. Gracie fitted the bill nicely. She was too polite to refuse to talk to him and too inexperienced to know how to get rid of him politely.

'I'm glad to have this chance of a word with you,' he confided, ingratiatingly. Caroline bit back a smile. If she closed her eyes she could believe she was talking to his mother. Perhaps she could believe it if she kept them open. He was a fat boy with rounded hips and breasts and a waddling walk and was beginning to suffer merciless mockery. She was sorry for him, remembering that Cavill had said he had elderly parents who overfed and over-protected him. The Almighty chose strange places to hide rather special voices.

The boy had an unfortunate habit of touching the people he spoke to to make sure he had their attention. She took a step away. 'What were you wanting to say to me?'

'It's about Gracie. She's being bothered by a yob called Shaun—on the canal bank, when her dad's working inside the cabin.'

'She can speak to her father about it, can't she?'

'You don't tell tales of Shaun, or you wish you hadn't.'

'Shaun Grant?'

He brightened. 'Yes, do you know him? Now he thinks Gracie's scared of him he messes her about at school as well. Not when

I'm around though.'

Caroline kept her expression solemn. 'I think you'd better leave us to deal with Shaun.'

Mark's relief was palpable. 'Well, if that's what you advise.' He moved closer and, without thinking, Caroline stepped several paces back. The boy felt the slight and was embarrassed. Staring at his feet, he muttered and Caroline had to step towards him again to hear.

'Gracie thinks Shaun's working for Mr Patel. She's worried because everybody knows he's bent.'

Caroline smiled to herself. So, Shaun's attentions to Gracie were not as unwelcome as Mark would like to think. 'Is that so? What does everybody say he's up to?'

'A lot of people say drugs but my dad says you people ought to search his boats because he's bringing cabinloads of sambos into Cloughton.' He misinterpreted Caroline's frown. 'Sorry. He calls all black people sambos. He doesn't mean anything.'

This was an idea Caroline had not considered. She wondered if her superiors had. Guiltily, she realized that, since the opera rehearsals had got under way, she had done little more, as far as her job was concerned, than what she had been ordered to do. Second miles had been gone at the behest of Cavill and Lewis Blake rather than DCI Mitchell. She thought about it now, pushing the problem of her priorities once more out of her mind. She supposed Patel's business would be a very convenient way of moving illegal immigrants about. There was little danger of them suffocating in the cabins of narrow boats. They could live very comfortably there during Patel's off peak season, though, if that was what he was up to, he had been rash to hire Hal Benton to restore his little fleet to good order. Unless Benton was working with him, of course. She had better have a word about that with Adrian as soon as possible.

*   *   *

Mitchell, suffering an attack of paperwork, was glad to hear a tap at the door and to see Caroline come in. Mitchell glanced up, then looked again, harder. 'You look different.' After further study, he announced, triumphantly, 'It's your hair.'

Caroline grinned. 'Ten out of ten.' She settled into the chair he indicated. Mitchell was taken aback. A change of hairstyle or the parading of a new, fashionable outfit was something that he was quite used to in Jennifer—not that it ever interfered with her concentration on or commitment to her work. Caroline's preoccupation was with music and, to a certain extent, sport, when she was not on the job. All she tried to achieve, as far as her appearance was concerned, was to be clean and tidy with clothing suitable for the task in hand. She was an independent character. Surely the change of hair colour had not been made to please Cavill. Mitchell doubted whether the fellow would even notice, anyway. He decided it would be safest to make no further comment.

Caroline, however, was not done with the subject. 'I've dyed it a bit darker and the coating makes it look a bit thicker. Then I got Cavill to cut an inch off.'

'Why?' was all Mitchell could manage.

'To look more like Rosie Goldsmith. Has the lab released any of her clothes yet? If not, it doesn't matter. The trousers were only M&S, so I could probably get some. The shirt's more of a problem. It was covered in blood and Jennifer says it was Italian and incredibly expensive—'

'Are you telling me,' Mitchell cut in, 'that you're volunteering for some kind of reconstruction of Friday afternoon?'

Caroline grinned. 'Only six out of ten this time. That was easier. Rosie was wearing size eight loafers. They'd fall off me, but I doubt whether anyone was looking at her feet. You do think it's a good idea?'

Mitchell grinned. 'It sounds as if letting you do it will be a lot less trouble than talking you out of it. It's too late tonight, though.'

'No matter. I should think you'd have a different set of folk walking the canal bank on a week night from at the weekend. I thought of tomorrow to catch anyone who goes that way every afternoon and Friday because it's a full week after. Or I could go every day, if you like.'

'Just the two, I think and we'll have a couple of uniforms down there for back-up. Smithson for common sense and someone else for muscle. Get a shirt the right colour and I'll authorize that and the trousers on expenses. We'll need to . . .'

A further tap on the door heralded not Jennifer, whom he expected, but John Carroll. Caroline departed tactfully and Mitchell offered the superintendent his only comfortable chair. He embarked on a description of the team's progress and current activities.

Carroll waved a hand to stop him. 'Thanks, but I read the files too, you know.'

Mitchell grinned. 'That's yet another way you're an improvement on your last two predecessors.'

'I wouldn't know about that. As I said, I'm aware of all the hard work that's going on, but I'd be glad to have your views on it all—wild theories included.'

Mitchell was delighted. However much the paperwork had fallen behind, he could hardly be reprimanded for pushing it aside in order to bring his superintendent up to date with the team's thinking. He obediently abandoned it and gave this second visitor his full attention. 'Caroline was here to offer—'

'Not to do a reconstruction? Oh, good girl. I'd been thinking it was a good idea. I like it even better now she's volunteered herself. I take it there's more to come from Jennifer than she's written up on the Swiss Cottage flat.'

Mitchell fished in his top drawer and handed over the tape from Rosie's answering machine. 'You can listen to that when you've a minute. We've no idea who any of the three callers are yet. When we saw the school leaving party photographs and we realized that Miss Goldsmith had been pregnant, I got straight on to the station at Preston. Rosie's mother's in a residential home there. Rosie's agent told us that and Jennifer played with the computer to find out exactly where. The local force promised to send someone to see her today. One of us may have to go down eventually, of course. It depends what the old woman says.'

Carroll frowned. 'I think we ought to deal with it ourselves from the start.'

Mitchell nodded. 'Right then. I'll cancel the request and send Clement. He's good with the old folk. Jennifer's still reading the stack of Jane Felling's letters.'

'Jane Felling?'

'An old musician friend of Rosie's who set her on the road to stardom, apparently. She

192

seems to have written regularly since they parted. Now we're trying to contact her. Do you want to look at the letters too?'

Carroll shook his head. 'I'll be quite satisfied with Jennifer's summary when she's finished them. I've too much else on to get much involved with a case that's being perfectly well conducted without me.'

'Tell me about it. I like to know that the rest of the world's working as hard as I am.'

John Carroll took the remark literally. 'We've got funny money flooding West Yorkshire, quite expertly done and no sign of its source. Ditto crack, though we do know where to start looking for that, and the drug squad's coming in. Might as well call on their expertise.'

Mitchell was quite happy to hear this. It would force Clement to drop his obsession with the canal boats and concentrate on likely suspects for their murder.

'Then, just this morning,' Carroll continued, 'we've got a missing child, though he's been on his travels twice before and turned up safely. Then there was a call from the fire people about a suspected arson incident and a cellarful of illegal immigrants under Gaukrogers' mill—working for peanuts all day and down in the dungeons all night, poor sods.' He leaned back in his chair and smiled. 'Gross exaggeration, actually. We only found half a dozen of them . . .' He caught Mitchell's sharp glance. 'What do you know about it?'

'Nothing concrete. One of the children Caroline interviewed repeated a remark of his father's. Something about Patel bringing cabinloads of sambos to Cloughton. She'll tell you the child's name.'

'Yes, ask her to. I'll have to go in a minute. What I came for was some news of Tom—and Hannah, of course. I could call round there myself, but that seems to make him feel I'm hounding him about coming back on the job. How's his migraine?'

Mitchell shrugged. 'No better, no worse. I try to keep him in touch with things here when he wants to know, but he's preoccupied with his own problems.'

'Doesn't the local authority help much?'

'They do their best, but most of the health care staff have never met this disease before. They know less about what's needed than Tom and Hannah have worked out for themselves. At least they've managed to hang on to the same people, though. They learn as they go and they've worked out a care plan that suits Hannah rather than a treatment for the complaint.'

'He was angry about the delays and the paperwork last time I spoke to him.'

Mitchell nodded. 'Ginny thinks that's good for him, in a way. His days are filled with phone calls and letter writing and working out ways and means. It gives him a chance to vent his fury on people he doesn't know and doesn't have to apologize to.'

'What do you mean by "ways and means"?'

Mitchell considered. 'Well, all the painkillers and pills for a start. Hannah can't swallow them now in the form they come from the chemist. Tom thought of crushing them up in the coffee grinder and mixing them with soup.'

Both men grimaced and the superintendent got up. Mitchell wondered whether the time was right for a question about his own prospects. More than a year ago, he had been delighted to step into his father-in-law's shoes and become an acting chief inspector. Now, with Hannah's death drawing inexorably closer, he was wondering whether it had been a good move from a professional point of view. He had had a good deal of useful experience but, when Tom was free again to return to his post, Mitchell himself might wish he had sought his promotion elsewhere.

Looking back, though, he could not see how he could have acted differently. Ginny would hardly have wanted to move away from Cloughton when her mother was dying there and her help was needed. And there was no other way that Tom's job could have been held open for him. Mitchell decided that the end of a case rather than the middle was a better time for discussing his own future. He stood politely to see his superior officer out.

Carroll paused at the door. 'Come and see

me when this case breaks. We need to talk about what's going to happen to you. I don't want Cloughton to lose you.'

Mitchell was content. If he moved away, he was unlikely to end up working for such a decent superintendent.

*   *   *

Later on Sunday evening, Mitchell visited his in-laws with a message from their daughter. Virginia would not be seeing them tonight. He was to tell Hannah that, in obedience to her mother's instructions, she was attempting to write a magazine article.

Hannah was not there to receive the message. Having been particularly unwell that day, she was already in bed. Mitchell decided not to tell Browne that the subject of his wife's piece was her attitude to her mother's illness. He would tell Hannah later, though, and he knew she would approve.

Now he sat opposite his father-in-law in a room lit by real flames that licked hungrily at the log he had just fed them. The old-fashioned open fireplace was the result of a family pow-wow, the purpose of which had been to seek out every possible pleasure that Hannah could still enjoy.

Their deliberations had resulted in Cavill coming to play Shostakovitch on the piano, in a visiting hairdresser attending twice weekly to

Hannah's thick, brown, shoulder-length hair, her only vanity, and in Virginia reading daily from her favourite *Mayor of Casterbridge*.

It had been Alex who had remembered Hannah's determination to be rid of the gas-fed imitation coal fire that she had inherited with their present house. Other projects, of practical rather than aesthetic importance, had ousted this one. Now, in the midst of a houseful of technologies, wheelchair, special bed, suction devices, there was the smell of burning wood and smoke, the satisfying noises as the burning brands shifted and settled, and the flicker of proper flames.

Maybe soothed by them, and satisfied that Hannah was safely and genuinely asleep, Browne seemed willing, for once, to talk about his own view of his situation. Mitchell was content to listen. 'To me, the essence of the person Hannah is still there. Her voice is different but her personality wasn't confined to that. Her humour's still there. I do miss her grace of movement. She isn't the Hannah I know—and yet, she is.' He stopped speaking and closed his eyes.

When he opened them again he spoke in an angry tone. 'Ginny talks to her naturally, without hesitating or weeping, just as she always has done.'

'I assure you, she weeps at home.' Mitchell had no compunction in making his wife's one short lapse into despair sound like a regular release. He knew, though, that Browne would not feel that Hannah had had her due until his daughter broke down and wept with her mother in her arms. He knew, too, that such behaviour would be intolerable for both women.

Browne confirmed his son-in-law's suspicion that his defence of his wife had not been just unacceptable to her father, but unheard. 'How dare she not be affected!'

Mitchell was irritated. He knew that Browne had, possibly, the hardest role of all in the present drama but he found it hard not to be critical of him. When he had been a lowly DC and Browne his DI, he had respected his quiet, low-key authority. Now, he found it difficult to hide the impatience verging on scorn that he felt at his father-in-law's capitulation to his chronic ailment and his quitting of his job.

However, he managed to listen with resignation to Browne's unburdening. When he imagined his own likely reaction if Hannah's fate befell Virginia, his resignation became pity. When he remembered his father-in-law's unfailing tolerance and practical assistance to himself, when his own impetuous behaviour led him into trouble, both personal and professional, his pity turned to shame.

CHAPTER TEN

Sunday had been an interesting day for Shakila. If she discounted the boredom factor, she thought her plan was working quite well. She had unfolded her tale, even managing the odd simulated sob. Patel had immediately offered his assistance, though not, she had felt, his sympathy.

The boat he seemed to live on was called *Shahnaz*. 'She's my ex,' Patel had volunteered, before Shakila could ask, 'but we could easily paint in a new name. What's yours?' When Shakila had supplied her own forename, he had grinned. 'You'd better tell Hal how to spell it.'

His tone had been bantering rather than lascivious. He had invited her on a tour of his boat and she had followed him around it, wearing an expression of rapt attention as he extolled its virtues. 'The cabin is twelve feet long . . . Kabola oil-fired stove . . . central gangway running through the kitchen area.' Shakila felt little interest. He would hardly be showing her over a vessel that he'd stuffed with crack.

Nor was she inclined to devote much attention to any boat that Hal Benton was working on. It was possible that the two were in league but, if so, they hid it skilfully. They seemed to know no more about one another than was normal between employer and temporary employee. Nothing had been let slip by either of them—no nicknames, shared jokes or passed messages except those which concerned the renovation work in hand.

What she was finding very interesting was Patel's attitude towards her. Her original object had been just to make his acquaintance. Until her rather shaky story had occurred to her that morning, she would have been satisfied with a short interview on which to build greater familiarity. The situation she claimed to be in would be credible to him. It was the decision to appeal to him, a stranger, that he would have thought peculiar.

She was a good actress, though. Maybe her simulated distress had really taken him in— but there was nothing remotely paternal in his attitude towards her. Nor did she think she had succeeded in attracting him sexually, so why was he humouring her?

Now the two of them came out on to the roof of *Shahnaz.* Glancing across the water, Shakila saw Hal put his tea tray on the roof of his boat, which she estimated to be no more than eighteen feet long. At the opposite end, by the steps leading down to the tiny cabin, the girl, Gracie, huddled into anorak and jeans, licked at an ice-cream cornet. Shakila admired the result of Hal's morning's work, a beautiful, detailed wreath of bright flowers. When she had first arrived, the design had been faded and peeling.

Patel explained that tourists were prepared to pay a good deal more to hire these little, refurbished, older boats with few amenities. 'They say they're full of character and spend their holiday playing at going back in time.' He sounded contemptuous of this attitude and was grudging in his praise of Hal's work. 'You're too enthusiastic. He'll be wanting his fee put up. All right, come into the office and let's see what we can do.'

She allowed him to help her back on to the bank, finding the manoeuvre more awkward than she had expected in her unaccustomed clinging skirts. Patel rattled keys on his computer, then beamed at her. 'I've got a boat that I could lend you. No need to hire it considering how you're fixed. If that embarrasses you, there may be one or two little favours you can do for me in return.'

So that was the answer. She was going to be made useful. She wondered what kind of service he might have in mind for her. Housekeeping for him? Or, maybe, he would try to detain her forcibly, perhaps find her family and demand a ransom. That was only if he'd believed her, of course.

Patel led her over to a shabby but serviceable-looking boat and helped her aboard. 'Hal hasn't got his hands on this one yet, as you can see. Now, before I leave you

201

with a boat, you'll need some tuition. I'll take you out myself for half an hour, just to explain the mechanics, give you a feel for boat handling, show you how to moor and work locks.'

Shakila truthfully claimed some small experience in these matters. 'My brother took me for a weekend on the Grand Union canal once. He was in charge, but he let me try.'

Patel shook his head. 'Ah, but every boat is different and each waterway has its own characteristics.' He spoke English with the local dialect and no trace of an Asian lilt. Shakila accepted his last statement and resigned herself to a tedious hour or so. Patel's voice droned on on the subject of bilge pumps, stern glands and header tanks as they floated past a pretty row of cottages with climbing plants anchored to identical trellises beside each front door. In a gleam of metallic sunshine, a party of ducks preened on the bank, watched by a solitary moorhen.

Shakila forced her attention back to her instructor and found that his subject had changed. '. . . not the business it was. Bookings are down and companies are struggling to pay their annual licences—over thirteen hundred pounds for a sixty-foot boat. That's the fee from two, or even three weeks' bookings.'

'What about little ones like this?'

'Huh! Down at the starter end of the market, things are even worse. An eighteen-foot trailable cruiser has to pay in the region of two hundred and eighty pounds, quite out of proportion to its value, which is only three or four times that amount.'

Shakila saved her sympathy. He seemed to be able to afford to have Hal Benton doing time-consuming craftsman's work on a considerable number of his boats. Or maybe not. She wondered again about the possibility of a conspiracy between the two. Meanwhile, she tried to stem the flow of complaints and pointed to an implement lying on the cabin top. It was a sturdy, right-angled piece of metal, roughly eight inches long. 'I know what that is—a windlass to wind the paddles up and down.'

Patel scowled. 'Be careful when you use that. If the ratchet that holds the paddle up doesn't hold, the windlass can fly off. If you try to grab it and it catches you, it'll break your arm.'

Shakila nodded and promised to heed his warning. Privately, she was planning another purpose for her windlass. If her growing 'friendship' with Patel should lead to either forcible restraint or an assault on her virtue, it would make a handy weapon.

*　　　*　　　*

Mitchell had justified his decision to visit Porter's shop himself. There were already two matters that his colleagues were investigating in this location before the opera production had brought it to his own team's notice. Now, the matter of the threatening letters to Lewis Blake and his recent discovery that the actual proprietor's name was Patel was more than he could resist.

His argument had seemed rather shaky to him and he had clinched matters with his need for fresh air before he could work efficiently in his overheated office. The previous evening's mini gale had abated and the air was pleasantly damp and cool, lit with occasional gleams of metallic sunlight.

The shop, purporting to be a printer's and stationer's, was situated half-way along a shabby street that seemed to have no need of such a business. Mitchell knew that the people who lived in the nearby flats would communicate with each other by means of modern gadgets that they stole from each other. For such letters as they needed to write, they would buy a lined pad as cheaply as possible from Woolies.

The proprietors had obviously realized this. Being a poste restante centre was very likely their chief source of income now, but they had diversified further. The window into which he and a very dirty child gazed contained— possibly to humour the original sign writer— an old-fashioned typewriter, an assortment of envelope files in once garish, now faded colours, cards of cheap biros and one arch lever-type folder.

A poster advertising a Christmas club was sellotaped to the glass on the inside of the window. Boxed games of Ludo and Snakes and Ladders shared the floor with miniature human models, variously dressed Barbie dolls, coyly escorted by Action Men in inappropriate battledress. Mitchell wondered how long it was since a Cloughton child had played Snakes and Ladders.

With an eye to essentials, the window dresser had added a tin opener, a mousetrap and a pack of tampons to his display. The dead flies, dust and mouse droppings had been contributed gratuitously. Mitchell suspected that the shop's best-selling lines were not on display.

As he pushed open the door, his arrival was announced by an electronic bleep which brought an Asian youth from behind a rack of tired-looking birthday cards. The lad took up his station by the till, from where he examined Mitchell without speaking.

Mitchell did not feel that the appraisal was aggressive. He was merely being weighed up. He unbuttoned his jacket and came further inside. Huge black eyes followed his progress to the counter. When Mitchell wished their owner a good morning they looked surprised, as though a polite greeting in this setting were inappropriate.

Indicating the pigeon holes behind the boy, which were stuffed with an assortment of envelopes, he asked, 'Is there anything else for the opera buff? Now that the show's actually on, I'm his errand boy.'

'You're not. You're police.'

The remark did not seem confrontational. Mitchell grinned. 'How do you know?'

'I was watching you through the window. You weren't trying to look inconspicuous.'

Mitchell blinked. The boy's setting didn't match his vocabulary. He indicated his substantial person with some satisfaction. 'I don't do inconspicuous. I'm not built for it. Is that how your customers usually look?'

'If they've come for a letter they do. People whose business is above board get their post through their own letter boxes.'

'I could have come to buy.'

'What? That stuff?' He waved an arm in the direction of the window, stirring the dusty air. 'And you don't look like a customer for the other.' He jerked his head in the direction of a top shelf of pornography that Mitchell had already judged to be tasteless but not actionable.

'It's still a big jump from there to police.'

Now the boy produced the ghost of a grin. 'Nah, it's not.'

'You got something against the police?' He shook his head. 'So, you'll tell me who brought that letter in.'

The door beeped again. Mitchell turned to look at the middle-aged man who entered in time to catch the knowing look cast on himself. The newcomer strolled to the counter and asked for a magazine which was unknown to Mitchell. He suspected that it was also unknown to any publishing house. Solemnly, the boy apologized. The shop didn't stock it, but if the customer would like to place an order . . .? The customer shook his head impatiently and departed.

The boy raised huge eyes to Mitchell. 'That was code for "I'll be back later and, meanwhile, get rid of him."'

Mitchell perched on a dilapidated stool that creaked in protest. 'You were saying?'

He saw the boy capitulate, anxious to obey his unspoken orders. 'A mate of mine brought the letter in one morning last week. I wasn't here but my uncle told me later. Peter—that's my mate—said the woman who passed it to him gave him a fiver for his pains. He only had to cross the road and come in here. She watched him from the other side.'

'So, who's this mate?' The eyes dropped. Mitchell waited for some seconds, then changed direction. 'Shouldn't you be at school? And shouldn't your friend Peter have been the other morning?'

'He's not bothered. His mother probably thinks he was there.'

'And you?'

'Chance'd be a fine thing.'

'Chance to go to school?'

The eyes flashed in the thin brown face. 'Not all teenagers are truants—not even if they're Asian.'

Mitchell said, sharply, 'Watch your tongue! I'm no racist. My best PC is a Pakistani girl. Doesn't your father know it's illegal to keep you here in school time?'

'He can't do much about it. He's in Armley.'

'Your mother, then?'

'More scared of my uncle than I am. I'd have a go at him sometimes but it'd be Mum who suffered for it.'

Mitchell leaned forward, his elbows resting on the counter. 'I think we could help each other.'

The boy was wary. 'He'll kill me if he thinks I've been talking to you people.'

'It won't be us. It'll be social services. He'll think the school has set them on to him. Why aren't they making a fuss anyway?'

'He makes Mum write notes for me. He's invented a kidney complaint for me. I did think of talking to my form master, but he'd be sure to find out, and then . . .'

'Yes. Your mum.'

'I'm not off as much as some of my classmates, actually. Just enough to pull my grades down.'

Mitchell was genuinely interested in the boy. 'What are you aiming at?'

'Getting Mum away from here.' The boy's tone was bitter. 'Then uni, or art college. I want to be an architect.'

'Has your uncle some objection to that?'

'Not so long as it doesn't keep me from his beck and call. Usually my mum is in the shop but he's broken her wrist and she can't work the till. He'll not loosen his hold on her unless we get out of the country and that'd be complicated.'

Nervously, he looked at his watch and Mitchell stood up. 'OK, I'll go. Just give me Peter's address and your promise to speak to me again.' The boy was already scribbling. Mitchell read the note he was handed. After the address was the name of a wine bar in town. 'Tonight, about eight?'

The boy nodded, willing to agree to anything, provided that Mitchell left. Pausing in the doorway, he looked the boy up and down. He was slightly built but well muscled. 'It won't be long before you'll be able to make him frightened of you.'

'Yes, if he hasn't got a knife in his belt, or a gun, and if he wasn't in control of all the rest of the family. You don't know the half of it.'

Mitchell closed the peeling door, wondering whether the reproach was against his race or his profession. Probably both.

* * *

209

With his shift sent out on a fresh set of enquiries, Mitchell sat at his desk and appealed to providence to send him yet one more legitimate distraction from the paperwork that was mounting there. He must have prayed more fervently than usual, since his request was immediately granted in the form of a telephone message from the desk sergeant. A Mr George Tomlin would like to speak to the man in charge. Thankfully, Mitchell pushed neat stacks of papers aside and prepared to welcome his visitor.

Mr Tomlin arrived, clad in a jacket over a boiler suit and a flat cap. He introduced himself at length. 'We live over our shop on the corner of Trent Street on the Swayneside estate. It used to be the village store when Swayne was just a village. The estate was built round it, like, and they gave us a better bus service, so our old customers beggared off to town to do their shopping. We were going to close down but then the clog factory opened round the corner. Naturally, then we thought we could just do coffee and sarnies, pop and cake for the staff there, like. The missus bakes, her ma butters the breadcakes . . .'

Obviously leaving the old man free to entertain the police, Mitchell supposed. He was about to steer his witness gently towards the point of his visit, when the man asked, 'Can I have a look at a good photo of this murdered singer?' He took the one Mitchell offered in a grimy hand with black-ringed fingernails. Watching him study the picture, Mitchell made a mental note not to patronize the family shop.

Mr Tomlin studied the photograph for almost a minute before he handed it back, nodding with a satisfied expression. 'That's her all right.' Guiltily, he regarded the slightly oily thumbprint with which he had adorned it. 'Sorry about the muck. I was setting off for the cash and carry when I passed my mate on the corner by Swaynes' farm. He'd run into the ditch so I had to give him a hand to shove his van out and get it going. I glanced at his paper whilst he was test-running the engine and saw this picture of yon singer. It was too blurred for me to be sure. I'd heard that she'd been knocked off, like, but I hadn't seen her face afore.'

'But she's been pictured in the *Clarion* on and off for a year.'

'Ah, not on the sports pages, though. Doesn't kick a football, does she?'

'Is that all you watch on television too?'

'Nah. I watch darts as well. Not that I'm much of a TV fan. I prefer my radio. Keeps me up with the news, sport a'course, as you'd expect, but what's happening in the world as well. You can listen while your hands are busy, like.'

'I thought your womenfolk ran the shop for you.'

211

'Aye. So they do. I run my garage next door.'

Mitchell's files reproached him and, reluctantly, he brought his visitor back to the point.

'Miss Goldsmith? Well, she was in our shop a'Friday.'

'Last Friday?'

He nodded importantly. 'Came up on the estate bus that gets to the corner at eleven, so she said. She didn't strike me as no bus-riding type but that's by the by. Wanted Richards Road, she said. The driver'd put her out at the nearest stop but she couldn't find it. She'd counted Brunswick ginnel as a turning, so when the driver said second on the left, she . . .'

He caught Mitchell's expression and moved the story on. 'She came in to ask but she couldn't resist the wife's cake. Stopped for a coffee and a sarnie as well, cheese and salad bap she had, and a bit of Doreen's coffee and walnut, which I'm partial to myself. She said nowt about being an opera singer. Just wanted Richards Road.'

The name was ringing a bell at the back of Mitchell's mind. He associated it with Clement and he tried to review the long list of witnesses he had sent his DC to question in the last few days. 'You were in your shop, not your garage?'

'S'right. I'm allowed my dinner hour, aren't I? Our eldest lass looks after the office whilst I have my dinner. She fetches me if there's owt urgent.'

Mitchell nodded. 'Did Miss Goldsmith say what she wanted in Richards Road?'

'No, but she was wanting to know what it was like, round about, like. Well, there are posher places where I suppose her sort live but there's far worse an' all. T'missus told her how to get there and she beggared off. Not before she'd bought a whole coffee and walnut cake off Doreen, though.'

'How long is Richards Road?'

Mr Tomlin shut his eyes to calculate. 'Not very. 'Bout forty or fifty yards.'

'How many houses?'

The man shrugged. 'Couldn't tell you but they're only on one side. There's the infant and junior schools on the other and their playing fields. That should have told her it was a nice district, plenty of grass and such.'

'True. Well, Mr Tomlin, I'd almost run out of lines to follow up so you've been very useful.' Mitchell rose from behind his desk to see his visitor out but the man seemed reluctant to go.

He stood up but held his ground. 'Don't you want to hear about when she called back?'

Mitchell gritted his teeth and yanked the smile back on to his face. 'I certainly do.'

Mr Tomlin resumed his seat with a smirk. 'We asked if she'd found who she was looking for. She didn't give quite a straight answer to that, said it had been a worthwhile journey. Then she asked how to get on to the marina, you know, on the canal, from our shop.'

'How do you, without your own transport?'

'Well, it'd be complicated. Anyway, I was taking a customer's car out for a spin, to make sure we'd got it ship-shape, like, so I said why didn't she hop in and I'd run her down there.'

'Where did you drop her?'

'On the far side of the industrial estate from the canal. It was as near as I could get a car to the marina, so she said she'd walk from there. I pointed out where she should hop over the wall and on to the canal bank. It's only a low wall. She was wearing trousers and her shoes were a damned sight more sensible than them my lasses wear. She'd have managed it all right.'

'Did she have a camera with her?'

'Mm. Might have had. She had a big handbag cum shopping bag thing. She'd have had room for the crown jewels in it. She seemed a nice woman, like. Can't imagine why anybody should want to do her in. Hey!'

'Yes?'

'It comes back to me now. Should have known who she was. She was so pleased to be getting there easy like, she burst into singing when we got going. It was only an ordinary song, not classic. One of Ella Fitzgerald's, but real loud she sang. It was hot, but I shut my window, like. Neighbours would have thought

I'd got a madwoman in there!'

*   *   *

Jennifer's first job on Monday morning was to interview Gwen Evans. She was one of the three chorus members Blake had employed as drivers, specifically, the one who had refused to be chauffeur to Rosie Goldsmith. Subconsciously, Jennifer had assumed from her given name that Mrs Evans would be verging on elderly. The woman who answered the door could be little more than thirty, though a rather harassed thirty.

Jennifer had heard screams when she rang the bell and had had a longish wait before the door was opened. 'Have I called at a bad time?' she asked, apologetically.

Gwen shook her head. 'No, the last crisis has just finished. No one knows when the next one will blow up. You may as well come in. Molly and I are getting used to each other. Eventually, she'll learn to feel safe here and I'll learn, in more detail, what she needs.'

Jennifer followed as Gwen went back to her kitchen. 'You're fostering her?' she hazarded.

Gwen nodded. 'Yes, with a view to adoption. It's a bit of a struggle. She's retarded and confused. No one's ever loved or disciplined her. We're making progress, though.' She sank on to a stool with a sigh. 'Sorry about the mess.'

Jennifer looked around. Basically, the place seemed well cared for. The dishes were stacked, unwashed, but there was no long-standing grime. The cooker sparkled. The child's tantrum had merely thrown the usual routine awry.

'We'll have a few minutes' peace soon. Dave's taking her to the park.'

From out in the hall, there was renewed shouting, this time over sensible shoes. When the screamer paused for breath, a calm male voice said, 'Either you wear them or we stay in.'

Jennifer smiled. 'He's good with her.'

'Yes, better than me with this child.'

'How many have you fostered?' Gwen shrugged. 'Don't you work?'

Gwen answered over her shoulder as she got up to fill the kettle. Jennifer sighed. More coffee! She thought that this inevitable offer from every witness was a defence mechanism, an attempt to turn their interview into a social occasion. They were trying to pretend that the conversation was entirely voluntary and that the police officer was merely a guest.

'I've done all sorts, between children,' Gwen was saying. 'Teaching driving was the last. I passed the exams. I'm patient.'

'You'll need to be with a disturbed child.'

Gwen plugged the kettle in and sat down again. 'I've worked in a shop—well, several shops. I did some typing for an elderly

216

romantic novelist who couldn't get to grips with word processing.'

'You sound like a useful person to have around.'

'I suppose so.'

They could hear happy chatter as, with Molly persuaded into her shoes, the park visit was declared back on. The door slammed. Jennifer saw that she now had her witness's full attention. It occurred to her that Gwen could have tried modelling as one of her odd jobs. She was not beautiful, but, in jeans and crumpled sweatshirt, trainers and a pony tail, she looked fresh and attractive and moved with a careless grace. She would like to have made general conversation with this woman. Fearful, however, that the young rebel might remove her shoes or offend in some other respect and so curtail her excursion, Jennifer plunged into her questions. 'Basically, we're asking everybody the same thing. What can you tell us about Rosie Goldsmith?'

Gwen lifted her hands, indicating that the question was too general for her to answer. 'You must know a good deal about her already. What can I add?'

'Tell me what you thought about her, what everyone thought. Tell me why anyone would want to kill her. Most of our witnesses keep telling us how charming she was.'

Gwen sighed. 'Obviously, I've seen her around a good deal but it was Tim who was looking after her, driving her. I was doing it for Miles—Mr Cranmer. I've plenty to do here, as you've seen, and my opera part to cope with. I've had no time to socialize.'

'But you've rehearsed a lot with Rosie. You must have. You and she and—Marian, is it?— have several scenes together.'

'OK. As you say, she was charming, so we got on quite well.'

'Gwen, why did you refuse to drive her?'

She made no pointless protest. 'I didn't like her.'

'But you wouldn't have known that when Mr Blake asked you.'

'Oh, but I did. We go back a bit further than the last few weeks. We went to school together in Preston. I haven't liked her since back then. Not that I've seen or thought about her much in the meantime.'

'And you weren't prepared to let bygones be bygones? You must have had some good reason to dislike her that much.'

'Chemistry, I expect. I don't suppose she liked me much either. I thought it would be more—well, convenient if I drove one of the others. There'd be less awkwardness.'

'Was it because you disapproved of her behaviour? Because she had an illegitimate child?' Jennifer could see that her witness was startled. 'You did know about the pregnancy?'

'Oh, yes. It wasn't that. We were all a bit wild in that last year at school. It could have been any of us.'

'I presume she had the child.' Gwen nodded. 'Did she keep it?'

'They moved away to avoid the scandal. She wrote a couple of times, not to me but to a mutual friend. After a few months, though, we all lost touch.'

Despite several further minutes of Jennifer's cajoling, Gwen Evans refused to be more specific about her lack of sympathy for the murdered woman. Jennifer left her with a final warning. 'If we find that you have withheld information from us that is relevant to the case, you could be appearing in court yourself for contempt of it. Think about it, Gwen. Think about the effect it would have on Molly.'

*   *   *

After the evening debriefing, Clement sat in his car as he waited for Jonathan Stepney to arrive for their Monday night run. Even with the windows tightly shut, he felt chilly. The Indian summer was over now and autumn was compensating for it with a biting wind and flurries of rain.

He hoped the lad would be wearing the thermal garments he had accepted so ungraciously. 'I suppose you want somebody else to look as bloody daft as you do. I'm not surprised you was getting rid of 'em.' This story had covered the transfer of a good deal of expensive equipment from Clement's own collection. He was pretty sure the boy was naive enough to accept the much repeated excuse, rather than ungrateful for his mentor's generosity.

Presently, Jonathan arrived, clad in a thermal top but bare-legged below his shorts. He reached the car park, not by his usual method of vaulting over the wall, but walking through the gap in it a dozen yards out of his way. So, the injuries were still hampering him. No run tonight.

Jonathan took a dim view of this. 'I've done all the things you said, hot baths like, and rubbing in that stuff. I'm not limping!'

'Not since you realized I was watching you.' Jonathan scowled and Clement relented. 'We'll walk though—maybe a slow jog at the end if you're loosened up and moving easily. And you've still got to warm up.' Jonathan made none of his usual objections to this. 'Beginning to see the wisdom of it?'

The boy shook his head. 'Nah! But, if it keeps you happy . . . Any road, t'nights are drawing in now so we aren't so noticeable.' Having saved face, the boy performed the required number of stretches and the pair began to walk.

'How's the chess going?' Clement asked as they breasted the brow of the hill and he had breath to spare.

Jonathan grinned. 'I'm too thick to take it in. There's too many rules. Still, the old man likes winning. It puts him in a good mood. Lucky old Shaun, only having his mum to deal with. Women're easy—well, more than men, any road.'

'Is that right?'

'Yeah. You ought to get yerself one. They mek a lot o' stupid fuss but they do all the washin' an' cookin' an' that. An' my mum slips me a few quid when my dad stops my pocket money.'

Clement grinned. 'I don't think I'll find one who'll do that for me.'

'Huh! On a copper's pay, you don't need it. You've got brass to chuck away. Look at all this running stuff you chuck out that's got nowt wrong with it, just because you've gone off t'bloody colour or summat. It's a good job, being a copper.'

Clement quickened his pace as the most tactful way of dropping that topic. Jonathan, however, was not put off and Clement found that he was the one who became slightly breathless. 'I've been thinking like—about my future. I might go to police college. I've been a big help to you like, so I thought you could speak up for me.'

Clement was amused. 'Have you suggested this idea to your parents?'

Jonathan nodded. 'Me dad reckons I'm not clever enough. He wasn't nasty like. Said he were just saving me getting let down and disappointed. Me mum says she can't see no harm in having one more useless copper on't streets. She were in a bad mood because she'd seen me talking to Shaun—but that's because I were bein' a nark for you.'

'How old are you? Sixteen?' The boy nodded. 'Well, we don't like people straight from school. Concentrate on your exams at the end of the year, get a job for a while to get used to being a responsible wage-earner, then see how you feel. Anyway, I've got a strong objection to your being a copper.'

Jonathan's face fell. 'I thought you'd be on my side.'

'I am. I can't spare you as my nark—and, in any case, you need to concentrate on your running, so no more fights with Shaun, even in the course of narking!'

'Right. He tries not to tell me what he's up to. Says I'm too thick with the filth. He can't help 'imself, though. He can't keep his big mouth shut about what a clever sod he is an' what a dickhead I am. He allus bragged to me and he can't break the habit.'

'Not such a clever sod then.'

'No, and I'm not such a dickhead.' The boy's smug expression invited more questions.

'Got one up on him, have you?'

Jonathan nodded importantly, then bit his lip.

Tactfully, Clement slowed down to their

222

energetic jog. 'Don't know how your sore muscles are doing. The cold's getting to mine. Shall we call it a day? I've got some cans in the car.' They walked briskly to warm down, making their way back to the supermarket by the shortest route. The boy's face fell when he found the cans contained Diet Coke, but he cheered up when Clement demanded, 'What have you got for me, then?'

'Pass us me bag of clean clothes.' Clement obliged and waited patiently as the lad extracted the maximum drama out of producing a grubby brown envelope from his fraying haversack.

Eventually, he handed it over. 'It wa'nt stealing. I just took a couple, for you, as evidence. Don't touch 'em. I had me gloves on to deal with 'em.'

Clement lifted the flap and saw banknotes. 'Where did these come from?'

'Shaun's pocket. He only turned up at school to flash 'em around in t'playground. I sat behind him in RE. Mr Shaw made him sit at the front for fooling around. He left his jacket on t'back of his chair. It were easy.'

'As easy as it'll be for him to work out who robbed him. I reckon you're in for another beating up.'

'Nah! Way he's spending it, he'll have lost count. Anyway, he knows I don't pinch any more—except in the line of duty—and there are plenty in our class 'at do.'

'What do you want me to do with them?'

'Find crack and stuff on 'em—and Shaun's prints.' Clement wished it were so easy. First he would have to explain how he came by the notes and then he would have to persuade his superiors that the three notes would yield enough evidence to justify the expense of the tests Jonathan had in mind. And, even if he survived all that and the notes were significant evidence of major crime, the case would be taken out of his own hands, possibly even out of the jurisdiction of the Cloughton force.

He put the envelope in his pocket and forbade the boy to embark on any further criminal activity on his own behalf. He took the sting out of his rebuke by producing two further cans, this time of beer. When they were empty, he drove Jonathan home, noting how gingerly he climbed out of the car. 'I'll meet you on Wednesday, work permitting. It'll still be mostly walking though, probably till the end of the week.'

Jonathan nodded. 'Cheers. Thanks for the lift. Hey! I've just thought o' summat. You might try asking Shaun if he saw owt on t'canal bank. He's allus hanging round that kid what plays her flute on her dad's boat. I think he fancies her. Could have been there after school, Friday. I could ask him for you, if you like.'

Clement reminded Jonathan of his healing injuries and hoped it had been enough to put him off.

* * *

Shakila had decided against the Swan for their meeting tonight. It was close to the canal, and so where Patel or Benton might stop for a drink and see her in conversation with Galloping Pig, Shaun Grant's name for Clement.

He sat, therefore, in the nearest pub to his flat, his local, he supposed, though he had only once drunk there before. It was a small, comfortable, old-fashioned hostelry that soothed Clement as he sipped his half of bitter and waited. He felt conspicuous, being, apparently, the only patron of the place under pensionable age. As far as he could see, Shakila, when she arrived, would be not only the only Asian but also the only woman.

He nodded from time to time to people who recognized him as a neighbour but initiated no conversation. Shakila was late but not apologetic. In fact cocky was the only word to describe the expression on her face. When he rose to go to the bar, she asked for Coke.

Clement blinked. 'On duty, are we? It never stops the DCI having a pint.'

'It's not the DCI I'm thinking of. Patel thinks I'm a strict Muslim, or at least from a strict family. I can hardly go back breathing brandy fumes all over him.'

'Nobody's offering you brandy.'

Shakila's face became totally serious. 'When I've discovered what jiggery pokery is going on in those boats, high and mighty Carroll will. And I shall tell him he can keep his Christmas pudding.'

Clement shrugged, then fetched the Coke she had asked for. The landlord looked disappointed that his new customers were proving as abstemious and taciturn as his regulars, but he cheered up when Clement complimented his draught beer. Shakila accepted her glass and swallowed.

'Thirsty or in a hurry?'

'Both. I'm supposed to be taking refuge from my wicked family.' Quickly she explained how she was acting out Nazreen's plight as her own. 'So I can't let him know that I'm swarming off from the hidey-hole that he's so kindly provided to drink with my mates.'

'What's kind about letting you hire a boat?'

'I'm saving up to escape for ever, so he's harbouring me for free, though he did mention little favours I might feel inclined to do for him. I'm not sure whether he intends them to be sexual or criminal. I'd prefer the latter, I think.'

'Shakila . . .'

She waved a hand at him. 'It could be he's lined me up to make frilly curtains for the boats that Hal Benton's painting. He approves of my sari and I did find somewhere to tuck my phone. I've found a safe place for the windlass as well, close to the bed.'

'What's that?'

Shakila began to explain but he shook his head. 'Never mind. If I thought it was the slightest use, I'd apologize for getting you into this and try to persuade you to quit.'

'But it isn't and I have to get back, so here's a quick run down on what I think so far. Either Patel isn't using the boats to store anything illegal or else Benton's in league with him. There's something going on, I'm sure. He always answers his mobile out of earshot . . .'

'Could be because he wants to add you to his harem before letting on how many . . .'

Shakila ignored his interruption. '. . . but sometimes he's angry and shouts.'

'In Urdu or English?'

'In English and Hindi, but it's sufficiently like for me to cope if I could get nearer. Once I made out something about paperwork. It was all done, he was telling the caller, so why wasn't the caller here to collect it.'

'Paperwork? I thought he was boating round the canal system delivering illegal goods.'

'It looks as though he does. About every six weeks, according to Hal Benton.'

'You've questioned him?'

'Not openly. He just said, when I was asking about hiring, that I'd have to go on Tuesday or I'd miss him. He'd be gone a few days, not usually more than a week. I asked where he went. Benton just shrugged and said I didn't need to know that to hire a boat, did I?' She grinned.

Clement put his half-empty glass down with a clatter. 'Shakila, you aren't planning to go with him?'

'I haven't been invited—yet. There are just a couple more things. He knows I've got a phone. I said it was for my girlfriend to keep me posted about what's happening at home. If he finds out I've left the boat I'll say I've been to meet her, to pick up some precious thing I had to leave behind. Young Shaun's somehow got a finger in the pie. Hanging round young Gracie is his cover. She's half smitten and half scared of him. Her father chases him off. I think he brings something to Patel, or takes something away. He lets himself be seen, then wanders off up the canal bank. Then, a bit afterwards, Patel follows.'

'How can you see all this? Is your little tub actually in the marina?'

'No, it's moored further along in the direction of the Swan. Not far, though. I use binoculars.'

Clement banged his glass down again. 'You're mad. You can talk your way out of having a phone, but—'

'They're not mine. I found them in a locker. I can see him coming in plenty of time to put them back. Oh, and Hal Benton's father told

228

me Patel's got a row of garages somewhere that he rents out. I haven't found out where but I'll have a poke around when I do. I had my chat with the old man. We talked for ages and he was quite interesting. He knows a lot about the area in general but there was nothing that the team would need to know.'

'I wish you'd leave the garages to us.' He saw her consult her watch again. 'Shall I run you back?'

'Don't be stupid. How would I explain you away?' She strode loftily away to her self-appointed duties.

Clement decided that he needed another pint.

CHAPTER ELEVEN

On Tuesday night, Shakila was the first to arrive at the new meeting place. When Clement came in, she was in animated conversation with one of the regulars and waved aside his apology.

He took her to the bar and the old man, crestfallen, returned to supervising his friends' game of chess. As on the evening before, Shakila disposed of her drink quickly so that Clement had to rush his own. Resentfully, he took her out to his car.

'I'll have to get back quickly. He missed me

yesterday so I had to spin my tale. I'm not sure that he believes anything I've told him. He's keeping a pretty close eye on me.'

'Shakila, you're playing with fire.'

'Well, there's plenty of water around to put it out. You'll be glad to hear I'm not going with him on the mystery tour. I dropped plenty of heavy hints but he didn't bite. I was disappointed at first, but then I realized it would make poking round his garages much easier—and I can chat up Hal Benton, interrupt his work without getting told off. It'll mean I can spend more time in the pub with you while he's away.'

'I gather you've found out where the garages are.'

'Stibson Lane. I had a bit of luck there. I'd already invented a helpful girlfriend so I gave her a mythical brother—said that Urfan was thrilled with his new flat but he was scared his car would be vandalized because he had to leave it in the street two floors below. He just nodded and said nothing.

'Hal Benton solved the problem, though. He met Patel on the towpath and they talked about some left-over paint from one of the boat jobs. Benton suggested slapping a coat on the doors of the garages in Stibson Lane and then putting the rents up. Patel refused—said all the houses in the area were being pulled down so there'd be no custom. When Benton tried to persuade him, Patel got quite shirty, told him to mind his own business.'

Clement nodded. 'Sounds as though he doesn't want people hanging round there. I shouldn't think he's the sort to miss a trick or waste any paint dregs. He'd get more compensation if the garages were smart-looking when they had to come down.'

Shakila hurried on with her news. 'I had a quick walk around there. There's a dozen of them, two rows of six, back to back on what used to be allotments. All locked. Now I've got to dream up a way of finding the keys. He's got a ring with seven keys on it that he keeps in his working jacket. One's a boat key—for the one he's living in. The others hang on numbered hooks in the office.'

'Any chance of searching the office while he's away, after Benton's finished work?'

Shakila shook her head. 'It's always locked when he isn't there. Anyway, I don't think I'd find anything incriminating. He asked me to sit in there this morning while he went on an errand. I was supposed to take a phone call he was expecting. I didn't get excited. He'd use his mobile for any illegal business and I wondered if he'd be keeping watch somewhere to see if I did any snooping. I didn't just in case.'

'Maybe he was snooping around too—on your boat whilst he had you cooped up in the office.'

Shakila laughed. 'I never thought of that.

I've only got washing things, clothes and something to eat and drink. I've been wondering if he's gay. He's tried nothing on with me and there isn't a girlie calendar up in the office or boat. Then again, maybe he's a strict Muslim, lives by the Koran.'

'Except for his shady dealings on the canal, you mean?'

'Actually, sitting there, waiting for the phone to ring, I began to think I was wasting my time. There's nothing tangible to prove he's not a model citizen.'

'There's Shaun, in the money and on the scene.'

Shakila cheered up. 'True. Shall I have a go at him?'

Clement shook his head and Shakila was sulkily silent for a while, before agreeing. 'All right, but I'm going to visit Patel tonight, tell him I'll have a meal waiting when he gets back on Saturday. With a bit of luck I'll have a chance to have a good look at that key ring. Those garages might have keys with numbers, the sort you can buy at that stall in the market.'

'Not if he's got crack stored there.'

She shrugged. 'Well, we'll see. So, what's happening at HQ?'

Quickly, Clement summarized the team's efforts and what they had achieved, finishing with Caroline's unsuccessful repeat of Rosie Goldsmith's last walk to the seat by the canal.

'I haven't heard that there was any reaction,' he ended glumly.

Shakila was indignant. 'If you'd let me know I could have helped keep a lookout.'

'What, ring you up and let Patel hear a man's voice on the phone?'

She capitulated. 'OK, but he'll be gone tomorrow, so keep in touch.'

Clem was uneasy. 'I still think you're wrong to go on with this and right to think Patel doesn't believe your story. He probably knows what we're up to and prefers to have you where he can see what you're doing. Is Benton watching you too?'

She glared at him. 'He's no more than pleasant and friendly. Now, are you giving me a lift or shall I catch a bus?' She allowed him to drop her within a quarter of a mile of her new home. As she was climbing out of the car, Clement made a last attempt to persuade her to let him drive her home.

She would not deign to reply to his question, merely thanking him for the lift. 'Same place tomorrow. Eight sharp. If either of us can't make it we'll phone.' She walked towards the canal quickly and angrily. Clement had presented her with this adventure. Now, when she was beginning to enjoy it, he was trying to make her feel guilty. She had made up the plan to cook for Patel on the spur of the moment, just to defy Clement, but she would do it.

She arrived back at her boat, made herself tidy, then walked in the dusk up the short stretch of towpath to the marina. Most of the boats were dark shapes against a luminous sky but lights shone from the cabin windows of *Shahnaz*. Shakila climbed aboard before calling and Patel met her at the top of the short flight of steps from the cabin to the deck.

He was weighed down by a brown paper-wrapped load and she could see he was not pleased that she had turned up. She had startled him and the top package fell to the ground, its cover tearing. It seemed to contain nothing more sinister than a pack of A2 paper.

She spoke to him, keeping her tone light. 'Don't worry, I haven't come to stow away. Is this a sideline of yours?'

'What?'

'Delivering cargoes, keeping HGVs off the road, cutting down on pollution?'

He was recovering himself. 'It's certainly a thought. This delivery is a one-off, though. I found these in a factory skip. The paper's not clean enough for whatever its original purpose was. I've a mate in Sheffield, though, who has a small cutlery firm. I thought he could use it for packing.'

Shakila nodded. 'Recycling too? Good scheme. I'd never have thought of that.' She went on to explain her presence by delivering her invitation. 'Amrita brought me some more supplies when I met her. I thought I could begin to pay you back for helping me if I had a hot meal ready for you when you come back on Friday.'

He gave her a quizzical look, then accepted the favour and thanked her.

She beamed at him. 'I'll go then. You're obviously busy. Have a good trip.'

But now he became hospitable. 'I need a break. Stay for a drink.'

She smiled and perched on the cabin top. 'Thank you, but you know I never—'

'Neither does Shahnaz. She likes ginger cordial, though. That do you?'

'That would be lovely.' At least it would be a change from Coke. It was a little more palatable than she had expected and she had her reward for sipping at it when, a few moments later, he excused himself.

His jacket hung from a peg on the cabin side, the keys making the pocket bulge. Dare she? She heard Patel slide the noisy metal bolt. That assured her of a few seconds' warning before he emerged. If it was a trap, then so be it!

She lifted the ring carefully. She hardly had the time to remove even one. Which? She could discount the colour-coded Yales. She had noticed that all the garages were padlocked. She selected the smallest of the rest. It looked the right size and vintage and would be the easiest to slide out. She broke a fingernail prising the coils of the ring apart, but managed the job quickly, slipping the rest of the bunch of keys back into Patel's pocket. The WC conveniently flushed and drowned the clink.

A few minutes later, she let him escort her back to her boat and watched him through the cabin window as he returned to his own. She had plenty to think about. His story was as unlikely as her own. The paper in the parcel he had dropped had not looked at all grubby or damaged—at least, not before it fell. What could he be up to with reams of it?

Suddenly, she knew.

*   *   *

Hannah listened to the sounds from the hall as Tom showed out yet another well-meaning, embarrassed, tactless visitor. She understood that people found it difficult to know what to say to her. She had no further use for the language of survival. She had faced imminent death for herself but she could not summon up the energy to manage her knowledge in relation to others or to help them in their dealings with her.

She did not consider the prospect of death itself as totally unacceptable. She was fifty-four years old and had enjoyed, in the main, a happy and fulfilled life. She had no wish to prolong this final stage unduly, and felt more anxious about the mode than the fact of dying.

She was looking for a good death.

What did she mean when she thought that? It had to be in the right place, with the right people, but she was not sure which or whom. And she had to have completed her agenda, but what was on it? Personal hurts reconciled? Final goodbyes said?

Maybe it was too late for all that, now that she could communicate only through a mechanical contraption with its metallic tone and limited vocabulary. She wished she had forced the family, Tom especially, to discuss the situation when she had still been able to express herself freely. Tom had avoided heart-to-hearts, reluctant to admit to her how he really felt. He refused to face, at any rate with her, the consequences for him of her illness and death.

She knew he was afraid of giving the impression that he was waiting for her to die and stop messing up his life. He was convinced that she would be upset if she knew there were things he was planning to do afterwards. Now, she was deprived of the means of convincing him that she would be delighted to know that there was light at the end of his tunnel.

She felt impotent fury as tears gathered and ran down her cheeks. She could order her hands to wipe them away but her muscles ignored her. Tom would blame himself, try to comfort her, protect her against thoughts that were not troubling her. The tears fell faster.

On Wednesday, Mitchell sent Jennifer to talk to Lauren Hardy. Someone had told her that the journalist was twenty-nine years old. Whoever it was had surely been mistaken—or had she misheard? The woman's hair had no grey in it but the face told the sergeant that her witness was at least forty.

Miss Hardy invited her in and made her comfortable in an easy chair, then asked, provocatively, 'How long have I been a suspect?'

In the same tone, Jennifer told her, 'Along with two or three dozen other people, ever since Rosie's body was found.'

'So you'd like to drink my coffee whilst you persuade me to convict myself.'

'Well, yes—if you make good coffee.'

The woman grinned and disappeared to her kitchen whilst Jennifer examined the large living room without rising from her chair. It was considerably more soothing than its owner. Nothing matched anything else, but the contrasting styles and colours had settled comfortably together. Papers were scattered on most surfaces but there was no dust and the paintwork and windows were clean.

After less than five minutes, Miss Hardy was back with mugs of good quality instant and a plate of shortbread. Jennifer helped herself to both when invited. With her mouth full, she urged, 'Do have some yourself, Miss Hardy, or you'll make me feel greedy.'

Miss Hardy pushed the plate towards Jennifer and away from herself. 'I don't want any.'

Jennifer swallowed. 'There's no way you need to watch your weight.'

'I said I didn't want any!' The sharp tone softened as she added, 'My name's Lauren. What do you want me to tell you?'

Jennifer bit her lip, then smiled. 'I was going to approach it obliquely, but that doesn't seem the right line to take with you. Caroline tells me you used to sing with the company. Why did you leave?'

'Because I was ill. I had a long spell in hospital. When I came home again, I found my work was as much as I could cope with.'

'That's a pity. I've been told you have a rather good voice.'

'It's a pity Mr Blake didn't agree with your informant.'

'But my informant was Mr Blake.' Lauren gave a disbelieving sniff. 'I gather you two don't get on.'

Lauren scowled. 'You could say so.'

Jennifer was delighted by this aggression. It was quite likely to make her interviewee less discreet even than usual. 'How do you see him, then? Describe him to me.'

'How do you describe a person? I can give

you an inventory.'

'Fair enough. Do that then.'

'Well, for a start he can't see further than a pretty face. When I was nineteen, he put on a production of *Traviata*. Three of us auditioned to sing Violetta. I hoped to be picked and most of the chorus expected he'd give the part to me. He gave it to Marian, the girl who's singing Mercedes in *Carmen*. Blake came to me afterwards and told me that he couldn't use me. I was too fat to take the part of someone who was supposed to be dying of TB.'

'You must have been angry—but it's a long time to bear such a grudge about it.'

Lauren's tone was no longer angry, just miserable. 'That remark changed the rest of my life. I was nineteen, as I've told you, and already self-conscious about my weight. I went on a starvation diet—not to try to get the part back. That would have been unfair to Marian. It was because he made me see myself as gross. I might as well tell you before someone else does that I was hospitalized because I had anorexia nervosa. I can't eat normally even now. Inside my mind, food means flesh. Flesh means being unacceptable, whether for singing Violetta or finding a job or being in a relationship with a man.

'When I came out of hospital, before I was certified fit to work, I went to a few of the society's rehearsals. Blake welcomed me back

240

effusively. I'm sure now that that was because some of my friends had blamed him openly for what happened to me.'

'You told them about it?'

'I didn't need to. He was crass enough to make the remark after he had been reading the finalized cast list to the whole company. A lot of them were still around. That's why it was extra humiliating. Anyway, I gave him the benefit of the doubt and took his friendliness as his way of apologizing.

'Soon afterwards, I started looking for work again and I asked him to give me a character reference. I didn't go to church so I couldn't ask the vicar. I'd been off work for three and a half years by then, so any past employer was past history.'

'He wrote one?'

'Yes, wasn't it kind of him? He said I was unreliable, didn't always turn up when called for rehearsals. He omitted to say it was because I was recovering from an illness that he caused.'

Lauren was silent for a while, except for her heavy breathing. Finally, she looked up apologetically at Jennifer. 'Why the hell am I telling you all this?'

'Have you ever told it to anyone else?' She shook her head. 'Then it was high time you did. I hope you find it's helped you. Now I'd like to know what happened at a typical rehearsal.'

Lauren thought for a minute. When she spoke again she had returned to the ironical, half-amused tone in which she had begun the conversation. 'They were all different.'

'All right, tell me about one of them. How about the first one?'

Lauren paused to recall it. 'That was the hardest one to write up because it was so static. Blake just lectured everybody about the wonderful production he envisaged. He was wearing an arty-farty tunic over jeans and he sat eating an apple whilst the rest all arrived in dribs and drabs. There was an eternity of Continental double-cheeked kissing and they all introduced themselves.'

'What, the whole shoot?'

'The chorus wasn't called. There was a working model of the set on a table. Blake must have talked for a solid half-hour. The cast tried to pin him down to a period and a country. He parried them with vague suggestions—"after Kalashnikovs but before mobile phones", and a factory producing "more probably coke than cigarettes". Oh, and it was as early as that when they had their first spat.'

'Yes?'

'Blake said that at the end of the first scene Carmen would escape by climbing over the top of the whole structure. Rosie apparently had problems with heights. She was less than impressed with that part of the plan. He went on for ages talking about the dancing at Lillas Pastia's. It was to be sado-masochistic and desperate. Carmen was to cut her feet dancing on broken glass. We all thought the whole thing sounded OTT. I made notes on everything he said and I took down his last sentence word for word. "The final image of Carmen will be as a dead bull, like one killed by Escamillo." Rosie said, "Gee, thanks!" and there was a shout of laughter.'

'How did Mr Blake take that?'

'He announced their break and stalked off by himself. We all went off for coffee and Miles was mocking and misquoting him. "I want a timeless feel" and "Ambiguity is important."'

'Sounds as though he rather asked for it— Blake, I mean.'

'He always does!'

√ Jennifer made no further comment on Lauren's contemptuous tone. She consulted her notes and asked, 'Some of the singers have mentioned party games at rehearsals. Could you make that clearer?'

Lauren answered with a clever imitation of Blake's high voice and fulsome manner. ' "I want to establish a laid-back atmosphere in which everyone involved in the production feels that the rest are friends"—or words to that effect.'

'Could you describe one?'

Lauren's expression said 'If I must.' 'For

one, we all sat in a big circle and each of us was asked for three pieces of personal information, two of them true and one a lie. He took first turn himself.' She watched Jennifer's busy pencil and asked, 'You don't expect me to remember what they all said?'

'I thought you wrote everything down.'

She shook her head. 'He wanted me to join in the games.'

'OK. Did anyone say anything that struck you sufficiently strongly for it to stay in your mind?'

She grinned again. 'Yes. Miles claimed to have played hockey for his county as a youth. He didn't say which one and I can't remember whether he claimed it as true or false. It sounded a bit energetic for a lazy article like him. Steiger said she was an only child for her false statement. That was a bit of wishful thinking. She has a handicapped sister that she hardly ever mentions, and then never with any sympathy. She resents the attention the poor girl gets. Rosie said her mother was in a London nursing home . . .'

Jennifer made a quick note of this. '. . . and Blake said he failed O-level music, which is true, and that he'd been asked to tour Europe with this production, which, of course, wasn't. Oh, and he admitted that his father was furious with him for letting it be known that his money came from gambling, and for the gambling itself.'

'What did you tell them?'

'I really can't remember.'

Lauren's tone told Jennifer to mind her own business and she made a mental note to get this information from someone else. 'Tell me about when rehearsals really got under way.'

Lauren cast up her eyes. 'Cries of "Quiet please!" always got more frequent as the day progressed. Blake couldn't cope with the chorus. He's only conducted them up to now on little church hall stages. The principals acted and the chorus stood below and sang. Now, they have to take part in the plot, have their places on the stage and react to what's going on. Blake had never decided quite what he wanted them to do. It didn't seem to occur to him that fifty-odd people weren't going to stand there in silence while he thought it out.'

She waited for another question. When Jennifer said nothing, she continued, 'Neither side played fair with the other. Blake kept encouraging people to throw in their ideas so he could incorporate them, but, in the end, no scene had any input but his. They paid him out, though. When he gave specific instructions they went their own sweet way.'

'So, how did it ever come together?'

'They had to compromise in the end. They all had too much invested in the show to let it flop—money, reputations. Blake kept reminding them that they were being paid to take his direction. That just kept everyone wondering how much everyone else was getting and when the money would run out.'

'Were there arguments about money?'

'Not openly. There were plenty of others though.'

'Other arguments? What were they about?'

'Technical things. Mark, playing Zuniga, threw a wobbly because he had to sing "Yes", just by itself. You'd think translators would realize that singers can't sing that word alone without getting a laugh. Why can't they make it "Assuredly", or "Most certainly", or "I really do"? The big three kept wanting the words changed for easier singing. Sometimes Blake agreed, sometimes not. When they had been changed, the singers kept reverting to the original. They never got the notes wrong though. You can't mess about with them. There were rows about Steiger being wooden.'

'Was she?'

Lauren nodded vigorously. 'Her whole attitude on stage shouted, "This is me acting." When Blake suggested she tried to be more natural, she hit the roof, said she'd done exactly what Blake asked for, which she had. That was why it was wooden.'

'I don't understand.'

'Well, for Rosie, what she was told was just the starting point. She did it, but added to it, showed us how Carmen would have felt about it. Rosie was such a pro. Whenever one person was giving her instructions, three others were

246

queuing up to say something else. There were no pauses for it all to sink in. Blake and Cavill, Peter, the choreographer, Andrew, the stage manager—all of them were at her. And that included Miles. Whenever he was found fault with, he soothed himself by lecturing Rosie. She listened politely to them all.'

'And ignored them?'

'Well, discarded the advice she knew was not appropriate.'

'Didn't you ever get cheesed off with the whole thing?'

Lauren shook her head. 'No. There was always the music. It's no big deal to the pros—not in rehearsal. They're all here because of their remarkable voices so they're used to the sound of each other. They've mostly got the music right before rehearsals begin. No one stops to say, "Isn't this a marvellous tune, a wonderful musical moment?" You're more likely to hear, "These words have too many consonants," or, "No, there isn't any breath left for a portamento." Their commitment isn't sentimental. There's something very moving, though, about the disciplined, mind-battering wall of sound, coming from people dressed in jeans and orange jumpers at ten o'clock in the morning.'

Lauren fell silent. Jennifer let the silence continue for some seconds, then asked, 'You hate Lewis Blake, don't you?'

She smiled. 'Yes, I don't think that's putting

the case too strongly.'

'You've enjoyed getting your own back on him through your *Clarion* articles, haven't you?'

She nodded. 'I felt slightly guilty about that—not on Blake's account, don't think that. The music they've all been making has been worth a more fitting tribute.'

Jennifer nodded. 'Yes, but I shouldn't worry on that count. The reviews will give them that, if they do a good job. Lauren, did your revenge on Lewis Blake also include sending him a series of letters?'

CHAPTER TWELVE

Clement had been pleased and surprised when Mitchell had agreed without demur to send the banknotes that Jonathan had stolen from Shaun Grant for forensic examination. He was delighted, too, with his DCI's crumb of praise passed on to him by John Carroll. So, the big chief had noticed his sympathy with the elderly, was aware that he could persuade information out of them, hit it off with them. He had every intention of getting on well with Gertrude Smith, Rosie's mother, as he set off to see her on Thursday morning.

He had made his courtesy call on the local force. They had welcomed him on to their patch with the freedom of their canteen and had given him efficient directions to Rosegarth. According to their desk sergeant, the place had once been a vicarage and stood in the grounds of St Matthias' church in this well-to-do suburb of Preston.

The church tower was visible over a six-feet-high white-washed wall that surrounded the residential home and its garden—an imposing mansion and an imposing church. He could see little of the church from here but had passed it before turning into the Rosegarth drive. He wished he had time to explore it.

Lining his Escort up neatly at the end of a row of larger, smarter cars, he climbed out and took a moment to admire the garden. The DCI would approve. There were plenty of roses to justify the name of the house but no sign of a bloom. No washed out, blowsy October pinks and yellows. No tentative buds half unfolding and then changing their minds about opening their hearts to this unwelcoming day. The bushes had been pruned within an inch of their lives and within eight or nine inches of the ground.

It was certainly a top-of-the-range place. He wouldn't mind being put away in a place like this when his own time came. He climbed moss-free, dirt-free stone steps and rang a polished brass bell attached to a recently washed white door.

His summons was answered at once by a

neatly uniformed girl. Clement stepped, at her invitation, into a vast hall, furnished like the entrance of a flourishing commercial concern, which, come to think of it, this place probably was. There were framed prints on the wall and leather sofas on thick carpet. He was himself carefully vetted before being allowed to proceed any further.

He kept waiting for the mixed odours of mass catering, urine, disinfectant and old age to hit him. They didn't. Nor was there a masking of dreadful synthetic sprays. The place smelled only of fresh air, with a faint suggestion of polish and cleaning materials.

The girl, Louise according to a badge on her lapel, led him along carpeted corridors, doors on one side, windows and framed prints on the other. The elegance was spoiled a little by a handrail, running at waist level along each wall. 'You have told Mrs Smith to expect me?' Clement asked.

Louise nodded and smiled. 'She says she can't tell you anything but she'll see you since you've come all this way.'

'Did her daughter visit her?'

The girl shrugged. 'Yes and no. When she was in the area, she would call in every day but she wasn't around very often. We expected Mrs Smith to be very proud of her, show photographs, cut her pictures out of the musical papers. She didn't. She seemed quite unimpressed.'

250

Louise tapped on a door, waited for an invitation before opening it and raised her voice a fraction. 'Here's Constable Clement to see you, Mrs Smith.' Clement was ushered in and the door was closed after him. Covertly, he surveyed the room's inmate. She stared back quite openly, obviously taking an inventory.

'You'd better sit down,' she instructed him, when she was satisfied.

He did so, then offered his commiserations. Tears fell, but briefly and in moderation. Clement felt he could not interrogate her yet. He offered, instead, 'You seem very comfortable here.'

Mrs Smith perked up. 'Comfortable's the word. Posh place, private room, everything done for you. What sort of life's that?'

'You'd like to be more independent?'

'Well, if I could have my lungs decoked and my legs'd work right, I'd be out of here right away.'

'You'd like to be back in your own home?'

She shook her head. 'No. I know I couldn't manage there but I'd like to be back in the council home. There's real people in there, not stuffed dummies with lah-di-dah accents and their scalps showing through their silly blue rinses and their Polyfilla make-up.' She paused to catch her breath. Recovered, she explained, 'It was the mill that got me like this.'

Clement regarded Mrs Smith with respect.

251

She was dressed in a plain skirt and jumper, thick stockings and expensive-looking leather slippers. Her hair was shining clean but unstyled. 'Why do you stay here?' he asked her. 'You could go back to your old place, couldn't you?'

She smiled. 'When Rosemary got rich, I had to come here to stop her looking mean and uncaring—and she wasn't. I have to admit that. You're right though, young man. I don't have to be here any more.'

Clement wondered how much of her daughter's money she had inherited and whether Rosie's husband, or, possibly, ex-husband, and child would be found. He didn't think Mrs Smith would be interested—not, at least, in the money. 'Do you think we could talk about Rosemary for a while?'

'As long as you like. It's a pleasure to talk to somebody with an interest outside TV and those posh magazines. Have you decided who killed her yet?'

'I'm afraid not yet, but we're making strides. You seem a forthright lady. Can I ask you a blunt question?' She nodded. 'You don't seem as upset about your daughter's death as I expected. Why is that?'

She remained silent for an uncomfortable length of time. Clement wondered whether he really was good with old ladies. When she finally looked up again, her manner was softer.

'She was never really part of my life. It's

hard to be close to someone when you've got practically nothing in common with them. Wilf, her dad, he was working in an office when I met him. He went to evening classes to better himself. I didn't want him better. I liked him as he was, but it made him happy.

'He got promoted, went up in the world. He and Rosemary sometimes had conversations that I didn't understand. I just kept out of things, except to try to make a nice home for them. I kept putting my foot in it with my rough and ready mill voice. Their friends had to try not to look surprised when I joined in the conversations. Not that I thought I was inferior to them. They were like a lot of the folk in here.'

'You strike me as someone who talks a lot of sense, and anyway, you haven't got a rough way of talking.'

'Not so much now, I suppose.' Her breath was coming short again. 'Something's rubbed off from living in here. Anyway, I never let Wilf and Rosemary walk all over me. I made the rules at home, but I didn't go about with them much.'

'You're surely proud of what Rosemary achieved?'

She considered. 'I was at first, but I'm chapel. She was doing the solos in *Messiahs* and *Elijahs* that I knew because the chapel choir had sung them, even though it was in posh halls and tickets a wicked price. Then she grew out of all that and I didn't understand what she was doing. I've only been to one opera in my life and that was one too many.'

'Mrs Smith, can you tell me about Rosemary's pregnancy?'

She sat up as straight as she could and glared at him. 'Her what? Wherever did you get that story from?'

Clement produced a print of the relevant photograph and passed it over. Mrs Smith peered at it. 'Huh, it's just the way she's standing—or maybe she'd pushed a cushion up her skirt. You know how stupid girls can be at that age.'

'Mrs Smith, we've read Jane Felling's letters.'

'Jane? Nice woman.' She sighed. 'Well, I don't suppose you'll tell me how much you learnt from them.'

She waited to see. Then he decided on the converse. 'What we still don't know are Rosemary's married name and how to find her husband and daughter.'

'And you think I'll tell you? They've both had more than enough to put up with. I don't suppose you'll let that nice Jane off lightly but, whatever you threaten her with, I know she'll stand up to you. I've a lot less to lose than she has, so you can do your worst.'

Clement left, disarmed and uninformed. Low over everything, the sky hung, pale and unfriendly. Deaths-heads on a hydrangea bush had profiles angular and hard against the pallid light. He sat in his car and wondered how he could have managed the confrontation better.

*   *   *

By eight o'clock on Thursday evening, Clement was once more in his local pub, finishing his first pint. The same gathering of elderly drinkers sat around him. He was very aware of their silent interest in the reason for his presence in this geriatric assembly.

The old man who had chatted to Shakila the previous evening kept glancing towards the door. After a quarter of an hour or so, he strolled across to sit at Clement's table, opposite him. 'Your lady friend coming in tonight?'

Clement grinned. 'I'm expecting her. What about your chess-playing friends?'

'Over at the Swan. There's a chess tournament there tonight.'

'You don't go to support them?'

'They won't let me.' Remembering the way he had distracted them from their game with one another the night before, Clement didn't blame them.

Having reached the end of what they had to say to one another, the two men sat on awkwardly, each offering a desperate remark every so often and wondering how to disengage themselves. Eventually, ignoring the mobile phone in his pocket, Clement asked if there was a public phone in the building.

The old man nodded towards the sign for the cloakrooms. 'Out there in the draughty passage—so you don't spend too much drinking time in chatting.'

'I think I'll see if I can get her on her mobile, find out what's holding her up.'

'Right then. If she arrives in the meantime, I'll give you a shout.'

Finding that the draught in the passage was actually a howling gale, Clement retired to a cubicle in the Gents and wondered whether to carry out his stated intention. If Patel had gone off on his canal trip as planned there should be no harm in trying to contact Shakila. He jabbed buttons and waited.

Her phone was switched off. What had she said last night? Eight o'clock sharp. If something went wrong with the arrangement they would phone. Clement was worried. It was half-past eight now. Shakila had been annoyed with him when they parted last night—just in the mood to follow up a madcap idea to show him how clever she was. What if . . .? He didn't know quite what to imagine but none of his half-formed notions of what might have delayed her was comforting.

He went back into the lounge bar. At least it was warm in there. There was still no sign of Shakila, but he saw, to his relief, that his unwanted companion was at the bar, standing in the middle of a group and taking his full part in its argument. There was now no unoccupied table. Clement seated himself at one where the two other occupants were hidden behind sporting papers and ignoring one another.

After a minute he took a paper for himself, left it reserving his stool and went to the bar for another pint. He'd read the paper and finish his beer. If Shakila wasn't here by then he'd better think about getting some help. Twenty more minutes passed. Time to act.

He went across to his former companion and bought him a drink. Pushing it across the bar to him, he asked, 'Do me a favour, mate?'

The man raised his eyebrows, inviting more information, but waiting cautiously to discover the nature of the requested favour.

'I have to go. If my girlfriend comes in, will you ask her to ring this number?'

This was acceptable, and, the favour granted, the old man felt able to accept the drink. He took the piece of paper Clement was offering and promised to hand it over. 'I'll give this to the young lady and I'll keep her well entertained till you get back.' Clement grinned at the outsize wink that accompanied the offer. Shakila would be quite equal to any challenge that might come from that corner.

He went out to his car and pulled out his phone again. There was only one person he could apply to in his present plight. The call was answered immediately. 'Caroline? It's Adrian. I've got a problem. Are you busy or can I come round?' There was a pause. He went on hurriedly. 'It's not what you think. It's about Shakila.'

'Oh.' Caroline sounded both relieved and curious. 'OK, I'll put the kettle on. How long will you be?'

'I'll be there by the time it boils.' He set off on the five-minute journey, regretting his infatuation with Caroline the previous year— or at least his lack of self-restraint in letting her discover it. By the time he arrived at the flat, he had killed Shakila off in his imagination several horrible ways and was beyond letting a meeting at home with Caroline embarrass him.

Quickly he explained how he had called the young DC on to the present case and his suspicion that Patel had killed Rosie in mistake for Caroline herself.

'I know all this. What's the problem now?' He described their subsequent regular meetings, what Shakila had discovered and her current situation as far as he knew it. Now both of them were anxious.

Caroline pushed a steaming mug at him. 'What did you think I could do that you can't? I suppose no one but the two of you knows about this?'

'That's right. I thought you might ring her

258

mobile number again, pretend to be her imaginary friend, try to find out why she hasn't shown.'

'Why not ring yourself?'

'I did. She was switched off. Then, I thought, if Patel's still around—or one of his heavies—and recognizes a man's voice, Shakila would have to make up another story on the spur of the moment.'

Caroline considered. 'I suppose it can't do any harm. Am I supposed to be Asian?'

Clement shrugged. 'Probably. Play it by ear. Shakila's a Pakistani but she sounds like a local.'

Caroline nodded. 'Do I have a name?'

Again Clement shrugged. 'I shouldn't give your real one. Not till you know what's happening, at least.'

Caroline sipped in silence, considering their options, then asked, 'You have checked your own phone, your answering machine?'

Feeling very foolish, Clement shook his head. Caroline cast up her eyes. 'Well, you'd better go . . .'

'I can ring for messages from here.' Quickly he jabbed numbers, then held the receiver so that both of them could listen. The third message was Shakila's. 'Adrian? Sorry, I've lost your mobile number. The key didn't fit any of the garages. I was a bit fed up at first, but then I wondered what it did fit. I knew Patel had a house in Cloughton so I got the address from the telephone directory. It's in the Greenway. Wouldn't it just be? I waited till it was getting a bit dark and the neighbours' curtains were drawn. I knew the key was too small to be for the house doors but there's a shed, a biggish one, in the back garden and, bingo! I'm in. Obviously I'm going to skip the pub. I'll ring again in about an hour. Hope I've caught you in. It's half-past seven now. Cheers.'

Caroline looked at her watch. 'Five to nine. Let's go to your place if that's the only number she's got. We'll give her till half-past for the promised call. If we've heard nothing by then I think we'd better assume the wheels have come off and we'll have to tell the boss.'

Clement fidgeted as he finished his coffee. 'You blame me, don't you?'

She took the mug from him and put it in the sink. 'Yes. You picked on Shakila because she's young and ambitious. You knew what she has in abundance is courage and what she lacks is caution and discretion. I think your theory is one that should have more consideration, but why couldn't you have suggested it to the whole team at a briefing?' She stopped and turned away angrily.

Clement had expected nothing else. He had come for help solely for Shakila's sake. He prepared himself to blink away the tears that sprang shamingly easily since his family troubles. He was surprised when what he felt was a surge of anger and the ability to refute

260

Caroline's accusation firmly and calmly. 'You're wrong. I never meant to work through Shakila on her own. I gave her a bell for the same reason the DCI did last time, because she spoke Urdu. Actually, it turns out Patel speaks Hindi but that's irrelevant now.

'Neither of us wanted her out on a limb like this. I just thought the boss would follow up my idea more readily if she was on hand. Anyway, I like her and I think she'd be good in CID. Once she was off the case in general, I did all I could to get her to leave it alone—not that I expected her to listen to me. She's having the time of her life—at least, I hope she still is.'

He glanced at his watch again. 'Sorry I bothered you. I'll get home and wait for her to call.' Nevertheless, he was glad to see Caroline get up and grab a coat. She squeezed his arm and he grinned. 'Let's see if my coffee's better than yours.'

'No. Let's hope she rings to be picked up before we've had time to make any.'

*   *   *

Shakila had not anticipated the steady, unrelenting rain but it failed to depress her. If her adventure had been comfortable, it would not have been so exciting.

Realistically, her chances of finding anything incriminating in Patel's garden shed

261

were not high, but she had taken her chance of stealing the key. When he missed it, he would know that she had it. She was putting herself at considerable risk and she wanted some compensation for this, however small.

The shed's dimensions were about nine feet by six. It was screened to some extent by a sturdy trellis, but the plant that grew on and around it had died off for the winter. Its quality and condition were in keeping with the rest of Patel's property, as far as the feeble torchlight she dared use could show her. The sides and roof were made of preservative-soaked wood—heavy planks of it—and it had a stout door. Shakila was glad she had not had to break in. She could not have done that quietly. Probably, she could not have done it at all.

To her relief, the key turned sweetly and the padlock opened. At first she was surprised that this was its only protection. Then she realized that to barricade it with protective devices would have invited speculation about its contents. Closing the door behind her, Shakila picked her way round an assortment of garden implements, probably used by a hired gardener.

There were shelves running along each of the longer sides. She decided it would be safe to risk the more powerful torch now that she was surrounded by the thick walls. The only window faced away from the houses and on to

262

part of the municipal golf course. On the first side, the shelves displayed nothing more exciting than a can of motor oil and commercial-sized tins of paint. More work lined up for Hal Benton, perhaps. She was less suspicious of Benton now that it seemed that Patel's illegal activities were not centred on the marina—unless, in addition to what she suspected he was doing, he was also, as Clement believed, delivering drugs to canalside pubs.

At the back of the shed, below the window, a heap of something could be seen, covered in a green tarpaulin sheet. She turned from it determinedly. First she had set herself to finish searching the shelves. Methodically, she began on the other side, forcing herself to examine an innocent-looking box of forks and trowels, bottles of fertilizer and weedkiller, bags of lawn seed. She unwrapped and unscrewed all the containers, peering and sniffing and finding nothing untoward. Now, she would let herself lift the tarpaulin.

It was covering more packs of paper, in the same wrappings as those Patel had been handling at the marina. Shakila tore at them eagerly, then gazed down in satisfaction—no, in triumph—as she saw sheets of uncut twenty pound notes. She tried to make a rough estimate of the number of sheets in a pack to work out the value of the fifteen parcels. She gave up when she realized that the other fourteen could well contain notes of a different denomination.

Gleefully, she reached for her phone. Time for her DCI's congratulations and the superintendent's humble pie.

When Mitchell's first reaction was a reprimand, she was very angry. She managed to keep a hold on her tongue, though, remembering how she had regretted previous unwise behaviour towards him. Besides, she could hear him relenting, his excitement rising. Concisely, she put him in the picture, adding a warning. 'He said he'd be away till tomorrow afternoon but I don't believe what he says any more than he believes me. He could be watching me now, so don't come with blue lights flashing.'

While she was tucking her phone away, however, it was not Patel's voice that she heard. It was high-pitched and she whirled round, expecting to see a woman. It was Shaun Grant who stood in the doorway, a knife in his hand.

CHAPTER THIRTEEN

On Friday morning, Mitchell was a little late in arriving at the station. He had allowed himself the luxury of joining in the family breakfast as his reward for working far into the previous night.

Now, he had Shaun Grant safely in custody. Shakila, rescued from Shaun's knife and unreservedly forgiven, at least by Mitchell himself, was waiting to notify him of Patel's return to the marina. All the impounded materials were safely stored away and even the paperwork was completed.

Mitchell was met, as he arrived in the foyer, with the news that Jane Felling had been not only located but brought to the station to speak to him. She was in a wheelchair and since there was no access for it to Mitchell's office, John Carroll had offered his own where Miss Felling was waiting.

Having introduced her to his DCI, Carroll disappeared. Mitchell restrained an urge to tidy the superintendent's desk. Instead, he brought the superintendent's chair from behind it and placed it beside Miss Felling's. He regarded his visitor. He had been expecting a disabled version of Rosie's agent, but she was a surprise to him.

He saw that keen greenish eyes were busy making an estimate of him. Her mousy brown hair was cropped sufficiently short to be no trouble to arrange but its style was still feminine. The face appeared to be devoid of make-up, but its features were so well defined that Mitchell suspected that they had been somehow enhanced. Her voice was an educated version of the friendly south

Lancashire drawl. Her left hand was heavily bandaged.

Mitchell shook the other hand and poured the coffee his superintendent had already provided. He observed without surprise that John Carroll had noted the further and hopefully temporary injury and had mugs sent in without saucers to manage. He pushed the tray to where she could pick up her own and thanked his visitor for coming.

She apologized for her several days' delay in coming to them and held up her bandaged hand. 'I haven't had another accident. This is an attempt to put right a bit more damage from the last one. It should make my piano playing as good as it was before. Not that it was ever at performance level, but it will be good enough to accompany my pupils competently. I was using the short stay in hospital as time out—didn't read the papers or watch television but took in a huge pile of novels. One of the other patients came to my room to tell me what had happened to Rosie. He didn't realize I knew her except by reputation—just thought I would be interested in the news because I was a fellow musician.'

She put a finger on her lips, then drank from the mug. 'Sorry, I'm rambling.'

Always blunt, Mitchell merely asked, 'Why are you nervous?'

His directness seemed to reassure her. 'Because there's a lot of Rosie's past that she didn't want to be known. I can't decide what I need to tell you.'

Mitchell offered no further reassurance. 'All of it.'

'It's a long story.'

'We've plenty of tapes.'

She nodded. 'I'll start at the beginning then.'

In spite of his demand, Mitchell was startled when the account began with Rosie as a fifth former at school. He grinned to himself, remembering that he had instructed his team to check on the victim's O-level results.

Miss Felling's account was far reaching and detailed but concise.

Rosie Goldsmith, Rosemary Smith in those days, came from a good, working-class family. Her father was some superior kind of clerk in the local council offices, with ambitions for the family and particularly for his daughter. Her mother was an ex-mill worker. Rosemary at fifteen had not disappointed them.

Miss Felling's eyes twinkled as she remembered her early acquaintance with her pupil. 'She was a good student, sociable and popular, a bit of a good-time girl. She collected eight or nine good O-levels, but also an unplanned pregnancy. Plans for A-levels and university were abandoned and she left school.'

Miss Felling seemed comforted by the news that the pregnancy was already known to the police. She went on to describe the family's plans for their daughter in these new circumstances. Rosie had carried on with the musical activities that had always been her hobby. She had been a good violinist but competitive. When the National Youth Orchestra had turned her down, she had dropped the violin.

'She had just won a singing competition. It was run by a much less prestigious organization, but as she was rather in everyone's bad books, success felt sweet. That was where I came in. I attended the winners' concert where Rosie was the star turn. It was about a year after my accident and I was beginning to look round for something useful to do with the rest of my life. I offered to coach her.'

'With a view to singing professionally?'

Jane Felling shrugged. 'Who knows? Even at that stage I believed she could do it if that was what she wanted. There was the coming child to consider, though, and how to support it. I've described Rosie as a livewire, and she certainly was, but she was unsophisticated and still influenced by her parents. They were "chapel" and anxious to get her married.'

Mitchell's witness fell silent, staring at him, but obviously not seeing him. After some seconds, he prompted her. 'It didn't work out? She didn't get married?'

She blinked. 'Not to the baby's father. I

never knew who he was. I doubt if anyone but Rosie did. There was another boy, though, who lived nearby. He was well regarded by her parents—quiet, well-mannered, with some local fame as a sportsman. He wasn't really Rosie's type but he had a huge crush on her.'

'Sounds like a recipe for disaster.'

'Well, in a way. He was a couple of years older and she occasionally used him as an escort, especially if she wanted to make another boy jealous—or, if an affair had broken up, to prove she could easily find someone else. The lad was quite handsome and the relationship with him seemed to deepen as the pregnancy progressed. He proposed marriage and offered to accept the child, bring it up as his own.'

'Enthusiastically supported by Rosie's parents, no doubt.'

'The parents were delighted. They stayed in Preston for the wedding, then the whole family moved to Accrington where nobody had heard the scandal.'

'Maria Gonzales told us that Rosie was brought up in Accrington.'

Miss Felling shook her head. 'I expect Rosie let her assume that.'

'How did the young husband's parents react?'

'They weren't so thrilled. They thought he'd been used, taken advantage of. They'd been expecting him to go to art college but, with

Rosie and her daughter to support, he had to leave school and find work.'

'Did you go on teaching her?'

'Yes, in a haphazard sort of way.'

Mitchell smiled. 'You don't look like someone who would teach haphazardly.'

'I taught the best way I could in the circumstances.' Her grin took the stuffiness out of her words. 'The baby had febrile convulsions all the time she was teething. Rosie wanted to go on taking part in local productions and competitions. She'd got into bad habits doing what amateur producers asked for and they gave her a fair amount of stick for thinking she needed more teaching than she was getting from them.'

'But you didn't give her up.'

Miss Felling shook her head. 'She'd given me a new life and interest as a patron and coach. She didn't stay with me throughout her career, but I'm grateful to her for starting me off—as she was to me, for the same reason. Then she recommended my services to other people when she became better known herself. I had other contacts, of course, but she found herself recently in a position to do me some favours.

'She was always exciting to teach—and easy. She knew pretty much how a piece of music would sound from just looking at it. Then, once she realized her technique was all wrong, she was not only willing but eager to do spadework in the form of vocal scales and exercises . . .'

Miss Felling explained at length how she had set about the job and how her pupil had responded. Someone who knew Mitchell better would have realized that the rapt and attentive expression he now assumed meant he had disengaged himself from the present situation to concentrate on more pressing matters. He would get Caroline to listen to all this stuff later.

'So, where are the husband and the child?' he demanded, when his witness paused for breath.

She remained silent, her uninjured hand fiddling with the wheelchair controls. Mitchell waited. After a moment, she looked up and he saw that she was ready to tell the difficult part of the story 'Well, by now Rosie was being offered minor roles fairly regularly, and once, during a flu epidemic, when several of the cast were struck down simultaneously, she sang Papagena with English National Opera.'

Mitchell was glaring at her but she smiled at him. 'It is all relevant. By this time, Carmen was three years old—'

'Carmen?'

'Rosie saw the show for the first time just before the baby was born. Anyway, the child was upset by her mother's frequent absences, sobbing inconsolably when she left, then refusing to have anything to do with her when she came back. Singing in oratoria meant she was only away for a single night. She was being offered the better minor roles in opera by now, though. For an opera, she'd be missing for weeks at a time. Her in-laws moved in to look after the little girl when her father was at work.'

'What about her own parents?'

'Her father had died by that time and her mother had a minor stroke. She also had breathing problems from working in the mill before Rosie was born. She could do nothing. Rosie was becoming better known and was quite intoxicated by her success. One year she was home for only eleven weeks. She was working with ENO and had bought herself a flat in London.'

'In Swiss Cottage? She's still there.'

'Yes. Her mother-in-law was very angry and went up to see her. There was a showdown. Rosie was told to keep away and to stop upsetting the child. She refused, of course, but the next time she went back to Accrington she found strangers living in the house who didn't know where the family had gone. She came to me, very distressed—stayed for a while, more or less had a breakdown.

'She couldn't bring herself to organize a search, go through the proper authorities. I didn't know how to advise her. Finding a husband and child who didn't want her meant more grief for her. Anyway, she was too depressed to make any effort.

'Professionally, I was afraid that, while she agonized, the musical world would go on without her. Without consulting her, I persuaded an American director friend to offer her the lead in his production of *La Bohème.* It got Rosie back on her feet and the show got rave reviews.' Miss Felling scrabbled in an untidy handbag and produced a tattered newspaper cutting. ' "This performance could surely only have been given by someone who has herself been torn apart by conflicting loyalties. She lifted the silly plot into the realm of tragedy." Of course, all stories are far-fetched and arbitrary when they are stripped of their clothing of dialogue, setting, emotional expression . . .'

'So, the American producer was glad you'd twisted his arm.'

'He'd only humoured me to the extent of giving Rosie an audition. When he heard her he snapped her up and once she was part of the production he was delighted with her. She was a good team member—all her directors have said so. When she was there, the others sang better. She seemed to have a gift for releasing the best in the rest of the cast. That's a very useful reputation to have when competition is so fierce. Her ambition was not just for herself but for the success of the whole production. After the first couple of days, no one is in awe of her, though their respect is tremendous . . .' Miss Felling paused, seeming suddenly weary.

Mitchell smiled at her. 'You don't need me to tell you how very useful this information is. I do thank you for coming. I'll send for Caroline in a few moments and she'll take you to the canteen for some lunch if you would like it. Contrary to popular belief, cultured and musical cops do occasionally exist outside detective novels. We pinched Caroline from the Royal Academy. She thought the concert platform would be too lonely for her, even if it was equally exciting.

'Also, in spite of all the moaning to save face, we're proud of our canteen. It's not bad at all. First, though, there are two more pieces of information I hope you can give me. Please tell me if you recognize any of these voices.' He switched on a tape recorder and Rosie's telephone messages began. Jane Felling's face lit up. She let the tape finish before she spoke. 'The first one is Roger Mills. He's in the ENO chorus and keen on Rosie. She liked him, often ate with him, but kept him at arm's length.'

'Wouldn't he have known that she'd be in Yorkshire?'

'Of course, but she's made several trips back during the two months or so of rehearsals. He'd know when she was likely to be around.'

Mitchell sighed. Another trip to London looked like being necessary.

Jane Felling continued her identification.

'Mrs Johns, as you've probably gathered, is the jewel who keeps the flat spotless. Now, Henry . . .' She paused to consider. 'I definitely recognized the first two voices, but this is guesswork now. Rosie was very friendly with Henry Hollingsworth. He's a director she's worked with quite a lot. I haven't met him, so I couldn't swear to that being his voice. I think he's working in Leeds with ON at the moment so he could have been hoping they could meet up whilst Rosie was in Yorkshire.'

'If this is him, it sounds as though they'd had a disagreement.'

'Yes, it does.'

'Who would he mean when he says "we're all" in Yorkshire?'

She frowned. 'I'm not sufficiently in touch to name names. You can imagine, though, that when a certain set of singers, director, choreographer and so on have collaborated on a brilliant production, they do their best to be hired by a company as a job lot so they can work together again. They like each other, understand each other. They get superstitious about what a flop will result if they split up.'

'All right, I can see that. What do you think he might be taking good care of?'

'I've absolutely no idea.'

'Any theory about why he didn't finish the message?'

'It could be any of a million reasons, maybe even a fault on the line. What was the second question?'

Mitchell felt that he had not been given the whole truth about the tape but he allowed his witness to move the subject on. 'I need as many details as you can give me about Rosie's husband and the rest of his family. Their names and whereabouts.'

'I prefer not to tell you.'

Mitchell had expected evasion but not this direct refusal. 'I'm afraid you have no—'

She raised her unbandaged hand to silence him. 'Oh, I do have the choice—and I'm quite prepared to pay a fine—or even to face a short spell of imprisonment rather than cause any more grief for those innocent people. Rosie's daughter will have grown up without her mother and won't miss her because she hardly remembers her. There's no need to spoil her life with resurrecting stories of her abandonment.

'Rosie's husband will have learned of her death from the media and be grieving for her. He really did love her. He can do without the added trauma of unjustified police suspicion.'

She withdrew her face from Mitchell's gaze and looked beyond him. 'It's strange that nature allows love that's not mutual. You'd think she would manage things better.'

Jane Felling refused adamantly to move from this stance. She also refused Mitchell's invitation to a canteen lunch. 'I think it would be unwise in the circumstances. Please tell your musical colleague that the concert platform is certainly lonely for a solo instrumental player and that I will be delighted to meet her when your efficient team has proved that Carmen's father did not kill her mother.'

*   *   *

Caroline reached forward and switched off the recording machine. At Mitchell's request she had listened to both long tapes of his session with Jane Felling. She wondered what the singer's own parents felt about their daughter's behaviour. It had deprived them of a grandchild, possibly their only one. It was interesting that Miss Felling had made no reference to them. Had they been so insignificant in Rosie's life? She would be interested to meet them. If she couldn't do that, at least she could study Clement's report on his talk with Mrs Smith.

Caroline glanced at the scribbled notes she had taken. She remembered that Maria Gonzales had told them Rosie was 'off men'. From her own observation she knew that Rosie had no problem either in attracting men or dealing with them. It seemed she had merely decided that she was a singer before she was a woman.

*   *   *

Some two hours later, Caroline, clad and coiffed for the second time as the murdered opera singer, had half an hour to spare before PC Smithson drove her to the industrial estate to begin Rosie's reconstructed walk. She elected to spend them in the canteen, in the company of a frothy cappuccino and a chocolate éclair. She arrived to find that Sergeant Taylor had had the same idea, varying it only with black filtered coffee and toasted currant teacake.

After a while, their desultory conversation moved round to Clement and, the subject having been broached, Jennifer launched into her customary attack. '. . . I grant you he's sometimes full of enthusiasm . . . can be almost manic . . . other times, and oftener, he's apathetic, hangdog, easily discouraged . . . seems totally lacking in self-esteem.'

Caroline liked Clement. So far, she had chosen to stand up for him against Jennifer's attacks by a calm support of him whenever she felt he was in the right. Not today, though. Possibly toppled out of her usual control by Jennifer's resorting to cheap, trendy pseudo-psychology, or maybe because she was a little nervous about her proposed exposure on the canal, she lost her temper. 'He's a nice bloke and he'd be a lot better for not having you consistently on his back!'

Several heads turned to look at them at the

sound of Caroline's raised voice. Not many people, even among her superior officers, dared to shout at Jennifer. Caroline was undismayed. 'At least he's well aware of his failings. A lot of us have only superficial confidence and authority. We're all unsure of ourselves, especially when we first join up. We're glad of the structure of the force and the uniform—and especially the baton—to give us courage and dignity. Underneath, lots of us are conformists. Being police officers gives us a value. Adrian knows that, admits it and battles with it.'

Jennifer was taken aback on two accounts. She dealt with the easier. 'Caro? You're engaged to Cavill. You're not still sweet on Adrian, are you?'

Caroline took a huge bite of her éclair and waited for her anger to drain away. She lowered her voice so that now only Jennifer could hear. 'I never was "sweet" on him. He's just had a rotten deal all round. Yes, he took a long while to settle to a career, came to policing late, but he's a damned good CID member in his own way. He can worm information out of some people better than I can.

'Then, just as he was feeling his feet, both Joanne and Richard died, in spite of the emergency section, and he upped sticks for yet another new start down here. Would you have managed any better in his place? I know he's

279

still a DC, he's not in a steady relationship . . .' She paused, hearing herself slip into jargon as irritating as Jennifer had used. 'He's got no sporting trophies, even though he's let running obsess him. There's no man in the regular shift to help him, except the DCI, and he's not in the best position.

'I felt touched and privileged when he offered me that diffident invitation to the police ball last year. We stayed till after midnight. He came home with me and, yes, we did sleep together that night. Unfortunately, he thought it was the start of something serious. By my normal standards it would have been. I don't sleep around casually.

'But Adrian needed sex. He'd tried to get to know other girls after Jo had been dead for a year but he always came on to them too fast and frightened them off. Eventually, he told me his real trouble. He'd got Jo pregnant to try to keep her. She didn't want children— they'd argued about it right from the beginning and she'd been on the point of leaving him. They had a sort of truce during the pregnancy. Then there were serious problems with it and she died, together with the baby. He thinks he killed them, and, in a way, he did.

'I don't know whether all that will help you to understand him or like him any better. What I do know for sure is that none of it will go any further—but don't forget about it. I don't suppose you've always got all your relationships right.'

Jennifer sat still, absorbing the information. Then she apologized, aloud to Caroline and silently to Clement. The two women chewed companionably without speaking, enjoying the few minutes' rest and their resumed good relations.

Conversation buzzed around them. As usual, the canteen was full. It was the hub of the whole station. A quartet of retired officers, working for the station as civilians, held a daily card school here. Serving officers were eating and drinking like themselves, or writing up notes and reports, holding informal meetings and briefings. The dartboard in the corner was in use and the Space Invader video game was being competed for. People in the queue, waiting to zap aliens, were reading the *Sun*. Two traffic wardens who habitually took refuge here had come in to avoid a shower. It was always the first place to look if you wanted someone.

Chiming in with Caroline's thought, Mitchell came in. 'Ha! Caught you. I'll forgive you both if you club together and buy me a coffee.'

Caroline looked at Jennifer. 'You earn more than I do.'

Jennifer grinned and went to the counter. When she came back, Mitchell and Caroline were poring over a chart showing Rosie's Friday timetable. '. . . So, at ten fifteen she answered the phone to Tim and said she wouldn't need him until rehearsal time. She got angry when he tried to persuade her to see the sights. Ten minutes later, she left by the back door, took a bus to a modest, respectable area and walked round it. She'd asked directions at George Tomlin's shop and bought and eaten her lunch there.

'A bit later, she came back and asked how to get to the marina. Tomlin took her there and dropped her on the edge of the industrial estate. Presumably she walked straight across it, found a convenient bench, screened from the towpath, and got out her camera. That's where we stop, at approximately four o'clock.'

Jennifer put a mug of coffee in front of him. 'Have you been staring at that all afternoon?'

Mitchell shook his head. 'I've been having another talk to Jamil Patel—in Porter's. I got absolutely nothing out of him on the subject of illicit drugs or illegal immigrants.'

'Does the porn get any worse than the magazines on show?'

'Yes. Knowing his uncle was on a "business trip", he took me into the back regions. I haven't time to deal with that at the moment, though.'

'If his uncle's away, why wasn't the boy at school?'

Mitchell turned from Jennifer to Caroline. 'His mother's not well. They daren't let the uncle hear that they closed the shop. Young

Jamil wants to be an architect.'

'Oh yes? Is he going to design minarets for Cloughton?'

They were all laughing at the idea when Smithson came in to collect Caroline. Another, much beefier, PC remained in the canteen doorway, the muscle that Mitchell had promised. Smithson addressed Mitchell as Caroline collected her props together. 'Poulter and Sarah Penney are down on the canal already, sir.'

'Hanging around looking suspicious, no doubt.'

'No, sir. They're on bikes. They've punctured Sarah's and they're both making a dog's dinner of an attempt at mending it.'

'Fair enough. What are your two going to do?'

'Mend the broken window in Patel's office, sir. Collier'—he gestured to the man still waiting in the doorway—'got his hand in at that sort of thing before he joined the force. I'm going to hold things for him.'

Caroline looked surprised. 'I ran past there at lunchtime. There wasn't a window broken.'

Smithson looked contrite. 'Bit of an accident a couple of hours ago. A stone went through, thrown from the bridge.'

As Caroline and her two escorts departed, they passed Clement coming into the canteen. Jennifer immediately got up to fetch another coffee, waving Clement to Caroline's empty chair. He sat on it, looking bemused.

Mitchell looked equally surprised, but merely remarked, 'At least we've sorted out Blake and his letters. He didn't get another one yesterday, did he?' Jennifer shook her head. When she had brought Lauren Hardy into the station, Mitchell had recognized the attractive but raddled face he had watched through his binoculars in the theatre on the previous Saturday.

'She's scared,' Jennifer said, 'that she's going to be accused of having carried out what the letters threaten. Do we suspect her? She says she was torn. When Rosie was killed, she wanted to come to us and confess to her harassment of Lewis Blake, but having issued the threats, she didn't dare. She was relieved in a way when I challenged her.'

Clement was shaking his head. Mitchell raised an eyebrow, inviting him to speak. 'I can't imagine a woman cutting someone's throat, especially Rosie Goldsmith's. She wasn't either small or weak. It would have been much safer, even for a man, to have stabbed her in the back or hit her over the head.'

'Or strangled her?' Jennifer suggested.

Clement thought not. 'That could have been quite noisy.'

Mitchell was off on another tack. 'We can't assume any more that Rosie was just on the canal because it was a nice afternoon. She made an unaccustomed bus journey in an

284

attempt to get to Swayneside without the opera people knowing. Then, whatever she found there sent her on a deliberate journey to the canal. So, what was it?'

'She got a message about meeting someone there? Maybe from the killer, but not necessarily.' Clement did not sound convinced by his own suggestion. He tried again. 'It could be as simple as some relative she'd discovered suggesting a week on a canal boat after the *Carmen* production was over—as a way of getting to know each other again. She could have gone down to book it. Something to keep her busy, distract her from her first night nerves.'

'To pick blackberries,' Jennifer suggested, facetiously.

'At this time of year?' Clement laughed. 'The kids will have stripped the bushes bare by now.'

Mitchell shook his head. 'Schoolkids don't do peaceful things like fruit picking any more.'

'There's nothing against her having had something to do with Patel's sneaky dealings. Being an opera singer doesn't make her a law-abiding citizen.' Clement's face fell as Mitchell vetoed this suggestion. Then he asked, 'Where does Shaun fit in?'

Mitchell relented. 'Let's bear that in mind. I'll give the lab a buzz and see how far they've got with the money your young friend stole for us. Let's hope it was covered in crack and

285

prints.'

'Have you had time to look at my report on Gwen Evans?' Jennifer asked, addressing the question to both men. 'I definitely got the impression she knew more than she was saying. I think she's protecting someone. I thought maybe she couldn't bear having Rosie around because she'd had an abortion. Gwen's fostering, so it's likely, though not certain, of course, that she can't have children of her own. She might have strong views about someone who can who's abused the privilege.

'Then I looked at the photograph again, though, and decided she appeared to be too far into the pregnancy for that.'

Neither of the men felt qualified to offer an opinion on so definitely feminine a topic. 'Would Gwen disapprove of Rosie having her child adopted?' Clement wondered aloud.

Jennifer thought not. 'Surely, if no one gave a child up, there'd be more grief for people whose only hope is adoption. She'd more likely be grateful.'

'I haven't had a chance yet to tell you what Jane Felling said. Rosie had the child and kept it.' Mitchell waited for his two juniors to take this in. 'Yes, Jennifer?'

She frowned in concentration. 'I'm trying to remember something Caroline told me. I'm vague because it was ages ago, well before the murder but after the production was in rehearsal. I think it was Gwen she was talking about. There was a failed adoption. Gwen—or whoever it was—had had a baby boy from birth because the teenage single mother was too ill to keep him for the usual six weeks. When she'd recovered and the baby was three months old, she suddenly decided she wanted him back.'

Mitchell was interested. 'How long ago was this? Would she still be upset about it?'

Clement's tone was bitter. 'I should think she'll be upset for the rest of her life.'

Mitchell led them on to another but perhaps no safer topic. After giving them a summary of Rosie's marriage and subsequent desertion of her family, he warned them, 'This isn't a substitute for you both reading it for yourselves.'

Jennifer nodded soberly. 'That's the kind of damage that Gwen's having to repair in the children she's fostering now. She might really have hated Rosie for the grief she's caused her daughter so carelessly.'

'Her husband,' Clement observed, 'probably hates her a good deal more. He's had to watch his child being—well, abused, in a way.'

'Going back to Jane Felling, she was helpful about the telephone calls on Rosie's machine,' Mitchell told them. 'She said she thought the third call might have come from a chap called Henry Hollingsworth. He's a director Rosie had worked with a number of times. I got the impression though that she was making him up. She was reluctant about it at first, as though she doesn't usually tell lies. Then she got more fluent when she'd made up her mind to go through with it.

'I was obviously being fanciful, though. Caroline checked him out with Maria Gonzales and Cavill knows of him, though they haven't met.'

Jennifer, her tone defensive, said, 'We haven't had a chance to get at that report or the tape. You asked Caroline to take them and work on them. Caro said she felt about Miss Felling as I do about Gwen, that she knew something relevant about someone and was protecting him.'

'The husband?'

'Very likely. All I can think is that, if two women are prepared to face a charge of contempt of court for him, he must be either a five-star charmer or else the salt of the earth type.'

'I wonder how Caroline's getting on on the towpath.'

Mitchell remained silent for some moments, then, ignoring Clement's comment, answered Jennifer's. 'I think I know who it is.'

They waited, knowing that he was checking his speculation against the facts, not pausing for effect. High drama was not the DCI's style. After almost a minute, he asked them, 'Who was the obvious person for Rosie to be watching and photographing from where she

288

sat? Who was so sure to be on the canal, that his neighbours could direct her to him there?' They stared at him.

'Come on, Adrian. Who lives in Richards Road? Whose child in the opera chorus is a promising young musician? What's the shortened form of the name Henry?'

'Hal Benton!' they answered together.

'I don't think he's a charmer,' Clement went on. 'Not even by a woman's standards. He seems a good bloke, though. Devoted to the girl, good to his parents, a fine craftsman, dependable.'

'You don't have to write him a CV!' But Jennifer was laughing. 'Was he the man the ticket office lady—Mrs Tyler, was it?—sold her single ticket to? We ought to get a shot of him, show it to her.'

They liked Mitchell's idea, were finding support for it themselves.

'Rosie did make a particular fuss of the three girls, asked them to tea and so on.'

'The senior Bentons are dead set against their granddaughter making a career in music. It is a chancy living, but what they'd really be afraid of would be Rosie and Gracie meeting up and Gracie realizing she'd been deceived.'

'And he maybe used his full name when he was younger, when they were still living together.'

'So the phone call could be from him— wanting to meet up so he could pay her out.'

'No! Wanting to meet up before she arrived in Cloughton so he could prevent it happening—but she never got the call.'

Mitchell had been enjoying the exchange. Now he interrupted it. 'Just a minute.' They looked at him indignantly. 'Jane Felling said the child's name was Carmen.'

'So?' Jennifer was scornful of this one, feeble objection. 'If they'd fled to Yorkshire to escape Rosie, they wouldn't want the little girl to have a way-out name. It could be quite easy to persuade a three-year-old that it would be fun to have the same name as her grandmother. It might be one of her given names anyway.'

Clement was strong in Jennifer's support. 'Grace is slightly out of the way too for a child her age, but it's less of a talking point than Carmen, less easy to trace.'

Now they began questioning one another. 'Did she—Rosie, I mean—accept Blake's offer so that she could come and get her daughter back?'

'But how had she found out they were here? Had she heard the phone message when Blake's offer was made?'

Mitchell shook his head and re-entered the conversation. 'That's silly. Rosie was engaged by Blake more than a year ago. The phone message can't be more than a week or two old, probably a lot less. I think Hal Benton read the papers and tried to set up a meeting with

290

Rosie before she arrived here. When that failed, he had to deal with her here. His family had lived in peace for eleven years with no contact from his wife. He wanted no more grief for either his child or himself. He wasn't having her upsetting them all over again.'

'So what,' Clement demanded, 'do we do now? Caroline's down on the canal bank, masquerading as his victim. Is he going to think she's a danger to him too?'

Mitchell weighed the odds before answering. When he spoke, though, he was reassuring. 'We've got four constables down there with her, including Smithson. I'll radio him to keep a particular eye on Benton.'

'Why not fetch him in now?'

'No. If all four officers are watching him, Caroline's safe enough. We might as well see if she can get a reaction from him that helps to justify an arrest.'

*   *   *

Friday evening was sharp and cold. Caroline had pulled out of her store of winter garments a thermal running vest to wear under the thin cotton shirt that had been adequate protection on Monday evening. Having given up her attempt to find a smaller version of Rosie's shoes, she had brought back into service the stout brogues in which she had pounded the beat before joining CID.

It had been a dispiriting walk across the business park to the marina. She had climbed the wall on to the slope above the towpath hurriedly, as Rosie had probably done, and looked about her for a vantage point from where there was little danger of being seen.

On her Monday walk, Caroline had been optimistic, sure that her likeness to the victim would stimulate recollection and produce new evidence. All week she had waited to hear of calls flooding in. There had not been one, 'Except,' Mitchell had told her, 'some wimp from the *Clarion* wanting to publish your lack of success.'

It was unlikely that this repeat performance would provoke any more of a reaction. Reaching the wooden bench at the end of her trek, she lowered herself gingerly on to it, avoiding the several dark stains that might or might not be Rosie's blood. The damp wood struck chill through the thin wool of her trousers and she resolved to sit there for a rather shorter time than she had on Monday.

She recognized several people that she had seen using the path then. The two unobservant young boys, making their return journey from school, were riding their bicycles sedately and in single file now their route had so much police attention. A friend of Gracie's, who had not been there on Monday, walked past and the two girls waved to one another a little furtively. Caroline thought her parents had perhaps forbidden this way home since the events of the previous Friday, but children smelt excitement rather than danger. A mongrel dog, unaccompanied, trotted purposefully from right to left in front of her, its fur clinging wetly to its thin body. Caroline shivered on its behalf. It was a bit chilly for a swim.

Hearing footsteps behind her, she turned to see an elderly man approaching her. She did not recognize him. As she watched, he quickened his pace to a shambling run, calling out in a keening wail. As he came nearer, she saw his lips drawn back to show his gums and realized that his incoherent words were directed to her. He stopped a couple of feet from her, pointing a veined finger. She was not sure whether the face was contorted with anger or with fear, but she wished that just one of her supporting quartet was in view.

'You she-devil! Get back to hell! You'll have to kill me to get them back.' The poor old thing was out of his mind. Should she try to restrain him forcibly or talk to him? His mouth was shooting out spittle and his screamed words, making no sense, were certainly threats. As she stood and backed away, the man's pointing hand was withdrawn. He reached with it into an inner pocket. Had he got a knife? Or a gun?

When the hand was withdrawn, it held a bottle of beer. Not to offer her a drink,

Caroline decided. The bottle crashed against the bench. Liquid spilled as the demented creature came towards her, green shards held in front of him in bleeding fingers.

Backing had been a mistake. The ground between herself and the wall behind her that meant escape was covered with tangled brambles. She should have gone forward, down the slope, before he got so close. She must do that now, surprise him, push past him to the smoother grass that led to the towpath and her colleagues further along it. Why weren't they in sight now?

She knew the answer. They were where she had asked them to be. This manoeuvre had been intended to jog memories, not to force a confrontation with a killer. She suspected now that the man was frightened rather than insane. Unless he was a psychopath, the killing would have preyed on his mind. On top of that, to find what he thought was the woman he had killed back again a week later to haunt him had overturned his reason.

He was standing, quiet now, just in front of the bench. She would have to dash behind it and round him. He anticipated her and she found herself alongside her attacker, trapped between the bench and the wall. She put up her arms to protect her face, but too late.

Thankfully, she realized she had pulled the man's arms lower than her eyes but that was all she could manage. She felt the glass slice into the flesh of her cheek, first a cold line of numbness, then a burning and a burst of pain. She tried to scream but could force no air from her lungs. Still silent, her attacker raised his arm again.

Suddenly, there was a flash of scarlet and gold, a sickening sound of metal on bone, and Caroline's assailant dropped to the ground. She was dimly aware of a magnificently sari-clad Shakila, wielding a lethal-looking weapon. She put it on the ground whilst she lowered Caroline to the bench and yelled for assistance from the two constables below.

Hal Benton appeared on the roof of a narrow boat. 'Did you say someone was hurt? I've got a well-stocked first aid box on board.'

'Bring it!' one of the constables ordered tersely.

Benton leapt neatly from his boat to the towpath, ascended the bank, offered his box to the officers surrounding Caroline and turned his attention to the prone man. He gave a cry of dismay as he recognized the figure lying on the brambles, receiving attention from a third policeman who looked up.

'His pulse is strong. He's in better fettle than the lass he felled.'

Benton lowered himself to the bench, at the opposite end to Caroline. Tears streamed down his cheeks as he looked from one casualty to the other. 'My God, Dad. What have you done? Whatever have you done?'

CHAPTER FOURTEEN

For once, Mitchell was free to leave the station at the end of the shift. He was looking forward to discussing the events of the day with Virginia and he knew that it was Jennifer who had made this possible.

Unreasonably, he was annoyed with her. She had set them up. He couldn't talk naturally to his wife about all his theories. He felt as though Jennifer had written lines for them to speak.

When he tried to explain, Virginia understood immediately. 'We can rewrite the script if we don't like Jen's version.'

He grinned. 'OK. It would be useful if you could supply the answers to the following. Should I be applying for DCI jobs outside Cloughton? Am I worrying unnecessarily about Shakila? How did we sort out this case without any of us having a music degree?'

'All right. That's enough to last us through supper. Which is most important?'

'To you and me, the job. To our present situation, I'm not sure.'

'Then talk to Carroll about whether you'll be keeping Dad's job. Then you'll understand what your options are. What's the problem with Shakila? I thought she was safely back at home.'

'She is, but for how long?'

'Till the next time you need someone to break the rules to crack a case.'

'Yes, but . . .'

Virginia grinned. 'You're just jealous because a high and mighty DCI daren't take the risks that she does. She won't worry you any more than you used to worry my father. He survived.'

'Guilty as charged. That means, as far as I'm concerned, she's got her ticket back. Let's hope the super agrees.'

'He will, after he's huffed and puffed a bit. As far as the music degree's concerned, Caroline got near enough.'

'Caroline's another problem. I'm really sorry about what's happened to her on her own account. From my angle, it's going to push her the way I didn't want her to go.'

'You mean that, because she got hurt, she'll want to pack the job in—with Cavill and music as her excuse.'

'When you put it like that, I don't think so. Caroline's the sort to dig her heels in—"I'll give the bastards as good as I get." '

'So it'll push her the right way?'

Mitchell threw up his hands. 'Who knows what the right way is for her? I don't think she knows herself. The attack won't make any difference. Eventually, she'll decide without reference to it.'

'How is she?'

'Physically, she's doing well. Thanks to Shakila, there were no life-threatening injuries. Her face is a mess, though, and they've told Cavill, though not Caroline yet, that there'll be no avoiding scars, though they'll fade.'

'Huh, when she's too old and wrinkled to care one way or the other.'

'How's your mother been today?'

Virginia smiled. 'Sleeping a lot. I hope her dreams are more cheerful than what she wakes up to.' She got up from the table. 'I'll start supper.'

Mitchell waved her down again. 'I'll get it. I like to have my hands busy when I've a lot to think about.'

'Dad's hoping you'll go round later to give him all the details.'

'Fine. I was going to anyway.' He raised his voice to call his offspring in from the next room. 'What do you want for supper, you lot?'

Caitlin's face broke into a beam. 'Are you cooking it, Daddy? Can I ask Sarah to supper? She won't come when it's Mummy cooking.'

Mitchell raised an eyebrow. 'I did tell you that Kat doesn't do tactful.'

*   *   *

The interview room was miserably small and lit by a suspended neon light. Its walls were dirty, their paint stopping at the picture rail, and the

298

only decoration was a map of West Yorkshire. There were cigarette ends and a dead wasp on the floor.

At a table, facing Mitchell, sat Harry Benton. He was unrepentant, sitting up straight and looking Mitchell in the eye. 'Don't expect me to be ashamed—or sorry except about personal matters. I'm sorry Grace will be on her own for a long while. I'm sorry about the dog. Poor little bugger will pine. He even sleeps with me.

'I'm sorry for poor stupid Hal—never could recognize a bad egg. Took that little slag on when she was carrying another lad's child, carried a torch for her all these years while the ungrateful cow was striking it rich and leaving little Gracie to cry herself to sleep. Almost came to blows with him when I realized that he actually intended to go to that theatre and watch her strutting her stuff, caterwauling, prancing about, lapping up the applause.'

The man's voice was rising hysterically and Mitchell cut in to ask, 'Don't you think he might have been going for Gracie's sake?'

The man sat, tense, his fists clenched, fighting for self-control. When he spoke again, his voice was tight but calm. 'I think he encouraged Gracie to ask Cavill Jackson to let her sing. It was Hal's way of getting into that creature's favour again. Not that she ever did favour him. He was only her meal ticket, her rescue from disgrace.'

Mitchell asked, 'Did you plan to kill her? Did you follow her, hoping for an opportunity?'

He shook his head. 'I'd feel more pleased with myself if I had. No. I went fishing as I told you. Caught nothing and got sunburnt. Then I thought of Hal on the boat deck getting equally hot and fed up. Thought I'd pick him up and we'd have a jar together—and a Coke for Gracie. Then I saw Rosemary taking photographs, trying to get her feet back under the table, shower presents on the child, get round her when we'd done all the hard work of bringing her up.

'Worse than that. Making us out to be liars because we'd told her her mother was dead. Was there any harm in that? Should we have told her that her bloody cow of a mother wanted fame and money more than she wanted her daughter? Now the poor kid's got worse to face. All that, and Rosemary's funeral, and the case against me and not being able to trust what we tell her any more.'

His composure crumbled and he began to sob.

*　　　*　　　*

As he sat in his father-in-law's chair and drank the home brew that Browne had prepared in happier times, Mitchell wondered how to bring Harry Benton alive for him in words. He did his best, trying to remember exactly how the old man had justified himself and to let him be his own apologist.

Browne listened intently, taken out of himself and his troubles. 'I'm surprised no one realized that this might be the work of an ex-marine.'

Mitchell accepted the reproach. 'I didn't read Clement's report carefully enough. He did make a note about it.'

'I'm surprised too that a marines-trained man didn't look further ahead, have a fall-back plan to protect his family.'

'But he acted on the spur of the moment. He was shocked by seeing that Rosie had the audacity, as he saw it, to spy on Hal and Gracie. He thought she was trying to re-establish her position as a mother.'

Browne was unforgiving. 'Marines are trained to think on their feet. So, what about the other business, the money?'

Mitchell perked up. 'It was a bit of luck for us, getting the breakthrough on our patch. The intelligence people have been keeping tabs on it for more than two years. They had a hunch that most of it was coming from just one ring. They even had a fair idea of who was behind it. What they really wanted to know was who was printing the stuff.'

'Where's all the evidence?'

'Stacked in the closed circuit cell. We aren't taking any risks. If you meant what have we got to produce in court, the answer's quite a lot. The notes taken from the lad, Shaun, tally with some we've confiscated—loads of his prints and a few of Patel's. We found fragments of torn-up notes in Patel's vacuum cleaner.'

'What about at the garages?'

'The middle two on each side had been knocked together internally and extra insulation put in. That deadened any noise and protected the gear. There was a four-colour litho press and computer-controlled guillotine, six feet tall and eight feet wide, for cutting large sheets.

'He'd tried to tidy up a bit. Shakila knew he was on to her. The image areas had been snipped out of bundles of copper printing plates but he hadn't got rid of the rubber blankets that cushion the rollers on the press. One showed the Queen's head, clear as day.'

'You raided the garages on Thursday?'

'Yes, once we'd rescued Shakila from Patel's garden shed and dealt with young Grant. I don't think he'd have done her any serious harm but I'm thankful she'd got her call through to us before he decided to walk in on her.'

'What is it about that boy?' Mitchell looked puzzled. 'He needs banging up for a good long while but every time you get hold of him you make excuses for him.'

Mitchell laughed. 'There, but for the grace

302

of God . . . My teenage career is probably Shaun's blueprint. I had the luck to get into the force before the force got me into reform school.'

Browne sniffed but made no further comment. 'You sent Shakila back to the marina. Why not just lock up Patel?'

'He didn't show till the middle of Friday afternoon and I sent Shakila nowhere. She's on holiday and that's where she chose to be without asking my permission. She thought she might pick up more clinching evidence before we arrived to collect him.'

'Surely he didn't just sit on his boat and enjoy the spectacle whilst Shakila was doing her rescue act.'

Mitchell chuckled. 'He was laid out on the roof of his cabin. Shakila hit him with the windlass before setting about Harry Benton. She said, "I had no choice, sir. If I hadn't he'd have scarpered." He knew she was one of us but not how fast she can run or what defending yourself in race riots, even minor ones, can teach you.'

Browne reached for the jug and refilled their glasses. 'Well, let's hope both Benton and Patel get safely locked up. We've lost some before when the evidence seemed just as watertight.'

Mitchell sighed. 'I'd like to get Patel, certainly. I have a lot of sympathy with the other poor sod. He was . . .'

'What? Protecting his family? What about slicing up Caroline's face?'

'He thought she was a ghost—but, don't worry, I won't be asking her to give evidence for the defence.'

EPILOGUE

On the first Saturday of the following December, Hannah Browne took an afternoon nap. She never woke. It was a good death, by Hannah's own definition. Tom Browne considered that his daughter's tears were not before time.

Cavill Jackson cancelled a prestigious engagement to play Shostakovitch on the organ at her funeral. Declan Mitchell played his recorder as the coffin was carried out of church. After Christmas, he was to begin piano lessons with Mr Jackson.

Caitlin Mitchell missed her grandmother for many months. The twins, Sinead and Michael, whose boisterousness Hannah had not been able to support, missed her hardly at all.

Alex Mitchell returned to hospital nursing at St James' in Leeds. In the New Year, he intended to propose to the prettiest student sent that term on placement to Jimmy's. He had good reason to believe she would accept him.

Acting Detective Chief Inspector Benedict Mitchell heaved a sigh of relief that Hannah's struggle was over. He took care to do it out of sight and hearing of his family.

*   *   *

Later in December, in a quiet church ceremony, Cavill Jackson and Caroline Webster were married. Since the surgeons were still repairing her face, Caroline declined to wear white with all the trimmings. The music, provided by Cavill's students, past and present, was superb.

* * *

Shakila Nazir was accorded all due credit for her part in the apprehension of Minesh Patel and the rescue of her colleague, DC Webster, from possible death by glassing. She could see no reason why she should not be drafted forthwith into CID. Neither could her superintendent. She had learned her lesson and he intended to support her request for transfer in the New Year.

Sergeant Jennifer Taylor also felt she was overdue for promotion. She searched the various publications where inspectors' posts were advertised. DCI Thomas Browne intended to leave Yorkshire, at least temporarily. By February he had two interviews lined up for posts in the Met where he had walked the beat in his early days. Superintendent John Carroll had no plans for his own advancement but counted his blessings in Cloughton. He set himself to find a way, against protocol, to confirm Acting DCI

Mitchell as his father-in-law's permanent successor.

*   *   *

In January, Lauren Hardy obtained a post on the arts section of a London-based national newspaper. Once she felt settled in her new position, she intended to join the London Bach Choir. She hoped to reach the stage where she could write a letter of apology to Lewis Blake and wish him well in his future productions.

*   *   *

At the end of the academic year, Jonathan Stepney finished his inglorious school career. After county trials, he was representing Yorkshire in middle distance and cross-country running. Of less importance, but nevertheless pleasing to him, was the offer of employment in a local factory. In view of these circumstances, he informed DC Clement that he could no longer spare the time to be his nark.

Shaun Grant was serving a term in a young offenders' centre. He had not yet decided how to turn this circumstance to his advantage, but he felt sanguine about his future.

Gracie Benton began the new academic year at Chetham's School in Manchester. Not

307

discouraged now from singing, she was discovering her voice. Her musical studies were a refuge from her jumbled feelings about her abandonment by her mother and the protective falsehoods told by her father and grandparents. Father and daughter had moved out of his parents' home. Rosie's money was providing his daughter's school fees. Hal Benton both dreaded and gloried in the future when Gracie too would become a performer and music would divide them.

*   *   *

Harry Benton was faithfully visited by Grace. She considered it was only his due when the state had left him to punish the much greater sins of their daughter-in-law.